MI5 N

[spooks]

ADAM CARTER REVEALED

Available from Headline

Spooks: The Personnel Files
Spooks: Harry's Diary: Top Secret
Spooks: Adam Carter Revealed

MI5 NOT 9 TO 5

[spooks]

ADAM CARTER REVEALED

headline

First published in Great Britain in 2008 by
HEADLINE PUBLISHING GROUP

1

Cataloguing in Publication Data is available
from the British Library

ISBN 978 0 7553 3401 8

Typeset in Letter Gothic by Avon DataSet Ltd,
Bidford on Avon, Warwickshire

Printed and bound in Great Britain by
Clays Ltd, St Ives plc

Headline's policy is to use papers that are natural, renewable and
recyclable products and made from wood grown in sustainable
forests. The logging and manufacturing processes are expected to
conform to the environmental regulations of the country of origin.

HEADLINE PUBLISHING GROUP
An Hachette Livre UK Company
338 Euston Road
London NW1 3BH

www.headline.co.uk
www.hachettelivre.co.uk

Foreword

Three decades in espionage have given me access to the full range of humanity, high and low. I have advised prime ministers, conversed with presidents and shared tea with monarchs. I have met terrorists and soldiers, war criminals and their victims, traitors and heroes. I have witnessed remarkable displays of courage, both physical and moral. I have been fortunate to work with many remarkable colleagues, and unfortunate to share an office with a few dreadful ones.

But of all the people I have encountered – professionally or socially, abroad or at home, young or old – there is no one more remarkable than Adam Carter.

I first met Adam in July 2004 when he was seconded to Section D from MI6. He appeared instantly likeable, instantly knowable. Tom Quinn, his first-rate predecessor, was a closed book: introverted, complex and, occasionally, cold. Adam, on the other hand, managed to distinguish between taking his job very seriously and not taking himself seriously at all. 'Just let it all crinkle out.' That seemed to be his motto.

For the most part, this adage worked well for him, as he neutralised myriad threats and kept the section going through some of the hardest times in its history. But it was often a difficult time for Adam as well. In January 2005, he lost his wife, Fiona, and struggled more than any of us really knew with post-traumatic stress disorder. Colin, Danny and Zaf all died on Adam's watch, along with countless, nameless innocents.

But if Adam was anything, he was a survivor. He lost Fiona; he found Jenny. Jenny left; he devoted his time and his love to his son, Wes. Ros distanced herself; he found solace, if not professionalism, in the arms of Ana Bakhshi, the wife of the Iranian Cultural Attaché. And through it all he maintained a constant, loyal devotion to his country, his comrades and his friends.

Adam was like Teflon: you could throw anything you chose at him and none of it would stick. Question his loyalty and he would prove himself four steps ahead of you again and again. Question his sanity and he would perform almost superhuman feats of cunning and bravery. If we cut him a lot of slack it was because we had no choice. Section D without Adam Carter is almost unimaginable.

But the unimaginable has come about. However indestructible Adam Carter appeared, he was not immortal. On 11 November 2008, he died as he had lived: serving his country without thought for his own personal safety.

And that, as they say, might have been that. We have had deaths before in Section D. It is a regrettable, inevitable consequence of the work we do, the business we're in. There are funerals — quiet, private affairs which the families often ask us to stay away from. Sometimes, there is a bit of a legal row. Then it's back to work, back to reality, back to the next disaster and a new colleague. Terrorism allows no time to grieve.

It might have been that way with Adam Carter. It would have been that way, were it not for the meeting I had with a lady called Lucy Dempsey a few days after Adam died.

I went to visit Lucy so I could find Adam's mother. When Adam was young we knew that he had been very close to Lucy and her brother, Richard, who also grew up to be an MI6 officer (once a suspected traitor, he disappeared again on an operation in the Balkans last year, having regained Six's trust, and has not been seen since). I hadn't, however, realised just how close this relationship was. Lucy told me that Adam was the son of a single mother who worked as a housekeeper for the Dempseys at Fleetwood House. Adam's expensive education had been paid for by Richard and Lucy's father, Simon. Adam's initial MI6 application form was factually accurate. Yet, as soon as he was recruited, he broke into the system and gave a false address, false telephone number – false everything – for his mother. He also changed other details about his childhood. On the hard copies, he forged the signature of the Director General himself.

My initial reaction was one of amusement. Was Adam Carter – the charming, good-looking, self-assured man we had grown to know and respect – an inverted snob? I know that Six's recruitment methods – the service Adam joined initially – are a little archaic. I'm aware that, despite all their show of placing advertisements in *The Times* and the *Economist*, they still enjoy an old-fashioned tap on the shoulder in a quiet Oxbridge quadrangle. But Adam already had all the advantages that they were looking for – poise, self-confidence and a first-class brain. He had something more besides: the grit and determination which many products of his adopted upbringing lack. He was the perfect candidate in his own right, on his own merits.

So why erect this elaborate smokescreen over his background? We no longer live in the 1930s. My amusement turned to bemusement. Surely Adam was more than a character from McEwan's *Atonement*. What else was he hiding? What if everything we thought we knew about him was false? What if Adam Carter himself was just another one of his aliases, another one of his many boxed identities?

Lucy had no idea, however, where Eleanor had gone since leaving Fleetwood. Just as I was wondering how I might track her down – there were no records in any database for 'Eleanor Carter' – she called on the public line and asked for me specifically. I was given an address in Blackpool and immediately took a day off work to investigate. I drove myself there, found the quiet detached row of houses and rang the bell. The red, solid door opened immediately.

'You must be Harry Pearce,' said Eleanor. 'It's good to meet you at last.' Her face was lined with age, her back slightly stooped with years of manual work but the charming, steely look in her eyes said, 'I am the mother of Adam Carter.'

We sat and made small talk for a while. Then she beckoned me into a small dining room.

4

'You'll be wanting these, I suppose. For the files.'

She opened a large wardrobe, stacked from top to bottom with carefully filed, handwritten letters. Some of them tumbled on to the floor.

'Yes, Adam was quite the letter writer,' she said, bending down to pick them up. 'Here,' she added, thrusting a file at me. 'You better start at the beginning.'

What follows is the true story of Adam Carter, as related in his correspondence with his mother and other important people in his life. These letters are accompanied by my own notes and interpretations on their veracity and impact. Where there are gaps — and there are many — I have attempted to fill them with my own, thorough research, including interviews with his mother, Eleanor, and a number of other key people whose lives touched the young Adam.

The story I've unearthed is shocking but ultimately, I believe, noble. It is one man's struggle with many things, not least himself. Perhaps most of all, it is the story of a man's man, a spy's spy, a spook from first to last. From me, there can be no higher compliment.

I repeat: I used to think there was no one more remarkable than Adam Carter. Now that I know the real truth about the man, I am sure of it.

Harry Pearce
London, February 2009

1
Childhood

St. Paul's School
London
9th October 1985

Dear Mum (sorry, I know it annoys you, but I absolutely refuse to call you anything else now that I'm at secondary school),

I'm sorry it's taken me such a long time to write. They don't stand over us in the same way as they used to at prep school and make us knuckle down to letter-writing every Sunday. But it does mean we can write whatever we like when we do get down to it. They don't check our letters, 'for grammar and spelling', here like they used to.

Things have been really busy at the beginning of this term. I've made it into the rugby team – playing inside centre. Richard plays blindside flanker. We're both missing Lucy, even though she's just down the road at the junior girl's school. We don't get much chance to mix with them in the first year. 'There will be plenty of time for that later,' says Mr Campbell, our form master.

Work is not going quite so well, although I'm enjoying geography, which Richard says isn't a proper subject. He prefers history, especially the battles. Please don't imply to Mr Dempsey that I'm not working hard, because I am. I just feel that some of the other boys have a slight academic advantage over me having spent five years at prep school instead of two. Still, I am very grateful and catching up fast.

Last week we had our first rugby match against Tonbridge. Richard . . .

Love from Adam

Letter continues in similar vein for some three pages
HP

St. Paul's School
London
1st November 1985

Dear Mr Dempsey,

Thank you for your birthday card. It was kind of you to write and ask how I'm getting on at the new school. I wanted to reply straight away and thank you once again for all your support. I know you have repeatedly told me that it's the least you could do but I can't express my gratitude enough. I am working very hard and not letting

sport get in the way of my studies. I will write again
soon.

    Best wishes,
    Adam Carter

St. Paul's School
London
3rd December 1985

Dear Lucy,

    I'm sitting next to Richard in double maths and we
couldn't be more bored so decided to write to you. Sorry,
that doesn't sound very nice, does it, but you know what
we mean! Thank you so much for your letter which arrived
this morning. Richard thinks we write to you far too often
but there's just so much to tell you that I couldn't wait.

    Anyway, we have to go now as
it's almost the end of the lesson

> Letter continues
> in similar vein for
> five pages
>   HP

and Mr Levenson is beginning to
get suspicious. He has that evil look
on his face which means our
homework this evening is going to
be twice as long and twice as difficult as normal.

    Richard is punching me on my writing arm – I think
he's a bit jealous – so we're going to sign off here.

    Love from Adam (and Richard)

9

Note from Harry Pearce

If Adam was an avid letter writer, his mother, Eleanor, was an equally avid collector — to the extent that she even collected letters not actually addressed to her. (She claimed to have 'stumbled across' the letters to Simon and Lucy Dempsey while cleaning and have made copies — for reasons which will become apparent — for the files.) Adam's correspondence between the ages of eleven (when he was sent to boarding school under the patronage of Eleanor's employer, Simon Dempsey) and thirteen filled an entire file in her dining-room wardrobe. I did not see it necessary, or suitable, to include all of it for the purposes of this file. There were reams of match reports: ball by ball, blow by blow, accounts of football, rugby, cricket, squash and tennis matches which invariably ended in victory for Adam's team. The academic side received scant mention, although his school reports clearly demonstrate great potential. There were occasional signs of homesickness, but remarkably little considering the age at which he was sent away to board. Adam was always a 'coper'.

According to Eleanor — and there is no reason to doubt her account — Adam also led an idyllic, happy childhood before the age of eleven. He was a happy, loud baby and a happy, naughty toddler. From the hundreds of photos she showed me, the Adam Carter we knew as an adult was clearly discernible by the time he started primary school — a mop of blond, almost white, hair, those piercing blue eyes, a mouth that could turn into a sulky glower or a beaming grin in a moment. He was tall

10

for his age and popular at school, if his school reports are anything to go by. A picture emerges of a cheeky, irreverent and piercingly intelligent young boy. Several of his teachers also remarked on a sensitivity often absent in an alpha male intellect and physique. Adam was never a bully despite possessing all the attributes of one. He didn't suffer fools gladly, but he was often seen standing up for the weaker boys in the school.

This kindness was most manifest in his behaviour towards his mother. It was not a D.H. Lawrence relationship, still less an Oedipal one, but from an early age Adam displayed a fierce, protective pride in his mother. Having met Eleanor I would venture that this pride is not misplaced. As I have hinted, she is a formidable woman: formidable in appearance and outlook. Occasionally formidable, too, in her behaviour, as we shall see. Together, they lived a simple life in a small cottage attached to Fleetwood House, a large manor house that Eleanor cleaned and maintained and Adam played in and around with the Dempsey children.

Adam thrived at his local, rural school to the extent that Simon Dempsey, a hugely successful businessman, offered to sponsor him on a scholarship to the same preparatory school as his son, Richard. Eleanor, a proud woman, initially turned down the offer, fearing that it would put the family too much in his debt, but was persuaded by Dempsey that it was too good an opportunity to miss.

There was a degree of snobbery when Adam, a fairly rough

and tumble boy of eleven, joined Richard at his preparatory school. However, this was rarely, if ever, mentioned in letters home and seems to have been felt more acutely by Eleanor than Adam. One letter from an eleven-year-old Adam, which I haven't included because it would have taken the stenographers too long to decipher the handwriting, describes him beating up a boy with a double-barrelled surname (I note that the victim is now a junior cabinet minister, and a fairly unspeakable one at that) who had mocked Adam's background. It is interesting to see that the school took no disciplinary action, presumably accepting — and Eleanor confirms this from her conversations with the headmaster — that young double-barrelled had received his just deserts.

There is an account of a childhood escapade in Adam's personnel file — doctored by Adam — which is based on truth and is worth including here for the light it sheds on Adam's character. On 3 June 1984 (not 1982 as stated) Adam ran away from Ridley Preparatory School. It appears to have been some sort of 'leavers' dare' (the high jinks carried out by boys in their last year who had finished their exams) in which Richard and Adam competed to see who could put the most distance between themselves and the school. Adam has struck out all references to Richard Dempsey but otherwise the details are correct. The twelve-year-old Adam Carter really did have sufficient presence of mind to fool the school and railway authorities and make it to London from Berkshire. More importantly, perhaps, he appears to have been sufficiently proud of the fact to retain the salient details in his personnel file.

The early letters I have chosen for inclusion give a good indication of the backdrop to the story of Adam Carter. In the letter to his mother, we see the first indications of a young man coming of age and leaving aside the more embarrassing monikers of his childhood. There's evidence, too, of his competitive nature – sport is clearly a priority – as well as his desire to catch up academically on those who have had a head start by attending preparatory school from the age of seven. There's also an unwittingly prescient brush with early censorship. Amusingly for those who grew to know Adam in his twenties and thirties, there is also an endearingly naive innocence in his relations with the opposite sex. It wasn't a naivety that would last long.

More importantly, I have chosen these letters for they illuminate the key relationships in his early life. Writing to his mother, Adam is affectionate, chatty and open. In corres- pondence with Simon Dempsey, he is grateful but guarded, even a little duplicitous. With Lucy, he is gushing and, in retrospect, at least, somewhat smitten. The five pages I have omitted for the purpose of these files are almost unbearably childish in their devotion. It is difficult not to sympathise with Richard's desire to punch him on the arm by the sixth page.

Richard Dempsey is the common thread that runs through all his early letters and it is worth commenting on their relationship in a little more depth at this stage.

The two boys were born within a few days of each other in the same hospital ward in the Royal Berkshire, Reading. Eleanor met Sarah Dempsey, Richard and Lucy's mother, at pre-natal classes where they struck up a friendship. The mothers lost touch — while their social backgrounds were similar, their social circumstances were not — but they met again when Richard and Adam attended the same nursery school, at which point Eleanor started working for the Dempseys at Fleetwood House.

For Adam and Richard, it was the beginning of a lifelong friendship and rivalry. Their respective mothers fuelled this competitiveness, comparing notes on who had walked, talked and mastered their two times table first. For the most part, however, maternal pressure seems to have played little part in the lives of the two boys as they grew up side by side. Sport was an obvious common ground — both organised games and more imaginative capers. Eleanor recalls the two of them 'always playing wars and ambushing each other' around the extensive grounds of Fleetwood House. Adam was taller; Richard was stronger and stockier. Both made it into all the first sport teams. School reports show them leading the class at different subjects in turn.

If Richard felt any jealousy or sense of intrusion that Adam, the son of a single mother, his parents' housekeeper, was supported financially by his father, Simon, he didn't show it — at least in their early years. The two were inseparable, except on the frequent occasions when their teachers did attempt to separate them to ensure some degree of peace and quiet in their lessons.

It is said by psychologists — of whom we have more than our fair share around Section D — that a person's psychological make-up and personality is largely formed by the age of thirteen. It is mainly to reveal Adam Carter as he was — confident, outgoing and surrounded by friends and a caring family, both real and surrogate — that I include these early extracts from Adam Carter's correspondence. Suffice to say he had a happy, secure childhood.

In retrospect, it is fortunate that this was the case, for what follows would have broken any lesser person.

We rejoin Adam five years later, aged eighteen, as he goes into his final year at school and finds himself caught up in the events which would shape the rest of his life.

2
A Tale of
two Fathers

St. Paul's School
London
5th November 1990

Dear Mum,

Thank you so much for the birthday card and the cheque. You shouldn't worry at all about it not being very much. My old rugby boots are fine really and don't need replacing. It's who runs around in them that counts!

I'm also writing because Mr Hewson is organising a trip to Israel during the Christmas holidays. The plan is to take in all the main Biblical sites - Jerusalem, of course, Tiberius, Nazareth ... I don't think we'll be going to Bethlehem as the West Bank is still a little unstable. But we'll be completely safe. There's also going to be a bit of time at the end to go down to Eilat on the Red Sea and learn how to scuba dive, which I've always wanted to do.

They're trying to keep the cost down as much as possible. Ben Joseph's father is a board member of Labour Friends of Israel and is subsidising the trip. We're also going to be staying with friends of the school in Israel itself which will keep the cost of accommodation down. I'm putting your birthday cheque towards the cost and have also been working weekend shifts in shops in London to save up so there wouldn't be any need to trouble Simon.

There is space for about twenty boys, and it's going to be oversubscribed, so is there any chance you could sign and return the enclosed form as soon as possible? Richard has already got his name down on the list and I'm really eager to go.

> Adam started referring to Mr Dempsey by his first name in mid-1988
>
> HP

> This was a form asking for a signature to confirm the approval of the parent/ guardian
>
> HP

I hope all's well at Fleetwood. I know the Dempseys always have a lot of guests at this time of year so you must be very busy.

Love from,
Adam

St. Paul's School
London
8th November 1990

Dear Mum,

Thanks for writing back so quickly but I'm really surprised (and, I must admit, a little annoyed) that you're so adamantly against me going to Israel. It's really not 'slap bang in the middle of a war zone', as you put it. I know the intifada has caused a lot of unrest since 1987 – we've been studying it for politics A level – but the situation is very much calmer now. Also, as I said in my original letter, we're sticking to the holy sites and tourist destinations within Israel itself. The unrest is mainly confined to the Occupied Territories. And in any case, Ben Joseph's father is very well connected in Israel. We wouldn't go anywhere stupid and would have good security advice.

Thousands of Jewish British schoolchildren go to Israel every year on organised trips and come back unscathed. They go to get an idea of their heritage, their history and the struggle of their people. There are millions more living in the country who go about their daily business without showing undue fear.

So I don't see why you're suddenly so concerned about this. It's not as if you wrapped me in cotton wool when I was growing up. You were always letting Richard and me get into all sorts of scrapes when we were kids. You thought it would be good for us. And it was. And in any case, you seem to be quite happy with me living as a boarder in London where we have our fair share of terrorist bombs. There was that IRA attack this summer, if you remember, on the Stock Exchange. Israel is no more dangerous than that.

I know you're worried as well about my studies in this, my A-level year, but the trip takes place during the Christmas holidays so it's not as if I'd be missing out on lessons. In fact, I think I'd be missing out by not going. The others are all planning on writing their political dissertations – one of the A-level political modules – on the current situation in the Middle East. If I write mine without first-hand experience, it will stand out as completely amateur compared to the others. There's no other topic I want to write about and I think it's important for me to get an idea of life outside the UK. I can't wait to travel.

I hate begging like this but I really do think it's important. Please, Mum, sign the form and let me go. Or at least give me a decent reason why not.

Love from,

Adam

St. Paul's School
London
14th November 1990

Dear Simon,

I was wondering if I could ask for your help with something. As you know, the school is organising a trip to Israel during the Christmas holidays and I would really like to go. However, my mother is adamantly against signing the consent form. It seems faintly ridiculous to me that we still need parental permission to go on holiday now that many of us are eighteen. But in any case, it's what the school requires and she seems to have a real bee in her bonnet about it. I've received two letters from her now – the second even more strongly worded than the first – vehemently denying me permission to go. Perhaps she's already mentioned this to you?

I think she's mainly worried about the financial implications, even though I've assured her (quite truthfully) that I plan on saving up enough money to pay my own way. I think she's also worried that you're going to have to make up the difference which obviously concerns her when she's already aware of the huge debt of gratitude we owe you. But I promise you I'll be able to cover the costs myself. In fact, the recent weekend shifts I've taken in London have made me think that I'd like to pay you back, over time, for all the school fees you've kindly invested in me over the years. I know you'll argue about this, and say it wasn't why you did it, that you have more than enough money already, and so on, but it would make me feel a lot better about everything. It feels like the very least I should do. Perhaps we could talk about this a bit more over Christmas if you get a moment?

Anyway, back to Israel. I was hoping you might be able to have a quiet word in my mother's ear - tell her that it's safe, that I'd be paying, that it would be beneficial educationally etc. I know she respects your opinion and would listen to you. The more we bombard her from all sides with the same opinions, the more likely she will be to see sense and give in!

Finally, I don't think it will come to this - and I feel rather duplicitous for even bringing it up - but if my mother still refuses to sign, is there any chance you might be able to sign on her behalf? I've had another look at the form and it says 'parent or guardian'. Strictly speaking, I suppose you could count as my guardian, bearing in mind your support of my mother and the fact that my father died before I was born. We needn't tell my mother what's going on. I could pretend that I'd gone to stay with a friend for a week instead.

It would seem a shame to go to an amazing school like St. Paul's and then look a gift horse in the mouth - like this trip to Israel - when it presents itself.

Best wishes,

Adam

St. Paul's School
London
19th November 1990

Dear Lucy,

I'm not exactly flavour of the month at Fleetwood at the moment! I don't know if Richard has mentioned it already, but there's a school trip to Israel planned over the Christmas holidays which he is going on. We need parental permission - which your father has given Richard, of course - but my mum is being strange about not letting me go. I wrote a letter - a somewhat insensitive letter, in retrospect - to your father asking if he might sign on her behalf without telling her and now all hell has broken loose. He showed it to her and I am in double trouble for going behind her back.

It's all very annoying, I must admit. It was wrong of me to try to play them off against each other - even if everyone I know tries to do so with their real parents - but I also think it's wrong of my mum not to let me go. I'm eighteen, for God's sake! Eighteen! I'm allowed to vote, drink, buy cigarettes, get married, have sex and die for my country. If I lived in a tribe in Africa, I'd probably have fathered four children by now. If I'd been alive earlier this century, I'd be fighting in a trench. But no, here I need my mum's signature to go on holiday. I tell you, I can't wait to leave this place, with its forms and its chits

and its petty rules and its signing out and signing in
and archaic language and pathetic teachers.

Boarding school - as you're probably discovering now
that you're doing your GCSEs - is all very well and good
when you're twelve years old. It's fun when you can
stay with your friends at school at the weekends and kick
a ball about and act and paint and generally take
advantage of the amazing facilities. It's certainly a lot
more fun than going home and having to help your
parents in the garden. But boarding school after the age
of sixteen - particularly a boarding school as strict as
this one - is just plain wrong. Here we just sit around on a
Saturday evening wondering when our lives are going to
begin. I'm ready for mine to begin now.

That's why I really want to go to Israel: it will be
an adventure and my life is pretty bloody short of
adventures right now. I don't know why Israel has become
such an idée fixe in my mind. It's not just that Richard
is going, or that it would be useful for politics A level, or
that I've been saving up for it for so long. It's become a
symbol of something more in my own mind: freedom, perhaps
- that tiny island democracy surrounded by hostile
states. Excitement, too: my first trip as an adult, abroad
with friends. But there's something else which I can't
put my finger on. I just know that I absolutely have to
go so I've signed myself up and forged my mum's
signature.

And that was where I was wondering if you could help . . .

You mentioned in your last letter that you're going to stay at a friend's house in the Scottish Highlands at the beginning of the Christmas holidays. Is there any chance you could pretend that I've been invited as well to give me an alibi while I fly off to Israel with the others? You could perhaps tell your Dad that you felt bad about me being left all alone in Fleetwood while both you and Richard were away. I'll leave the details to you – I'm sure your lies are more devious and believable than mine.

In anticipation of your help, I've indulged in a spot of deviousness of my own. Earlier this week, I wrote off to the Scottish Tourist Board and asked them to send me a batch of postcards of the Highlands. As you can see, I've written on five of them and have added stamps and addressed them to my Mum. If you were able to post them from Scotland every two days, that would be brilliant. My Mum will obviously be slightly suspicious that my holiday with you and a younger girl's family she's never heard of happens to coincide with the Israel trip, but this should allay her fears.

I hope you don't think me too devious or presumptuous, but I just can't see any other way around this. I'll make it up to you, I promise.

Adam x

Transcribed postcard from Adam Carter

Hi Mum, Lucy and I are still having a great time in the Cairngorms. The Price family are really fun. We went cross-country skiing again today – much more tiring than the downhill variety. Will send another postcard before the end of the week. Sorry to keep on writing but I miss you all and thought you'd find this picture of a sheep amusing. Love Adam

Aviemore 17 December 1990

Jerusalem
Israel
17th December 1990

Dear Lucy,

Thanks so much again for covering for me so that I could come on this trip to Israel. It's definitely been worth it so far and I'm keeping my side of the bargain by writing to tell you all about it, as you asked. I was going to put this in a postcard but I realised that a) I have far too much to tell you; and b) it would be a little suspect if I sent a postcard of an Eilat beach to your home address. So I'm writing on airmail paper and I'll get Richard to write the address on the envelope so your parents recognise his handwriting and think it's from him.

Israel is the most fascinating country I've ever visited. You realise you're going somewhere special even before you leave the UK. El Al – the Israeli national carrier – has its own separate check-in area at Heathrow. Men with sub-machine guns patrol an overhead gallery as polite but scary-looking Israeli security guards from Shan Beth [H.P. Adam appears to be referring to Shin Bet, also known as Shabak, the Israeli equivalent of MI5] ask all sorts of personal questions. The process takes so long that they ask you to check in three hours in advance instead of two. Ben Joseph and Ariel Goldhagen – two guys from school in our group – were waved through pretty quickly. A boy called Ahmed bin Assadi was given a much harder time. After he had been strip-searched, the security officials offered him a voucher for a coffee and a biscuit as an apology. 'I'd rather my relatives had their country back,' he said, tearing the voucher up into little pieces.

For me, it was an excellent introduction to the intractability of Middle Eastern politics, its high-minded geo-political concerns and its low-level indignities.

It's a debate the twenty of us have conducted with some vigour during our first few days here. Who is right? The Israelis or the Palestinians? Are both of them wrong? Does right and wrong even exist in this context?

On the one hand, Israel is a sovereign country, a democracy, recognised as such by the United Nations. It has been invaded by all of its neighbours on a number of occasions, sometimes simultaneously. Terrorists, a minority of them home-grown Israeli Arabs, blow up its citizens indiscriminately within its borders. Six million Jews were systematically murdered in a Holocaust that took place less than fifty years ago.

Then you have the Palestinians, millions of whom were turned out of their own homes for a Zionist state that makes few allowances for their alternative claim to the land. They're hustled into refugee camps with no hope, no economy, no real leadership. Israel has billion-dollar military packages from the United States; the Palestinians have stones.

And then there's Jerusalem with its disparate claims from three separate religions, its pilgrims, its rival claims as a capital city . . .

I'm sorry - you don't want a history lesson from me in a letter! But this trip has been a real eye-opener, in more ways than one. I think everyone has their historical and political blind spot - mine always used to be the Middle East - but now that I begin to understand the area, I find it completely intoxicating. Until now, I've been unsure about what to study beyond A level. Geography, politics and history don't lead anywhere obvious, unemployment aside. But now I think I'm set on applying to read Arabic at university somewhere.

But please don't think that I'm anti-Israel. I love

this country – its macho militarism, the beautiful girls in uniform carrying machine guns on buses, its arrogance, its defiance, its climate, its kibbutzniks, its pioneers who irrigated and colonised the desert, its religious history (today we visited the Dome of the Rock, the third holiest site in Islam, the Jewish Wailing, or Western, Wall and two separate churches claiming to mark Jesus's crucifixion – all within twenty minutes of each other). It's just that being here has given me a taste for the region as a whole, a hint of Arabia beyond that has captivated me. I love the sound of the muezzin wailing out his call to prayer from the old city's minarets. I love the food – the falafel, the shawarma and the teeth-rotting sweets to follow. And I love the passion, the raised voices, the bartering, the smells and the respect for family that you don't often see in Europe. I want to climb above the rooftops of Damascus for sunset and haggle in the souqs of Cairo. I want to ski in the mountains near Beirut in the morning and swim in the Mediterranean from the capital's beaches in the afternoon. I want to ride around Petra and walk along the ancient Greco-Roman columns of Jerash.

Forgive me again – I'm getting a little carried away! Lawrence of Arabia syndrome, I think they call it. Or Carter of Arabia. Although it doesn't have quite the same ring, does it? Jerusalem is well known for having a funny effect on people. According to my guide book, there is an English lady here who climbs the Mount of Olives every day in expectation of the Second Coming. If the Messiah does return, she reasons, what would he like more than a nice cup of tea as a welcome?

I hope this letter finds you well, although I shall no doubt find you before it does. Still, it is nice to write these thoughts down properly in any case. I enjoy writing letters. You rarely get the time to think these things through in everyday conversation.

Adam x

Ben Gurion International Airport
Tel Aviv
Israel
23rd December 1990

Dear Lucy,

I thought after my last letter I wouldn't be writing again. However, something very strange happened at the

There was a second letter sent from Adam in Israel, postmarked three days after the first, and almost as adolescently enthusiastic in its contents. It contained further insights into the political situation in the Middle East and a breathless account of a scuba diving trip to Eilat. I saw no need to include it in the file.   HP

airport and I've got nothing else to do except write to you.

We arrived at the airport a full 36 hours ago now. You might think that the security procedures on leaving the country would be less intrusive than on entering - what does it matter, after all, if you're up to mischief outside Israel's borders? - but no, they're every bit as interested in the departures lounge as they are in arrivals. When you get here, they want to know where you're staying, why you're visiting, who you know and what you plan on doing. And when you leave, they want to know where you stayed, why you visited, who you met and what you got up to. It wouldn't surprise me if they had some way of corroborating your two sets of answers.

None of this should have posed any obstacles. We arrived as a school group, we travelled as a school group and we left as a school group. When we got here our teacher - Mr Hewson - answered everything on our behalf. Ben Joseph's dad also helped soothe over any ruffled edges.

But a few days ago, Richard and I did a fairly stupid thing. We'd grown a bit bored, to be honest, of travelling around in a large group all the time. Our minibus screamed 'tourists'. Our clothes screamed 'schoolkid tourists'. Mr Hewson never let us relax and actually enjoy ourselves, even in a cultured way. Every site had to be turned into an 'educational experience'. Often, it felt like only one step up from wandering around the Science Museum in London with a clipboard as a ten-year-old.

The last three days of the holiday were meant to be

spent on the beach in Tel Aviv, but considering we'd already spent two days in Eilat where it is much warmer, this didn't appeal much. So Richard hatched a plan to go and have a bit more excitement. Wracking his brain, he remembered that your father has a first cousin up the coast in Netanya. Mr Hewson said we could go and stay with him on condition that he could speak to him directly on the phone to check we'd be OK. Given that we had no intention of going anywhere near Netanya, this involved the complicated deception of Richard finding out the phone number of the public phone box round the corner from the hotel and dialling that number in front of Mr Hewson while I picked up the call and pretended to be Yitzhak Avi. If Mr Hewson was surprised to discover that your father's cousin sounded like a Welsh / Pakistani teenager with a cold and a barely controllable giggle, he didn't voice any suspicions. He is, 'al hamdu li allah', a very gullible man. Ten minutes later, Richard and I met, our bags packed, in the pub opposite the hotel and raised our bottles of dark Israeli Goldstar lager in a toast.

Arabic for 'thank God'

HP

'To Gaza.'
'To Gaza. And the West Bank.'
'Gaza and the West Bank.'
It was one of the best – and potentially worst –

things Richard has ever coaxed me into doing. In Gaza, we were, unsurprisingly, treated with outright hostility and suspicion by the Israeli Defence Force who patrol the border. They only let us through after Richard embarked on a made-up, but incredibly convincing, story about volunteering for Médecins Sans Frontières.

Once in Gaza, we initially found the Palestinians to be pretty unfriendly as well. Richard, as you know, is swarthier and darker than me and the people of Gaza initially mistook his broken nose and arrogant demeanour for an off-duty IDF officer. But once they realised that we were not that brave - or that stupid - and had only come out of curiosity, they were unbelievably friendly towards us.

> Sustained during a rugby match in 1987, according to Eleanor, and never set properly
>
> HP

It was a pretty humbling experience, I must admit. If you visited Leeds on a Saturday evening and its people were in a state of civil war with Sheffield, I cannot imagine them being particularly welcoming to an Arab from two thousand miles away. But in this inverse situation, their hospitality was overwhelming. When we realised we hadn't arranged anywhere to stay - the only hotels we could see in Gaza were five star for some reason - one of

> The reason is that Gaza is generally visited by diplomats and not student backpackers
>
> HP

33

the most expensive hotels offered to put us up for free.

We took them up on their offer and decided to go for a stroll down to the beach before turning in. When we got there, we met the local fire brigade who invited us into their beach hut for illicit vodka drunk from brown paper bags. They were very friendly until Richard brought up the topic of Saddam Hussein.

'Saddam emniih,' said one of the firemen. Even if he hadn't accompanied the statement with a thumbs-up, we'd already picked up that emniih meant 'good'. You heard it a lot.

'Mush emniih,' said Richard. 'Very bad.'

'La,' said one of them. 'Saddam very good. George Bush very bad. Margaret Thatcher very bad.'

'Saddam Hussein is a manyak,' said Richard. 'And so is Yasser Arafat.'

I stared awkwardly at the ground and murmured under my breath, 'Shut the fuck up, mate.' Two of the firemen started to fidget ominously. One of them stood up. The one who had spoken didn't take his eyes off Richard. Eventually, it was me who broke the ice.

'Yes,' I said, raising the vodka bottle again. 'They are all manyak. Arafat, Bush, Saddam and especially Thatcher. Politicians all manyak. And my friend here, he is a manyak as well.'

Everyone laughed and we were all friends again. But on the walk home, Richard and I had a fight.

'I hate the way you just gave in like that,' he said.

'And I hate the way you think you can be that insulting.'

'You were just scared of them.'

'I was scared by you. Scared that you could be so crass.'

'But what I said is true. Arafat is a wanker. I mean, look around you. Do you think that the outside aid pouring in goes to making these people's lives better? Or does it go into arming militants and providing Yasser with plush houses and expensive helicopters? And Saddam? Well, he's a wanker, too. They only like him here because he's a rogue element who sticks two fingers up at the West. They admire him because he's not one of the corrupt Gulf Sheiks. But that doesn't excuse what he does to his own people. It doesn't excuse invading Kuwait or threatening Israel with Scud missiles. It doesn't excuse taking British children hostage and parading them on the news.'

'That may all be true. But you can't just come to someone else's country and tell them that.'

This incident took place on 23 August 1990 in the lead-up to the first Gulf War

HP

'It's not a country. It's a strip.'

'And that makes it OK, does it?'

'I'm just stating a fact.'

'A subjective one. Your problem is that you hate these people. You don't feel sorry for them; you're disgusted by them. Their poverty, their lack of sophistication, their political impotence.'

'And your problem is that you lionise their situation like a classic Western liberal. There's nothing romantic about subjugation. There's nothing heroic about children throwing stones at tanks. It's pathetic, that's what it is. Pathetic and weak.'

'And you can just stand there, with all the privileges of your upbringing, and write them off like that.'

'It's your upbringing too. The difference is that my own father paid for it and you're a bastard without a father.'

Lucy, I'm sorry to say that I hit your brother at that point, right on his crooked nose. And hit him pretty bloody hard, too. I'm sure he'll tell you the story himself, with his own particular slant. But I wanted you to hear it from me as well. It wasn't an unprovoked attack. I know your family has been very generous towards me – your father has told me, more than once, to 'stop bloody saying thank you the whole time' – but I don't see why I should have to put up with him adding a personal angle to what was essentially a political argument.

Anyway, Richard staggered backwards clutching his

nose, shaped up to punch back and then let his fists drop again to his side.

'I'm sorry, mate,' he said, holding out a hand. 'That was out of order.'

We didn't talk about it for the rest of the trip. The next day, we went to Hebron and Ramallah in the West Bank (no wonder there is no state of 'Palestine' given that their two separate territories, the Gaza Strip and the West Bank, are 25 miles apart and only negotiated by travelling along a narrow road through Israel again). In Hebron, we saw the tomb of Abraham. Nearby was an American Jewish family – originally from Tennessee – who had decided it was their Old Testament calling to leave Nashville and settle in the middle of an Arab town. Their house was surrounded by eighteen young soldiers from the IDF, on permanent watch. I was about to say something to Richard but we'd decided to steer clear of political debates by this stage.

We were on safer ground in Ramallah – which we travelled to in a shared yellow taxi – where we found some young people smoking a shisha (like the one your Mum brought back from Morocco once, but keeps tucked away in the corner of the sitting room because your Dad hates it). These blokes were timing each other to see how long they could hold the apple-flavoured tobacco in their lungs. Richard and I joined in and came last and second last respectively.

Anyway, this all happened two days ago. Yesterday, we arrived at Ben Gurion International Airport in Tel Aviv, having joined up with the others in their hotel earlier. Richard told Mr Hewson that the bruise on his nose had been sustained after playing beach volleyball with some Israelis in Netanya. 'It was like the scene in the film Top Gun,' he explained. 'Except they took losing very badly.'

I don't think Mr Hewson had heard of Top Gun.

We checked in at the airport while Mr Hewson answered the standard questions on our behalf. Where had we been? Had we visited the Occupied Territories? Who had we met? Had we packed our bags ourselves? Had we left them unattended? And so on.

Mr Hewson appeared to give satisfactory answers but they still decided to do a spot check of some of our bags. I was singled out, along with Ben Joseph and Richard.

They repeated the same questions. Richard and I gave the same answers as Ben. We had decided beforehand that there was no point creating more trouble for ourselves – with either Mr Hewson or the Israeli authorities – by admitting to our little excursion. There was no evidence to prove we had been anywhere we hadn't said we'd been.

'So you definitely haven't visited the Occupied Territories?' asked the security man again.

'No,' I said.

'Of course he hasn't,' said Mr Hewson.

'Then how do you explain this?' asked the security man, pulling out a large Palestinian flag from my rucksack.

I said that I had no idea how it had got there.

'And this?' demanded the security man, pulling out a framed picture of Yasser Arafat.

'And these?' he added, pulling out sweets with Arabic writing on them.

'I'd forgotten about them,' I said, blustering. None of the items were mine. 'I must have bought them in East Jerusalem.'

'Then why do they say Gaza all over them?'

Fuck.

'I think you better come with me,' said the security man.

He took me to another room, away from the main check-in area, which was clearly where they took all the suspicious-looking people: Westerners backpacking alone, Arabs, anyone with facial hair – they were all there, looking on anxiously as plain-clothed security personnel went through their belongings with plastic gloves and some sort of beeping machine – a radiation measurement, perhaps. In the corner was a small area, sectioned off with a curtain, from where people occasionally emerged looking shaken.

'Look, I'll come clean right away,' I said to the first security man. 'My friend and I did go to the Occupied

Territories. We were bored of our school trip and curious so we sneaked away without our teacher knowing. We spent one night in Gaza and one in Ramallah. We didn't meet any terrorists, none that we knew of anyway. We didn't have particularly political discussions. And as for the flag and other stuff in my bag, I can only guess that it was put there by my friend as some sort of practical joke. We'd had a bit of an argument – about a girl at home – while in Gaza and I think he wanted to get his own back. So you can look at the rest of my bag. You can ask me as many questions as you like. You can take me into that little cubicle over there and strip-search me. But that's the truth and I'd quite like to get on the plane with the others as my mother doesn't know I'm in Israel and I'll be in serious trouble if I get back too late.'

The security man – his name I discovered later was Ariel – looked at me strangely. Perhaps he didn't know what to make of me. Perhaps people normally showed more fear when they were brought to this room. Or maybe the straight-up honest approach had thrown him off guard.

'Well, you didn't take long to crack,' he said with a smile.

I smiled back.

'That's because I've got nothing to hide.'

His face fell again.

'We'll see about that.'

Ariel then proceeded to question me in depth about

40

my background. I told him about my mother (although I soft-pedalled her opposition to my visiting Israel) and your family. He was particularly interested in my father. When had he died? What had he done for a living? Had I known him? No, I answered, truthfully; he died just before I was born and my mother rarely talks about him - which was, of course, a lie. As you know, she talks about him the whole time. She always wanted me to feel as if I'd known my father, even though I'd been denied the opportunity. But I don't see why I should share that with a stranger.

Ariel then started asking about politics, bombarding me with questions to which there was no correct answer, like a particularly sadistic version of one of Mr Hewson's lessons. What did I think of the PLO? Did Israel have a right to defend itself? And to what extent?

I must admit, I laid on the flattery with a trowel: Israel was a wonderful country, a beacon of democracy in a dangerous part of the world, a sanctuary for the oppressed and downtrodden etc. etc. Even your ardently Zionist brother would have blanched at some of the nonsense I came out with. But I didn't care: I just wanted the questions to stop so that I could get on the plane with the others.

Eventually, Ariel stopped the interrogation.

'Good,' he said with a nod. 'Wait here.'

I had to wait so long that I started writing this (very long) letter to pass the time, hiding it under my bag whenever someone looked over at me. As luck would have it, there's a rip in my rucksack where something caught while we were hiking. The rip is almost impossible to spot and the gap between the two bits of material is paper thin. Whenever I've suspected Ariel is about to return, I've simply hidden the letter in that gap. In any case, they don't seem interested in the contents of my bag any more. It's me they're interested in now, which, if anything, should be significantly more alarming.

Later

I have no idea why they left me to stew so long - Ariel returned and led me into a private room where another, much older security officer sat behind a desk. He introduced himself as David, with a roguish twinkle in his eye that I rather liked. But behind it was steel, pure steel.

'So this is our young adventurer?' he said to Ariel in his Americanised accent.

Then he turned to me. 'You wouldn't believe how difficult it was to persuade your teacher to abandon you and join the flight. And your friend, Richard. He kept on jumping up and down and saying the flag was all his fault. Very loyal of him.'

'So why aren't you talking to him as well?' I asked.

'We're not interested in practical jokers,' said David. 'This is a serious business and we're interested in you.'

'Then for God's sake, tell me what it is so I can go home,' I snapped. 'Because I'm bored of sitting here on my arse telling Ariel about what I did on my holidays. I'm bored of our political tutorials. I'm bored of watching your colleagues picking through backpackers' smelly underpants. And I must admit, I'm pretty fucking bored of this airport as a whole.'

Ariel and David made eye contact and smiled. 'I told you so,' said the look on Ariel's face.

'That's exactly what we like about you,' said David with another of his smiles. 'You have courage. Nothing frightens you, does it? You lie to your mother so you can come on an exciting school holiday. Once you get here, you're bored so you and your friend go looking for excitement in a war zone. And then you get to the airport – where you're caught with pretty compromising materials in your possession – and you just brazen it out, head high, clear-eyed, with the truth.'

'I don't see what's so compromising about a flag,' I said. 'Especially when it's not even mine.'

David chuckled gently. 'To you, it might be just a flag. Black stripe, white stripe, green stripe, red triangle. But to us it's a whole lot more. To the Palestinians, of course, it's a lot more too. A symbol of resistance to be waved at terrorist rallies . . .'

He let the notion hang in the air for a bit before continuing.

'Then, of course, there's the problem of the picture of Arafat, a man we have spent a rather long time and devoted a lot of manpower and money towards trying to assassinate. What's the relevant article of domestic law, Ariel? I'm a bit hazy. But there's definitely something there about "by their behaviour, or financial activities, conspiring to support an act of terrorism". Yes, I'm pretty sure that constitutes a crime.'

'A crime?'

'How do you think your customs officials would feel if I walked through Heathrow carrying a picture of IRA leaders?'

'I very much doubt you walk through customs at all when you visit my country.'

David laughed, a full-throated roar this time. 'Witty as well as insightful. What a combination. Of course, it's likely you'd laugh less if we sent you to an Israeli jail for ten years.'

'Ten years. For possession of a flag?'

'And cocaine,' said David. 'Don't forget the cocaine. Especially when it's in sufficiently large quantities to constitute dealing.'

He produced a large bag of white powder. It might have been cocaine. It might have been sugar for all I knew. He was, I suddenly noticed, wearing a pair of gloves. I hadn't even seen him put them on.

'That has nothing to do with me and you know it,' I

said, sounding almost as indignant as I was, but nowhere near as frightened.

'Of course I know it,' said David. 'But will the judge when he sees your fingerprints all over it?'

Ariel grabbed my hand and put it on the bag.

'I'll tell the court the truth,' I said. 'You can't force me into anything. I know my rights.'

David smiled that same charming smile.

'Adam,' he said, calling me by my name for the first time. 'You can tell the court anything you like, for we do not exist. Do you really think my name is David? Is Ariel really Ariel? Do we have family names? My young friend, we operate in the shadows. We are vapour. We are invisible. We are nameless.'

'No, you're not,' I blurted out. 'You're Mossad.'

David's face went hard for the first time.

'Where have you heard that word before?' he demanded.

'In politics. At school.'

David relaxed again. 'Well, you can call us that if you want. It doesn't really matter what you call us, for you won't see me again. But if you want to see your family and friends again within the next decade we're going to have to come to a little arrangement.'

'Blackmail. How original.'

'Don't get clever with us, Adam. And trust me when I say you have no idea what you're dealing with here.'

'We're recruiting you,' said Ariel, softly, suddenly good cop to David's bad. 'We're recruiting you because we like you, because you're plucky, because your politics are right and because you can be useful to us. We're recruiting you because we've spent the last eight hours making inquiries through our sayannim - our sleepers - in the UK and we're assured that you'll go far, that if we invest in you now, you'll be an excellent asset in the future.'

'And what do I have to do?' I asked.

'You will become a sayan as well,' said Ariel. 'You will continue with your normal life until we need you. One of our existing sayannim will make contact.'

'You're asking me to betray my country?'

'We'd never ask you to do anything against the interests of the United Kingdom.'

'And what if I don't want to accept your offer?'

'It's not an offer.'

'What if I call your bluff, demand a lawyer and face trial?'

David stood up from behind his desk and came over and squeezed my shoulder. In any other circumstances, it would have been a friendly gesture.

'Then, Adam, your mother, Eleanor, forty-four years of age, born on the ninth of August nineteen forty-six, currently of Fleetwood House, Berkshire, should watch her step very carefully if she's ever walking the Dempseys' family dog, Buzz, in the woods near the house.'

What choice did I have, Lucy? They seemed to know everything. They seemed to know everyone. Perhaps a braver person – I'm talking about moral courage here – would have brazened it out, told them to get lost, shouted louder about their rights and demanded a lawyer. After all, Israel is a democracy. Would they really have set me up as a drug dealer as they'd threatened? Any decent lawyer would have made mincemeat of them, surely. What evidence did they have beyond fingerprints which we could easily have argued were fabricated? We would have called in character witnesses – Mr Hewson, your father, your mother, other teachers at school – who would have dismissed the entire idea as preposterous. Any jury would have acquitted, I'm sure.

But as I sit here in first class on the plane – they've treated me very nicely indeed after I said yes – it is easy to be wise after the event. At the time, I was terrified, if I'm honest with myself. All that bravado, the brazening out, the quips – they were all just a defence mechanism. Inside, I was quaking; I just chose not to show it. There are few things I'd gamble for the risk of spending ten years in an Israeli jail. Even an English boarding school wouldn't prepare you for that. It's impossible to explain if you weren't there, but there was just something about Ariel and particularly David that made it impossible to say no.

Then again, if I'm honest - really honest - with myself, I said yes for exactly the same reasons as Richard and I decided to go to Gaza. It was not so much the path of least resistance as the path of most excitement. I wanted adventure and what more adventure could you have than working for the world's most professional intelligence agency? They've assured me I won't be working against the interests of the UK - and who knows, at some point in the future it might be very much in the interests of the UK for me to have the ear of Tel Aviv. I know I've written earlier of my sympathy for the Palestinians but this is balanced by my admiration for the Israelis and their right to exist.

We're flying over Poland now - soon we shall be over Germany, scene of the worst holocaust in human history. It seems rather unlikely that I shall post this letter now, given that you'll already be at home - I wonder how you and Richard have explained my absence between the two of you - and I'll see you before it would arrive. But I just had to write this all down. I'm bursting to tell someone and you're the only person I can trust. Richard will envy me for it. Your father wouldn't believe me. My mother . . . well, don't even get me started on my mother.

Love from Adam

Note from Harry Pearce

For the most part, these letters speak for themselves. However, it is still worth my drawing out some themes and elaborating on a few points.

In the first series of letters, we note Adam's combination of persuasiveness, duplicity and perseverance – skills (as we would view them; some employers might consider them vices) already developed at eighteen which would stand him in good stead for the rest of his professional career. 'I feel rather duplicitous,' he writes to Mr Dempsey, but the weight of this burden on his conscience doesn't appear to stop him continuing with his scheme regardless. He won't take no for an answer, even deploying entirely fabricated evidence to support his case. A-level politics, for example, had no dissertation module in 1990, according to my research, so Adam would scarcely have missed out academically if he hadn't joined the trip. In fact, he would probably have gained from additional revision time spent at home in the Christmas holidays before his A levels.

On a re-read, I was, perhaps, a little harsh in my textual notes on Adam's political naivety. His summary of the Israeli-Palestinian situation is actually remarkably astute for a young man. What is more worrying – or, simply, more jarring – is the speed with which he 'goes native' with regard to the Middle East. God knows, we've seen it happen enough times with our own Arabists in the Foreign Office. You only have to pluck a young Rupert with a double-barrelled name out of Oxbridge, put him through the civil service exams, send him out to language school in Damascus and give him a first posting in Cairo and three months later he'll be decrying the influence of British colonialism in the region, criticising the Americans for keeping military bases in the Gulf, quoting Salah Ad-Din in memorandums to King Charles Street and opining that maybe General Nasser did have a point after all.

What makes Adam Carter more interesting than the Ruperts of the diplomatic corps is the evident confusion of his own loyalties. If anything, he 'goes native' twice over, simultaneously lauding the Israelis for their ruthless arrogance and romanticising the Palestinians for their heroic resistance. It points to something deeper in Adam's psyche: an ability to see the merits of strength while still appreciating the cause of the underdog.

Another notable attribute, which we have seen displayed on numerous occasions in Section D, is Adam's ability to talk himself out of a situation. My superiors have often referred to him as a blunt instrument, whereas I've always pointed out his ability to charm as well as cajole. The incident with the firemen in Gaza City is a case in point. Richard speaks his mind; Adam may not be aware of his, but he's sufficiently alert to neutralise a situation that may have escalated out of control.

A subsequent incident – the fight with Richard – reveals the more pugilistic, short-tempered side of Adam. It would not be the last time that a loss of control led to physical violence.

While this was not the first time that Richard and Adam had fought, it is interesting to note that this appears to have been the first time that Richard showed any resentment concerning his father's financial support of Adam. While growing up, Richard took it for granted that Adam joined him at the same expensive school and was included on family holidays. To all intents and purposes Adam and his mother were part of the Dempsey family. It was never questioned and never resented. This incident, however, was symbolic of a slight distancing in relations between the two – believed, by Eleanor, to have been provoked by Adam being selected for the Oxbridge preparation classes at the beginning of their final year in the sixth form (Richard had been left out). Understandably, perhaps, Richard felt jealous that his father's money had helped promote Adam ahead of him academically. Furthermore, the two Dempseys, father and son, had recently had a blazing row when Simon had rewritten his will after a short but worrying illness and told his son that he intended to include Adam as a beneficiary of his estate.

We return to the relationship between Adam and Mr Dempsey again later. Suffice to say, the triangle of Adam, Richard and Simon became increasingly complicated during this period. Richard calling Adam a 'bastard' was not only inexcusable but also, it would appear, technically inaccurate. Again, we shall return to this later. But it is interesting to note that Adam's reflex reaction is to lash out with his fists. It is also revealing that in his letter to Lucy Adam doesn't dwell on

Richard's motives for using this word.

On returning home, Richard apparently remained silent about the cause of his black eye — still bruised three or four days later (Adam must have hit him fairly hard). When pressed by Lucy, he told her he had fallen on an uneven paving stone. Lucy, who doted on Richard as much as she admired Adam, suspected he wasn't telling the truth. She was always the reconciler between the two, the go-between when they fell out. She hated being excluded.

Then, of course, we come to the really interesting development: the apparent haphazard sequence of events and circumstances which led to the conclusion of Adam's letter. Richard, the security officers claimed, put the flag and the other incriminating items of Palestinian paraphernalia in Adam's bag. It appeared to have been a joke to mock him gently for his pro-Arab sensibilities. It was also a peace offering — a manly joke between two particularly masculine friends — to draw a line under the violent argument in Gaza. Adam later found a note from Richard with the sweets. 'Sorry, mate,' it read. 'I shouldn't have said what I did.'

There was no evidence that Richard deliberately placed the items in Adam's bag in an attempt to set him up — although Adam could be forgiven for reaching that conclusion. However, the senior officer's comment to Adam that Richard was upset in the airport about causing him trouble appears to be accurate.

The Adam Carter we see here under light interrogation is in many ways the same Adam Carter we knew almost a decade later in Section D. There is an interesting combination of honesty and distraction, charm and defiance, giving his interrogators just enough to keep them interested. He showed a youthful recklessness, however, in starting to write to Lucy halfway through this process (although, ironically, the discovery of this letter might have let him off the hook with regard to their interest in him. No intelligence agency wants an avid correspondent among its employees.) And the older, wiser Adam would not have been quite so complimentary about Israel. If he really did lay on the flattery as thickly as he claims, it is surprising that neither David nor Ariel smelled a rat. But perhaps they were blind to that. Here was an engaging, intelligent, fiercely combative young man who appeared to have fallen in love with their country while compromising himself in the most secure airport in the world — it was too good an opportunity to pass up.

A quiet word with some of our more trustworthy friends in Tel Aviv has ascertained that Ariel (Orlev) did indeed work for Mossad but in one of its more shadowy branches, which dealt with black ops. Certainly, the methods on display here tally with Mossad's MO: coercion, charm and threats. There is no record, however, of the more senior officer, 'David'.

It's not in any way unusual for intelligence agencies to use blackmail to recruit agents. Agent recruitment relies on MICE: money, ideology, compromise (i.e. blackmail) and ego. The least trustworthy agents are often the ones doing it for their ego. The best — but the most sensitive — are the ideological converts. Money is an incentive but it leads to greed. The blackmailed can sometimes give up altogether, deciding that the risk of exposure is better than the double life they are forced to live.

Adam, clearly, was compromised. But was there also an element of ego there? And ideology – although not in the way his new handlers suspected?

At this stage, no one knew. Adam himself didn't appear to know. There was a definite relish with which he related the tale in his letter to Lucy and Adam's mother believes the two were a couple by this stage, or at least on the verge of being so. Lucy was an exceptionally attractive teenager, perceptive and intelligent, with no shortage of admirers. Adam stood out, not only by virtue of his long-standing association with the family but also because he was so different from the bland types her other friends in the school lacrosse team met. There is no doubt that he wanted to impress her in his letter.

On returning home, however, he appears to have thought better of being so open. He never handed the letter to Lucy but kept it in his room and, much later, passed it on to his mother for safekeeping. We can be grateful it survives for it provides a vividly compelling first-hand account – the only account, as it turned out – of his blackmail in Tel Aviv.

In the event, Lucy's powers of deception did not match Adam's, or even Richard's. On returning from her holiday in the Scottish Highlands – all pre-written postcards duly posted – she was asked at length by her parents and Eleanor about

Adam's whereabouts. She held out long enough — Adam had decided to stay on a few days to visit some friends in Edinburgh etc. — for Richard to get home. But when she saw Richard without Adam she burst into tears and confessed everything to her parents.

Eleanor, apparently, had in any case already guessed that Adam was not on holiday with Lucy in Scotland.

'Call it a mother's intuition,' she said to me with a wry smile. 'That and the fact that I looked up the weather and snow reports and there wasn't any snow that year for him to go skiing as his postcards said.'

When Adam eventually walked in the door at Fleetwood, a full day and a half after Richard, and three days after Lucy, he was met with a huge hug from his mother.

'I thought you'd be livid,' he said, judging, accurately, that she was aware of where he had really been.

'I am,' she said. 'But more than anything else, I'm relieved. Just so relieved. I was so worried. You see, your father…' She trailed off and caught Simon Dempsey's eye. He also knew.

'Darling, you better read this,' said Eleanor, putting a letter into Adam's hands.

'I already have,' said Adam. 'Why else do you think I was so keen to go to Israel?'

There follows a copy of the letter Eleanor handed to Adam, a letter she'd worked on a hundred times with a hundred different drafts, a letter Adam himself had seen on her desk at half-term, before the Christmas trip to Israel, broken into, read disbelievingly, and replaced.

Copy of letter from Eleanor to Adam Carter, Christmas 1990

My darling Adam,

I cannot tell you how many times I have started this letter, only to rip up the pages and throw them in the bin. I first wrote this all down at the time, as it happened, so I wouldn't forget anything. But time has moved on and so has the story and the way in which I want to tell it.

I know that what follows will be upsetting, even harrowing, for you. That is why I've had to write it down. Some of these things should not, could not, be spoken of out loud. But now that you've had your eighteenth birthday, you are a man – a strong, good man – and I feel you should know the truth. Indeed, you need to know the truth for I am scared and need you. Just please, please, remember one thing as you read this. Everything I did, everything I have done, was because I love you and will stop at nothing to protect you. As a girl, I used to hear my own mother talk of a mother's love for her child and it never made any sense. Now I understand. You are the sense of my life. I am very proud of you. Always remember that.

Adam, you will have often have heard me talk of your father. There is no easy way to put this, so I shall have to say it bluntly: the father I have often spoken to you about did not exist. There was no

David Carter as such. We did not meet at university as I described, him with his long hair pulling up on his motorbike outside my halls and taking me to the pictures. We didn't get engaged in Florence, neither was our wedding featured on the front page of the local newspaper. The fatal motorbike accident, when I was six months pregnant, was a fiction too. No promising engineering career was cut short. David Carter did not die, because he never lived. He did not exist.

Why would a mother invent such a callous untruth for her son? The answer is that I wanted to protect you, not only from the truth, which is far worse, but also from your real father who is alive and a very dangerous man.

Let me start at the beginning. Everything else I've told you about my life is true. My parents, both of them teachers in Manchester, married late. He was the headmaster whom everyone had previously taken to be a confirmed bachelor; she was the pretty Head of Music who hadn't yet met the right person. My mother was in her late thirties when she married and they struggled to conceive. I was an only child. My father died – in his mid-seventies – of a stroke when I was halfway through my French A-level exam. My mother died of a broken heart soon afterwards.

Although it was my father's greatest wish that I should follow them into the teaching profession, it wasn't what I really wanted to do. I wanted to be a nurse, or a ballet dancer, or any number of other childishly foolish dreams. But losing one's parents makes you grow up fast. I felt I had a duty of honour to my father in particular. So I applied to do a teacher training course at Homerton in

Cambridge. It was, I believed, what they would have wanted.

Cambridge was fun – this was the mid-sixties – and my
friends and I got up to all manner of mischief. I won't embarrass
you. Children don't want to imagine their parents when they were
young. But you can imagine that I found that the actual teaching
horribly dull after the excitement of university.

Initially, I was posted to a posh school in a leafy suburb of
London where none of the children could be bothered to learn. Many
of them were horribly rude – almost as rude as the rich fathers who
would attempt to flirt with you on parents' day and the silly mothers
who fussed like mad over the slightest sniffle. After a year in this
prison, I moved to a rough, inner-city school where I naively thought
I could 'make a difference'. But the other teachers were old cynics
looking to knock the stuffing out of any idealistic young graduates.
Some of the pupils were fantastic – we got a number into good
universities during my time there – but the majority were
troublesome and uninterested. Any degree of job satisfaction was
cancelled out by the stress of exams and marking and internal
politics, not to mention the daily stress of keeping control in the
classroom for those who did want to learn.

At the end of the summer term of 1971, I handed in my notice
and went to work, pretty much on a whim, in a kibbutz in northern
Israel with a friend called Hannah I'd met at university. She was a
bit older than me and had spent six months working in another
kibbutz during her gap year before coming up to Homerton. She was
also fed up with teaching.

Well, we had the most amazing time during that long, hot

summer holiday – not that it was a holiday of course. Kibbutzim work pretty hard and they like to work their guests even harder still. As newcomers we were given the worst jobs, such as getting up at dawn to collect the eggs and clearing out the pens.

But I didn't mind. It was so different to my staid 1950s upbringing, so different to the boring life I'd fallen into in London, different even to the wilder excesses of university, the selfishness of only living for yourself. That's what I liked about the kibbutz. Goodness knows I'm no communist – neither was anyone in their right mind during the Cold War – but there was something in that small-scale community spirit that appealed to both Hannah and me. We all ate together in the same large canteen, doctors, lawyers and labourers alike. Those on manual shifts changed places every month or so. Everyone took their turn at washing up, cooking and cleaning. The children were educated together in the same kibbutz school.

Much of this has changed now, I'm told. The kibbutzniks who believe themselves responsible for building the modern state of Israel – it is not much of an exaggeration – have become embittered. The ideology has gone. Those working outside the kibbutz want to keep what is theirs. At that time, however, for Hannah and me, it was intoxicating.

All this, of course, you know already. I have often spoken to you about my time in that kibbutz. But I need to repeat it here so you can understand better the context of what followed.

By the end of August, Hannah decided that she didn't want to go back to her job either. One glorious morning, we crammed into a payphone at the end of the road where she rang her headmaster and told him exactly what he could do with his blasted school. The money ran out before he had a chance to say anything. We hurtled out of the phone box, giggling and free, and took a bus for a weekend away in Tel Aviv.

We got very drunk, of course, that Saturday afternoon in a bar near the beach. Israel was, still is, a very open culture in which women are fully emancipated in most walks of life. It is almost inevitable in a society where they, along with the men, are expected to do at least a year's national service after leaving school. The sight of two women having a good time was in no way unusual. We did, however, attract the attention of some men in their thirties. A couple of them – David and Yuri – broke away from their group and came to chat to me and Hannah. They were both good-looking (nearly all Israelis are; it must be something to do with the climate, or the genes, or the years in the army) and very charming. They had known each other since school. David said he 'still worked in the military'. Yuri claimed to be a civil engineer.

Poor Yuri and Hannah had absolutely nothing in common, but they stuck at it gamely, making small talk and polite observations, for the sake of David and me. We hit it off instantly. He was very charming, as I've said – attentive, sure of himself (a little too sure of himself) and intelligent. He was interested in me, too. The four of us moved on to dinner – a place way out of our price range and incredibly exotic to our palates after months of kibbutz food. David and Yuri must have been pretty rich, we concluded excitedly, when they took us on to a private club after dinner. It was as if we were backpackers again, naive, young students, happy-go-lucky and in love with being alive.

David became what you might call my boyfriend. He was based in Tel Aviv although there was no way of getting hold of him there. No work address, no work telephone, no permanent home address even. In the early days, he told me that he was moving flat so there was nowhere we could go. Later, he made up pathetic excuse after pathetic excuse about the boiler being broken or the electricians not wanting to be disturbed. I should have seen through it, of course. But either I didn't or I didn't want to. I thought he was something of a cad with a girl in every kibbutz but at least at the time he was my cad. He was different from anyone I had ever met before. I suppose what I'm trying to say is that I fell in love with him – quickly, naively and, ultimately, dangerously.

I'm sorry. You don't want to hear this sort of thing from your mother. I don't particularly want to share it with my own son. But it's important – vital – that you get the whole picture.

David would often come and visit me at the weekends – in a different car each time, I noticed later – and whisk me away from the kibbutz. It was always a welcome escape. Mucking out chickens seemed exciting and different in July. By September, it had lost any appeal it once held. It was growing colder, too, in the hills of the Galilee. Many of the friends we'd made over the summer had returned to their universities and their jobs. The relationship between me and Hannah had also grown a little cold as we spent too much time in each other's company. I think she was probably jealous of David. He had not been part of her plan. In any case, David and I spent some glorious weekends together – in Netanya, mainly, a fun-loving coastal town, as well as the more cosmopolitan Tel Aviv. I never met any of his friends, or his family. It was just me and him, and that's how I wanted it to be.

But after three or four months, our relationship turned sour. I don't think it was my fault. I never asked anything of him. I never pushed him for commitment, but it was as if he had grown disgusted with me. He became surly and uncommunicative. The charm went and was replaced by something altogether scarier: contempt. I began to suspect he was seeing someone else. One day I confronted him with this suspicion directly. He hit me. Afterwards, he tried to apologise in the only way he knew how – sexually. I refused, of course. He forced himself on me.

The next day I told him I was leaving him. He didn't seem to believe me. You're leaving me? He was incredulous. I said I was leaving him and if he didn't accept it, I would go to the police and tell them what had happened the night before. He just laughed at me. You'll go to the police? And you think that bothers me? The police are scared of me.

I didn't want to know what he meant by that. He never talked about his job, merely alluded to it. I knew it was something to do with the military but that was nothing special in Israel. Everyone was something to do with the military. In a war, they'd all be called upon to fight. Half the country had fired a gun in anger.

That same day, I missed my period. I didn't tell David. I just went back to the kibbutz and said I'd have a think about our relationship and see him the next weekend. I was suddenly terrified of him. I told Hannah everything. We discussed every option. And in the end, she persuaded me that I had to tell David the whole situation. I still couldn't face him, so I rang the number of a friend he'd finally given me as a way of contacting him in emergencies. His friend put me through – God knows how – and I explained what had happened. David erupted. This was all my fault, he shouted, illogically. This would ruin him if the service knew he had a goy (how I hated that word) child. It would have to be terminated. It wasn't my decision to take, it was his, and so on . . .

But somehow, nothing he said mattered any longer. I could hear his words in the receiver, I could hear the outrage in his voice, but none of it really penetrated. It was suddenly clear what I had to do. I had to get away from him, for my sake and for the sake of the new life I now carried. I hung up on David – something I should have done months previously – and made preparations.

Hannah – always good in a crisis – took control. An unkind part of me thought that she had been waiting for this opportunity for months. This was her I-told-you-so moment. But that was an uncharitable thought because I'm not sure I would have made it out of the country alive, were it not for her. Within a few hours of hanging up on David, one of the young kibbutzniks who'd just returned home on leave from military service came bursting into our room and said there had been a full-scale alert put out for someone matching my description at airports, ports and land borders.

'Who have you offended?' asked the young man, Daniel. He had a charming confidence which Hannah liked. He seemed to like Hannah, too.

Hannah rolled her eyes. 'Don't ask.'

'Then it's lucky for you that I can't stand that man,' said Daniel. 'No offence meant.'

'None taken,' I said.

Daniel leant forward and squeezed my shoulder, in a brotherly fashion.

'We kibbutzniks stand and fall together. Don't worry, we'll get you out of this.'

It was the nicest thing anyone had said to me for what seemed a very long time. I felt like I belonged. Why couldn't I just stay there, I wondered, in the kibbutz, among friends who had come to feel like family? What had I done wrong? What was this power David held over me, over the whole country, it seemed? If anything, he should be the one running scared, not me. I hadn't broken any laws.

'Trust me,' said Daniel. 'If you stay here any longer, you'll be dead by nightfall. I know what kind of man David is.'

I just looked at him blankly.

'I'll explain in the car,' he said. 'Come on.'

Daniel reasoned that the airports were far too conspicuous – there would be no room to manoeuvre there and we would be trapped if anything went wrong. You have to remember that the land borders didn't exist as such at this stage. Egypt didn't make peace with Israel until 1979; Jordan not until 1994. Just over a year after the events I've been describing took place, Israel was invaded in a surprise joint attack by Egypt and Syria on the Jewish holiday of Yom Kippur. Five years previously, they had been invaded on three fronts during the Six Day War.

Getting me out of Israel by land over a heavily guarded border would therefore have been complex enough. Surviving on the other side would have been nigh on impossible. I spoke no Arabic, had a Jewish sounding first name, an Israeli stamp in my passport and the sunburned physique of someone who had been working on a kibbutz. If suddenly deposited the other side of the Golan Heights or the Litani River, I would probably have been executed as a not very good Israeli spy. Even if they had smuggled me over the border and I hadn't been caught or questioned, how would I have got home with no proof of how I'd mysteriously arrived in the country?

This left me with the only option of attempting to leave the country by sea. Daniel had a friend in Haifa who knew people among the fishing community. For the right price, he said, they would do anything for you. Daniel, Hannah and I jumped into Daniel's Ford and set off at breakneck speed — even faster than most Israelis drive — for the coast.

'What did you mean by what you said earlier?' I asked Daniel. 'What do you mean by saying, "I know what sort of man he is"?'

Daniel looked me straight in the eye through his rear-view mirror. I couldn't see his lips move, just the intensity of his pupils as he spoke.

'There is an organisation in this country called the Mossad,' he said, his eyes never darting back to a road he was travelling down at over 100mph. 'All countries have their equivalent. The Americans have the CIA, you British MI6, the Russians the KGB, the Syrians the Mukhabarat. The Mossad or, simply, Mossad are similar: they, too, are an intelligence agency that principally operates abroad. Their officers sometimes work under diplomatic immunity as cultural attachés and the like, sometimes not. But Mossad has one crucial difference: they do not play by the rules. Intelligence for them is not "the great game" that your Kipling described. Mossad does not just recruit from the most expensive schools and the best universities. It does not indulge in little games of Cold War hide and seek with outdated code words.

'No, Mossad recruits thugs as well as intellectuals. It has to, for its game play is serious, its mission is survival. We are an island country, an island of democracy surrounded by neighbours who want to destroy us. They don't want merely to fight us, or take a bit more of our land, or our natural resources. They don't want peace conferences and treaties and trade agreements. They want to push us into the sea. They want to destroy us. So, intelligence for us can never be simply the great game, exciting though it is. No, it is about survival. And Mossad will do whatever it takes to ensure the survival of our country. Assassinations, sabotage, defamation. It is all in a day's work. It is fighting on the front line of the Jewish people's ongoing war with the rest of the world.'

'You're saying that David works for these people?' I asked.

'Of course he does,' said Daniel. 'I worked in the intelligence corps in the army for a while. And I've been there long enough to spot them. The arrogance, the coldness, the calculated charm, the unmarked cars, the suits. He's Mossad to a T. A high flyer, too. So if you've crossed him, he will stop at nothing to ensure that you're taken care of. That is the kind of man he is.'

'He is a bully and a coward,' I said. 'That is the kind of man he is.'

We sat in silence for a while. Then I spoke again.

'I understand everything you've said. I sympathise with a lot of it, as you know. Of course you have a right to defend yourself. But I still don't see how I fit into the equation. What am I to David? I'm just another one of his ex girlfriends. I'm hardly a threat.'

'Then you haven't understood everything I've said,' replied Daniel. 'As far as Mossad is concerned, you're either with them or you're against them. If you know anything about this man David, then you're a threat. If you have a grudge – even the potential to have a grudge – against this man David, then you're a threat. And if you have his child – a child that will grow up to know what kind of a man it has for a father – then you're even more of a threat. A threat not just to his career but, as he will try to justify at least, to the country.'

Daniel slowed down a little and swivelled in his seat to face me. 'Eleanor, you're a threat just by being alive.'

There was a roadblock ahead as we neared Haifa. They were fairly routine in Israel but I was still ordered to get into the boot by Daniel and cover myself up.

I could feel the car slow to a crawl and then stop. There was the sound of an electric window being wound down, the radio being turned off and voices speaking Hebrew. Every muscle in my body had tensed up, ready to flee or fight. I caught a few words of the conversation, my understanding hampered by the foul-smelling military blanket over my head and the natural language barrier. The voices rose to shouts — Israelis were always shouting — and then there was a smack on the boot. I thought it was all over. I started to pray, to any god, Jewish, Muslim or Christian. Then the car was moving again, at a slower, more sedate pace. The thump on the boot had been a signal that we could continue.

Still secured away under the blanket, my body bruised from the uneven road surface and Daniel's chaotic driving, we entered the port area. I could smell the fish and hear the sea. Daniel opened the boot and grinned down at me. Hannah, too, stood there, grinning.

'It's not a bloody game,' I said, attempting to stand up.

Hannah started to giggle.

'But it is,' said Daniel. 'And sometimes, it's the best game ever.'

We all collapsed into nervous laughter. The hard part was over. Within an hour I would be stowed away on a fishing boat and en route to Cyprus — Europe. Daniel had more friends there. He was a very well-connected man, it seemed.

'How can I ever thank you?' I said to him.

Daniel smiled and put his arm around Hannah.

'You can leave this one for me as a present.'

'No, seriously. How can I pay you back for everything you've done for me?'

Daniel looked serious.

'Look after that baby,' he said, gently patting my stomach. 'Bring him up well. Teach him that not all Israelis are like his father.'

Adam, that baby was you, that man, Daniel, and his wife

Hannah, are the godparents you've never met, and your father, David, is, as far as I know, still a serving Mossad officer.

[Later]

That, then, darling Adam, is the true and complete story of how you were conceived. I wonder how you will react. Perhaps you will think it very exciting and glamorous. Or you will be livid with me. I can't tell you how scared it makes me to be sharing this with you after all this time. But I must admit that it is also a huge burden off my shoulders, to know that there will be no more secrets between us.

You will want to know why I didn't tell you earlier. But there seemed to be no need. It was a pleasant fiction we lived. When I returned to the UK, things finally seemed to work out OK for me. You know the story: I taught again in a nursery school until you were born (I thought the practice with children would do me good; I had never been very good around children). Sarah Dempsey and I met at pre-natal classes and struck up a friendship. A few years later, she sent Richard to my school. You and he became inseparable, Sarah was often away for work and so I moved into Fleetwood House as a housekeeper cum nanny. The Dempseys have always been very good to us. We were happy.

You were such an outgoing, brave young boy, Adam. Nothing fazed you. Nothing put you off your stride. You'd fall out of trees and split open your head and play football and graze your knees and do all the other Just William pranks that I previously thought only happened in books, but you would always come up smiling the other side. So I never wanted to spoil these moments. You were happy with me and the Dempseys. You were happy imagining that a father you'd never known had loved me and cared for me. So why spoil it? A grotty Israeli kibbutz seemed a very long way away from Fleetwood House.

While I'm being honest with you, I had a huge fear – an obvious fear, I suppose. Now that you know the truth, it might be a fear that you'll share yourself. You see, I worried that you would turn into your father. It was only natural to worry. What would I do if my charming, happy-go-lucky boy turned into a monster? What if the charm turned to manipulation, the warm confidence to cold-hearted arrogance? Occasionally, I'd see glimpses of David in you, but they were only small things – tiny mannerisms, a way of running your hand through your hair. I often wondered whether I had imagined them. After all, I hadn't known him for very long. What little I did know I had attempted to block out. As far as I was concerned, you grew up as my son and no one else's. So I want to reassure you of that. People make their own futures; not genes, not circumstances.

Of course, I always intended to tell you the truth at some point. I discussed it with Simon Dempsey, who knew the facts. He thought sixteen was an appropriate age. Sarah thought I should wait until eighteen (I remember thinking how grown up you were even at thirteen). But every year, I would think of one more reason not to, one more reason to postpone the inevitable date. We felt safe in Fleetwood. Sometimes, I even wondered whether you needed to know at all. I began to believe that your father had made his own assumptions. Maybe he thought I had had an abortion. Or that I'd disappeared. Or perhaps he had simply made a few inquiries and realised that you and I were no real threat to him and had concentrated on his career. Or perhaps we had slipped so successfully under the radar that he had forgotten about us. For all I know, he could have been in similar situations with countless women. I was just small fry.

But then, at the beginning of September this year, some very strange things started happening. When I first arrived home from Israel, I was highly paranoid. I would check my post carefully to see if it had been tampered with. I would try to vary my routine as much as possible so that I didn't leave work at the same time or always drive the same route. Daniel's description of Mossad – I'll never forget those eyes, framed in the rearview mirror – had terrified me, however much I'd tried to pretend the opposite at the time.

This state of nervous tension – I suppose that's what you'd call it – lasted around six months. Then I relaxed and stopped seeing shadowy figures everywhere. Eighteen quiet years, if 'quiet' is the right adjective to describe bringing you up. Then, in September, just after you went back to school for the autumn term, I became paranoid again – and not, I think, without good reason. I saw the same unknown car outside school two days in a row. The bulky men inside definitely weren't picking up nursery school children. On days when I was at Fleetwood, there were strange phone calls which didn't make any sense. Well-educated, well-spoken people would ring up several times per day – sometimes from the same utility company – and ask self-consciously innocuous questions that went well beyond the remit of their jobs. I'm sure I've seen people in the woods around

Fleetwood as well. This is a small community, as you know, and strangers stand out.

Adam, darling, I know that you'll need time to read and digest this. You can take as long as you like. Please remember how much I love you. And please talk to me about everything in your own time.

All my love,

Mum

3
Samuel Joseph

Note from Harry Pearce

Eleanor's account in her letter is full and frank with only a couple of omissions, which became clear while talking to her more recently. For instance, she makes no mention of how or why she gave Adam the surname Carter (her own maiden name is Gordon). It transpires that Carter was a name plucked from the phone book, not, as I had briefly wondered, chosen as a tribute to the thirty-ninth President of the United States, a particularly involved supporter of the Israeli-Palestinian peace process. (President Carter did not become President, in any case, until 1977, five years after Adam was born.) Eleanor changed her name to Carter soon after returning to the UK via Cyprus (a remarkable feat in itself). It was part of the process she describes of disappearing under the radar: a new name; a new life.

This omission aside, this is a lucid and compelling account of events in the year before Adam's birth. Eleanor may express her concerns that Adam might have turned out to display some of the nastier characteristics of his father but we can certainly discern a case of 'like mother, like son'. In fleeing

Israel and standing up to the mysterious David, Eleanor displayed a moral and physical courage which we have come to associate with Adam. She brought him up well.

On re-reading her letter to Adam, it is interesting to note the way it divides into two unequal halves. The first part, the account of her time in Israel, is cogently structured and well written. This will not be evident from the typescript but it was also entirely without crossings-out or revisions. Eleanor really had gone through draft after draft in an attempt to tell the story as she wanted. I will probably not be alone in spotting that she tells it with some relish, complete with dramatic pauses and a thriller writer's turn of phrase, however hackneyed. Perhaps she knew Adam well enough to know that the best way to get him onside was to appeal to his sense of adventure — already well marked at this stage. If she made it exciting enough, she might have reasoned, he would be swept away by the glamour of the unusual circumstances of his conception. But I think there was something else there as well. I think Eleanor really did enjoy the episode at the time. The passage where she, Hannah and Daniel break into nervous laughter is telling. She might have taken refuge in a quiet life since but it was indeed the 'great game' for her at the time. She missed the sense of excitement — she told me so herself. She certainly enjoyed reliving it, whatever her protestations to the contrary.

The second part of the letter, however, is very different in its style. Again, it is not evident from the transcript, but it was riddled with mistakes and corrections and clearly written in a great hurry by someone in a distressed state of mind. Eleanor's paranoia over a sudden burst of interest in her situation appears to have been well founded, as we shall see. What was exciting in her youth had become terrifying in middle age, especially as it was no longer just herself she was protecting.

Clearly, this letter — and the fact that Adam had read it before his trip to Israel (he claimed to have seen the first half lying on his mother's desk in the October half-term) throw open some wider issues.

Firstly, did Adam go to Israel with the intention of tracking down his father? It would appear not, at least according to the story he related to Eleanor when they sat down after Christmas to discuss — at some length, obviously — the contents of her letter. Adam claimed, as he had done in previous letters, that he did not even know himself why he was so keen to join the trip. Partly, it was so he could be with his friends (it certainly had very little to do with his politics A level). Partly, it was because of the letter, although he claims — and this makes sense from a psychological point of view — he didn't really believe its contents until he had it confirmed in person by his mother on his return. It is all very well for outsiders to read this correspondence with the benefit of hindsight and discern what is clearly truthful from what is fabricated. But we have to remember that this concerns an eighteen-year-old boy who was being asked to turn his entire life story on its head. Adam went to Israel out of curiosity, certainly, but until he was challenged on his return, he seemed to believe that the whole thing was some kind of strange make-believe of his mother's, a bizarre fiction to keep herself busy when bored of cleaning Fleetwood House and teaching in the nursery. This was his defence mechanism at least. Eleanor, I don't think we need to be reminded, is not the sort of person to indulge in make-believe.

Also, it should be noted that the letter doesn't actually give many details for Adam to go on, however curious he might have been. Haifa, of course, is mentioned but it is a big city with a large port. It was unlikely that any fisherman would remember a young English woman who had been smuggled out of the country almost nineteen years previously. Similarly, David, Hannah and Daniel are only referred to by their first names. The kibbutz in the Galilee isn't even named. It's not as if Adam could have simply marched into the country and announced he was looking for his long-lost father.

What Adam actually did was a lot more cunning than that.

His first inkling that the letter he had chanced upon might be truthful was the night Richard called him a 'bastard' in Gaza. As I've noted earlier, it appeared strange – at least without further evidence – that Richard chose this particular insult. Richard and Adam certainly called each other a lot of names throughout their friendship (which two young boys don't?) but this particular choice of abuse was telling. Richard did not mean 'bastard' as it is used, inaccurately, in the modern sense of the word. He meant 'bastard' as the word was originally conceived — a person born out of wedlock. Was this intentional?

According to Eleanor — and I have referenced this in passing earlier — Richard had a blazing row with his father during the autumn half-term of 1990 when it was mentioned that Adam was to be included in the Dempsey family will. 'Why can't he get his own bloody family?' Richard had shouted. 'Why do you have to be his surrogate father the whole time, just because his own stupid father died in a road accident?'

David Dempsey was so shocked by the strength of his son's reaction (a large part of which was born of jealousy of Adam's academic achievements) that he told Richard the full story of Adam's background. At the time, he believed Richard was placated, stunned into feeling sympathy for a best friend who had been born into very difficult circumstances. Clearly, though, as events in Gaza reveal, the waters ran rather deeper than that.

The knowledge that Adam had already read his mother's letter puts his reaction to Richard's taunting in a new light. It would certainly explain the instinctive ferocity with which he retaliated.

More importantly, this incident sheds more light on Adam's behaviour at the airport. The accidental discovery of his mother's letter, Richard's insult, which seemed to confirm his suspicions — it all conspired to make Adam feel as if everyone, even his closest friend and his own mother, was holding out on him. It wasn't paranoia as such, more a frustration that he didn't seem to be fully in control. He had became a passive player in his own life.

So when Adam found the Palestinian paraphernalia in his bag – he wasn't stupid enough not to check and pack it himself when about to pass through the most security-conscious airport in the world – he made an active decision to leave it there. It was a calculated risk, of course. And a blind one, too. Would they even bother searching his bag? And how much would they care about its contents? The way he attracted the interest of Mossad was an unlikely stroke of 'luck'. But it was the sort of luck that follows someone like Adam Carter – a charming, intelligent chancer who was always willing to take risks.

This, then, was the situation as it stood at the beginning of 1991. Having read his mother's letter, Adam gave his mother what can only be described as a full and frank account of his trip to Israel, an account that matched the letter he wrote but never gave to Lucy. There was evidently a lot to talk about.

According to Eleanor, she was pleasantly surprised by Adam's reaction to her revelations. The two of them had always been close, but the sharing of secrets – perhaps inevitably – represented the beginning of a new era of openness. Before going back to school at the beginning of January, Adam solemnly vowed that he would tell his mother everything that happened from that moment on. There were practical reasons for this: it was her life as much as his on the line.

We re-join Adam in the first week of the Easter term.

St. Paul's School
London
16th January 1991

Dear Mum,

It feels so strange being back at school. I can't get over how normal everything is - or how normal everything appears, at least. My locker is still there, the teachers haven't changed, my friends are still my friends, the rugby season continues, so do my lessons. I'm not sure what I was expecting, but it's as if nothing in Israel ever happened. It feels like the whole experience was a short, sharp, non-existent nightmare, an illusionary episode that never actually took place. I walk around the school and look at people and feel they must know - Mr Hewson especially, he was there, or Richard or Ben Joseph - but no one seems to care. Of course they all know I was kept behind a bit at check-in, but as far as they're concerned, it was no more exciting than that. Security. Check-in. Delayed flight. End of story. I've had a bit of teasing about it - Adam the security risk, international terrorist etc - and that's it. Ironic, really.

But I really can't stand this waiting around the whole time. I know we've agreed that it's best for me to continue as planned, but there are quite a few moments when I just want to go and talk to someone in the British government about what happened, get it all out and hand it over to them. I'm back safely on British soil now. I'm a student, for God's sake. No one can blackmail me.

But then I think about what you said about my father and I'm sure you're right. The government would just laugh at me. As far as they're concerned, he doesn't exist. We have to smoke him out. So I'll bide my time, just as you (and Ariel) advised, and see what happens. I wonder who my sayan contact will be. I wonder what they'll ask me to do, to prove myself. I wouldn't say I'm becoming paranoid as such, but every time I meet someone with a Jewish name or see someone with Middle Eastern features, I wonder if they're going to approach me with some sort of strange code phrase I've forgotten to memorise.

In the meantime, I've been throwing myself into work. You might have thought that having this strange thing hanging over me would be distracting, but I've found the opposite to be the case. It's given me a new energy to study, so I can be ready for whatever gets thrown at me.

In any event, I've never been busier with school stuff. I've been on to Cambridge to ask if they would be happy for me to swap to Arabic. They've said yes in theory, but they're quite oversubscribed for Arabic at the moment so my offer would be changed from two Es to three As. I know I'm predicted three As – and they would have been pretty

> Adam received an offer to read history at Trinity Hall, Cambridge, during the Christmas holidays, following a successful interview
>
> HP

unhappy with me if I had taken them at their word and turned up with two scraped passes – but it's really going to focus my mind over the next few months. I can't afford to slip up in any subject.

> The standard Oxbridge offer in the 1990s for candidates they liked
>
> HP

You'll be pleased to know that Richard and I have made up – in as far as we needed to make up. He's come round to thinking that Oxbridge isn't the be-all and end-all of life, although I know he originally had his heart set on it as he really wants to be in the Foreign Office and thinks that they only recruit from those two universities. I think he's got an insurance place at Bristol but might reapply next year if he gets good marks and can persuade someone to write him a decent reference. It would be strange to go to a different university to Richard after all this time.

Anyway, we're friends again and things are easier

now that I'm able to talk to him a bit about David. Still, I hate not being able to share the whole story with him. He feels bad that his pranks meant I missed my flight - and caused trouble at home - but as far as he's concerned, there's no more to it than that.

It was good to read in your letter that you think the odd phone calls and trailing have stopped. Maybe it was all just a strange coincidence. Or perhaps they were just performing those checks which enabled Ariel to blackmail me more convincingly at the airport. Maybe this is a sign that we are now going to be left in peace for a while. I have been paying rather closer attention than normal, as you might imagine, in the espionage parts of Mr Hewson's history lessons. Many of these intelligence agencies appear to operate sleepers which they leave alone for years, decades even. It's an insurance policy more than anything else - they know they can call upon them if needed and there's a two-way channel of communication if the sleeper comes across anything - but most of the time there is no need.

As you'll see from the envelope, I've taken the precautions we discussed. Probably unnecessary but better to be safe than sorry, I suppose. I'll write again soon.

Love from Adam

Note from Harry Pearce

Over the Christmas holidays, Adam had discussed with his mother how they would continue communicating by such an insecure method as letter. This was, obviously, before the day of email when it would have been simple to share access to the same web-based email account and write and save unsent draft messages — a method that is almost impossible to intercept.

According to Eleanor, Adam came up with the remarkably astute idea of writing two sets of letters home. In one set, which were sent as irregularly and infrequently as you'd expect from a teenage boy writing home to his mother, the envelopes were correctly labelled and the contents were bland and uncontroversial, mainly limited to sport and requests for pocket money. This set was intended for any hostile elements intercepting the letters. Eleanor wrote similarly predictable, if slightly more frequent, letters back to Adam, checking to see if he was eating properly, studying diligently, washing behind the ears, etc. Eleanor kept, and showed me, a few of these early samples and there is no need to include them in the file.

The other set of letters was posted from a different postbox every time by Adam. This posed a clear test of ingenuity for a young man at a boarding school in a relatively quiet suburb where all the school's external post was collected from the same sorting bay at the same time, but it was a challenge Adam met with customary aplomb. Some were posted on the way to rowing or rugby practice, or on any school trip that took them outside the usual environs. Others were slipped directly into sorting offices and mail vans. Adam even took up a sixth form social services option instead of the Combined Cadet Force which you might, more naturally, have expected him to join, so that he had the option of visiting elderly people around London and posting his letters en route.

Years later, in Section D, we came to view Adam as someone who could be lax with his own security. Assets were 'debriefed' in safe houses which were no longer safe by association. Informants were treated so badly that they could quickly compromise cover stories. Rules were only there to be ridden roughshod over. But aged eighteen, when it came to the safety of his own mother, Adam's amateur tradecraft was faultless. Innately aware that the first rule of espionage is the eleventh commandment — Don't get caught — Adam never courted more risk than he needed to while keeping his mother informed of developments.

Rather ingeniously, Adam bought a large number of generic A4 envelopes and sticky labels from a mail order company and disguised his sensitive letters home as junk mail from a non-existent holiday company, complete with slogans such as, 'Would you like to win a seven night Caribbean cruise?'

To distance his mother even further from the source, these were sent to Sara [sic] Dempsy [sic] at Fleetwode [sic] House. Eleanor, in her role as housekeeper, sorted the Dempseys' post, so always saw anything intended for her before Sarah did. And even if one day she didn't, they reasoned that the envelopes were so self-evidently junk that Sarah would throw it straight in the bin without a second glance. Unless anyone knew the exact scheme, the system was fool-proof. Adam and Eleanor even arranged that certain misspellings of Sarah's name on the envelope would mean different things. If the name and address were all written in lower case, for example, it meant that Adam was writing under duress.

Eleanor, in turn, tried to keep her sensitive letter-writing to an absolute minimum. When necessary, she addressed them to 'Johnny Baxter' – interestingly, an alias that Adam came to use on numerous occasions in Section D – care of the same boarding house at St Paul's. Adam was fortunate to have a fairly gullible housemaster who believed Adam's story that it was the nickname given to him by a girlfriend at a different school. The housemaster appears to have taken the attitude that it was best not to ask.

Of course, the system was not perfect – there is always an element of risk when sensitive information is communicated – but it was remarkably efficient for two amateurs who wanted to keep in touch in a risky environment.

[spooks]

Dear Mum,

It's happened. Contact has been made.

I was just coming off the pitch after a rugby match on Saturday when I caught sight of Ben Joseph's father on the touchline. It was strange to see him there as Ben is completely useless at rugby and has never made any sporting team higher than the fifths. Mr Joseph came over, clapped me on the shoulder and complimented me on the match.

I thanked him and asked, as politely as possible, what he was doing there.

'I'm a governor, remember, Adam,' he said. 'I like to take an interest in the school. And its pupils.'

I looked around. My team mates had slowly sloped off towards the showers and we were left alone. I'd never really got to know Mr Joseph on our Israel trip. He spent a lot of his time, as you might expect, with Mr Hewson. No doubt he didn't want to embarrass Ben by trying to join in too much with his friends. He left us to our own devices a lot of the time and we left him to his. Mr Joseph had plenty of friends in Israel.

'Shall we?' he said, gesturing in the direction of the school.

Mr Joseph is a somewhat bumbling man, with a reddish beard and thinning hair. He was a scientist, I think, before setting up his own business. It is difficult not to suspect that his disarmingly shambolic manner is a front for something more sinister.

'Now, you'll know, of course,' he said, 'that I'm here to talk to you about, you know . . . well, it's very good of you to agree to help us out a bit. You see, ever since nineteen eighty-eight we've been banned from operating in the UK, so it's useful to have loyal people who are entirely unsuspicious, the unusual suspects, if you like, har har . . .'

I'll spare you all the tortuous twists and turns of Mr Joseph's monologue. The crux of his message was that Israeli Intelligence is currently banned from operating in London after failing to warn MI5 of a Palestinian plan to have an Arab cartoonist killed. The cartoonist, who regularly lampooned Yasser Arafat, was shot dead in 1988. Scotland Yard subsequently arrested a Mossad agent who knew about the plot in advance and had failed to warn the British authorities. Thatcher was livid, expelling two Israeli diplomats and limiting Mossad's freedom to work in the UK. The Political Action and Liaison Department of Mossad – which deals with friendly foreign intelligence services such as the Americans and the British – was severely weakened. Apparently, it now only has one full-time Mossad officer working under diplomatic immunity at their embassy in Kensington.

As such, the Collections Department – Mossad's largest operational branch that deals with intelligence-gathering abroad – has turned its attentions instead to recruiting informers, or sayannim, among the British Jewish population. According to Mr Joseph, they have over two thousand active sayannim in the UK, mainly in London, who operate as a support network for any planned operations. A sayan can book a car or an apartment or get a part-time job for visiting Mossad operatives, while remaining beneath the radar. The Jewish community in the UK is close-knit.

However, this tight community also poses the obvious problem that Israel has very little intelligence on what is going on elsewhere. British Jewish sayannim are all very well and good at providing back-up support but they're unlikely, limited as they are by the circles in which they move, to come up with high-grade information on elements hostile to Israel. And that, apparently, is where I come in.

'But that's ridiculous,' I said to Mr Joseph when he eventually came to the point (this was several hours later and we had shifted to a quiet corner of a nearby pub by this stage). 'It's not as if I move in the most exciting circles myself. I'm a middle-class schoolboy about to go to university.'

'But that's exactly it,' cried Mr Joseph, dabbing at the Guinness which had become caught in his beard. 'Have you not lived through the 1980s? People like you are the future of this country. And when you go to university, you'll meet the future threats to this country. And Israel. And the world. Bright, bored, ideologically motivated young men. Second generation immigrants. Lapsed Muslims who thought they would fit in and never did and turned to religious extremism. You'll meet these people – especially now that you're switching to Arabic. You'll befriend them and then you'll tell me, your handler, all about them.

'I've been watching you, Adam. For years now. I know more about you than you can possibly imagine. You've made yourself noticed – and liked – by a lot of people at St. Paul's. You'll go far and, when you get there, we want to make sure that you're one of ours. We like to recruit people young.'

'It's still ridiculous,' I said. 'If these people are a threat, why doesn't the British government take them seriously? Why, in fact, should I be working for the Israelis at all?'

'The British have other priorities,' said Mr Joseph. 'The IRA. The imminent collapse of the Soviet Union and the possible end of the Cold War. The current war in the Gulf. They're completely unprepared for the future. Take a look at MI6, for example. It is stuffed to the rafters with

Russian speakers. Within five years, they will all be obsolete and MI6 will be scrabbling around for Arabists, wondering why they didn't see that the new – and only – threat to world peace will come from a seemingly unstoppable rise in Islamic extremism.

'So I'm not asking you to be a traitor, Adam. Who knows, one day you might work for British Intelligence as well as Mossad. It's not a mutually exclusive arrangement per se. I have British citizenship as well as Israeli. I am a patriot. I love this country. Yet I fear for its future because of its blinkered narrow-mindedness. If this country can't take sound advice from its long-standing allies such as Israel, then others must do its work for it.'

Mr Joseph sat back on the pub bench, evidently convinced by the convincingness of his own case. I was, I must admit, fairly convinced as well. But I wanted to call his bluff. I wanted to see the lengths he would go to in order to support his arguments with action.

'And what if I don't want to do it? What if I'd rather have a quiet life. What if I tell you that none of this has anything to do with me? That I'd rather go to university and have a good time and a quiet life like everyone else?'

Mr Joseph stood up, brushed down his trousers and started putting on his coat.

'It's your life, Adam. Do what you want. There are

others. But I think you know as well as I do that you're not going to say no to this.'

He made as if to walk to the door, then turned, walked back to the table and whispered in my ear.

'I think you know what I'm referring to.'

And that was that. He was gone, out of the door, leaving me bemused at my table, a half-pint in front of me, dried rugby mud still not entirely cleaned from my knees. On the one hand, I felt better about the kind of things I might have to do. They were not asking me to betray or murder or kill. There was no obvious danger in waiting until I got to university and occasionally telling a harmless middle-aged man with a reddish beard about who else I met at the Arabic faculty. Mr Joseph made a convincing case for the practicalities, if not the morality, of the set-up. What are countries these days anyway? Just lines on a map. Arbitrary divisions of customs, language and currency. If one country has seen the future better than another, who is to say that they are wrong by a simple accident of birth? I love my country. Passionately yet soberly. As a Brit should do. But I love it enough to do what is best for it. I love my life, too. And I love you. And if this is what it takes to flush out a potentially dangerous father and to protect the two of us, then so be it.

And yet. And yet ... There is something highly unsettling about Mr Joseph. I've already mentioned the bumbling manner which would be endearing if you didn't wonder about how much lay beneath. You don't get to become as rich or as influential in two separate countries as Mr Joseph without a great deal more nous and cunning than he lets on. Seen in this light, there is something a little calculating about his shambolic nature. The truth, you know, must be anything but.

Then there was the extraordinary way in which he left me. What did he mean by his parting shot? Was it a threat? Against you? Against me? Does he know about my father? Does anyone know about my father? Is this whole situation merely the most unfortunate string of coincidences?

There are so many more questions than answers. I have a feeling they will reveal themselves slowly, if at all.

Love from Adam

St. Paul's School
London
17th February 1991

Dear Mum,

I took the train up to Cambridge yesterday as the Arabic Director of Studies in Trinity Hall wanted to see me before finally accepting me on to his course. He assured me that it was only a formality, not an interview as such — I'd already been accepted by the college for history so this was just a chance to get to know me beforehand – but I was still nervous.

You've told me before how bitterly cold Cambridge can be in the winter but I'd never believed you properly until this visit. I must have hit upon a freakishly warm day when I went for my history interviews in December. Yesterday, the train rolled through the flat Fenlands – I hate flat; give me mountains and hills any day – and it started to snow as we pulled into the station. As I walked into the centre of town, I overheard one student telling another that there are no mountains between them and the Urals. So an easterly wind in Cambridge is pretty much a Siberian wind. Certainly, there was one cyclist ahead of me who seemed to be almost stationary, despite standing on her pedals and battling with all her might to make any progress.

I don't know how well you remember Cambridge from your time there, but I imagine it is the kind of place that stamps itself indelibly on your memory: the colleges, the river, the pubs, the atmosphere. No doubt it has changed slightly, but I'm sure the atmosphere itself stays the same: slightly fusty, self-consciously louche, at least when it's warm enough to be louche. I was early for my interview so darted into the Copper Kettle – that must have been there when you were – for a warming mug of tea. From my vantage point in the window, I watched students meander past, apparently oblivious to their surroundings. Maybe this is what happens after a while. Maybe you get used to walking past a fifteenth-century chapel every morning on the way to lectures, or vomiting in a fourteenth-century quadrangle fountain on your way home at night. I'd like to think not.

Trinity Hall, as you will remember, is one of the smaller, older colleges, tucked away on the river between its larger neighbours, Clare and Trinity, and flanked to the south by Caius. I think one of my teachers once compared it to Switzerland - or was that John's at Oxford - small, smug, old and rich. But that was probably forty years ago. Even in a place like Cambridge, stereotypes change quicker than that.

As I walked through Front Court, past the dining room and down towards the river in search of Dr Mark Roupell, lecturer in Arabic and Middle Eastern studies, and resident of N staircase on Latham Lawn, it was also, I remembered with a sudden thrill of ironic amusement, the college attended by Donald Maclean, one of the infamous 'Cambridge Five' who worked for the Russians in the 1930s.

Maclean had left Cambridge a traitor. Was I arriving as one?

I eventually found the right door at the top of N staircase. Dr Roupell - or Mark as he insisted I called him - is probably what the media would describe as a 'trendy don'. In his late thirties, he looked as if he had been born wearing a designer cardigan. He topped that off with crushed corduroy trousers – the trendy ones, not the beige grandad cloth – black rimmed glasses and slush puppy shoes. It was difficult not to take an instant dislike to him on appearance alone.

He gesticulated to the sofa and took his place on the worn armchair opposite, self-consciously crossing his legs and tucking his hands underneath his right knee. We sized each other up.

'As salamu alaykum, ya Adam.'

'Wa alaykum as salam, ya doktoor Roupell.'

'Ismi Mark.'

Was this going to be one of those interviews you read about in the newspapers where the candidate is thrown a rugby ball and has to catch it and throw it back in order to get a scholarship? Would I be asked to surprise him and reach for a lighter in my pocket and set fire to his newspaper? Would he tell me to throw a brick out of the window, requiring me to show sufficient presence of mind to open the window first, instead of smashing it?

Dr Roupell laughed, a light, tinkling, annoying sound that made you want to find a brick and smash it in his face.

'Very good, Adam. Very good. No flies on you. And don't worry, this isn't one of those mythical interviews you hear about where I ask you to do strange things. In fact, as I said in my letter, it's not even an interview at all. I just wanted to meet you and see if you really did speak a smattering of Arabic as you claimed. You wouldn't believe the amount of rubbish people write on their application forms.'

I slowly began to warm to the man. Perhaps there were worse crimes than being a trendy don. We talked about my trip to Israel and a little bit about the Gulf War. What were the coalition's true objectives in the region? Was it about Kuwait? Or disarming Saddam? Removing him, even? Were they motivated by oil? Or by a commitment to protect Israel? It was all fairly easy knockabout stuff. I'd read The Times every day for the last two months. There's little that's going on in the world that's not covered by The Times over a two-month period. It allows you to speak authoritatively on subjects you know next to nothing about, appropriating the carefully considered views of distinguished columnists as your own and marshalling the facts that someone else has gone out to gather. I'd also read a children's book on the history of the Middle East which gave a better overview of the region than anything else I'd seen.

When it came to Arabic itself, however, Dr Roupell's questioning became a lot more aggressive. Ostensibly, it might not have been an interview, but it certainly felt like one.

'Are you only changing to Arabic because you think it would be easier to get in?'

'Obviously not. I've already got a place and you've just made my offer a lot more difficult.'

'Won't you find learning a language a bit boring? Vocabulary tests, grammar rules, letters to non-existent pen friends in Cairo?'

'There's more to a language than vocab and grammar. There's literature, the culture, the religion, not to mention the opportunities to travel and meet new people. But if you're asking whether I have the dedication and presence of mind to apply myself to learning a difficult language, then my answer, obviously, is yes.'

'Won't you miss history?'

'I think history will probably carry on without me. I will still read history.'

'No, you won't. Be honest with me. Everyone says that, but you won't read anything outside your subject.'

'OK, I won't read history in my spare time. But there's a history module in Arabic, isn't there? I'll learn Arab history, which is more interesting than Western history in any case.'

Dr Roupell leant back in his chair, evidently still a little bit sceptical. Then he leant forward again.

'Adam, what do you want to do when you leave here?'

'Leave here? I haven't even arrived here yet.'

Dr Roupell smiled. 'Still. Do you have any idea what you might like to do as a career?'

I looked him straight in the eye. There was something

there which suggested it might be worth trying a blunt joke on him.

'I suppose I'll just have to wait until my final year when you tap me on the shoulder, invite me for tea and ask if I might be interested in a "specialised career that deals with foreign affairs".'

Dr Roupell looked momentarily shocked. Perhaps I'd gone too far. We'd been getting on quite well and now I'd pushed the boundaries. Then his features relaxed and he gave a little chuckle.

'Very good, Adam. Very good. We'll see, shall we? In any case, I'll look forward to seeing you in October. Ma salami.'

'Ma salami, ya doktoor Roupell.'

And that was pretty much that. Dr Roupell showed me to the door and I spent the rest of the afternoon – school had given me the whole day off – wandering around Cambridge. Well, I say wandering, but that implies a meandering pace, when in reality I had to march pretty bloody quickly to stay warm. It was also necessary – purely for practical reasons of survival, you understand – to visit most of the pubs between Trinity Hall and Peterhouse, and then a few the other side of the river as well, en route to have a look around the Arabic faculty.

I think I'm going to enjoy Cambridge.

Love from Adam

St. Paul's School
London
19th February 1991

Dear Mum,

I'm writing again so soon – it's turning out to be a bumper week for Caribbean holiday offers – because I wanted to update you on what happened after returning to school from Cambridge.

Mr Joseph is taking his gubernatorial duties very seriously, having acquired a previously unexplored taste for watching rugby matches. He came to the away match this afternoon and managed a few quick words afterwards.

'I hear it went well with Roupell,' he said.

'You know Roupell?'

'I know people who know Roupell. Roupell is the MI6 recruiter in Trinity Hall.'

'No shit. The Arabic tutor in a Cambridge college is the MI6 recruiter. I would never have guessed that.'

'Don't get smart with me, Adam.'

Anyway, I reassured Mr Joseph that I had done nothing to offend Roupell and pointed out that we had even struck up something of a bond.

'Good,' he said. 'Excellent, in fact. Now, so far we haven't mentioned payment of any sort. We don't expect you to do this for free, of course. So here's a little lump sum to tide you over. Go and have fun. Or save it up for university.'

Mr Joseph reached into his pocket and pulled out the largest wad of banknotes I've ever seen. Most were twenties, a few were tens and there was even the occasional fifty, all in non-sequential numbers. The total came to £1,000. From blackmail to bribery. Mossad certainly knows how to look after you.

I'm going to bring it home at half-term for safe keeping. And I think you should treat yourself to something. You never treat yourself to anything at all. At least something good can come out of this whole unpleasant business.

After he had handed over the notes, Mr Joseph said that they wouldn't be needing me again until after I'd finished my A levels. This sum of money was simply 'a little golden handshake, if you will'.

'You're not much use to us if you fail your exams and don't get into university,' said Mr Joseph by way of conclusion. 'So we'll leave you in peace for a while. Don't mess your exams up. And don't mess anything else up either, for we'll know about it.'

And with this cryptic, vaguely threatening, parting shot, he walked off in the direction of his car, probably relieved that the next sporting fixture he'd be obliged to attend would be a more congenial cricket match, in the warmer summer months after the end of exams.

Love from Adam

Note from Harry Pearce

Samuel Joseph was as good as his word, leaving Adam in peace for the rest of the Easter and most of the summer term. Adam also kept his side of the bargain by securing three As at A level, including a certificate of excellence in history for coming in the top three in the board. Judging from his school reports, it was a level of academic excellence achieved without too much exertion on his part. Adam was always — especially at this stage — a very last-minute sort of person. Faith in his own innate abilities gave him sufficient confidence to rely on last-minute cramming.

On reading these letters home to his mother, we can also discern a more general, rising confidence in his own abilities. Here is Adam playing devil's poker with the representative of one of the world's most feared intelligence agencies and seemingly relishing the challenge. The tone of some of the letters is potentially worrying when you stop and imagine the anguish that Eleanor must have been suffering, both on her own behalf and on Adam's. But from talking to her, she appears to have been happy that Adam was facing the challenges with his head held high. His confidence appears to have rubbed off on her. The suspicious activity around Fleetwood House hadn't returned. If anything, she assured me, she was somewhat jealous that Adam was having all the fun and there was nothing active she could do to contribute.

Adam kept his promise to hand over the money to his mother at half-term. Eleanor, however, pointed out that if he was serious about his offer to pay back Simon Dempsey for his school fee investment, this was not such a bad way to go about it. He would also have to fund his way through university in some way or other. The government was more generous with grants in those days but it was still fairly difficult to live on a grant alone. Some survived by working in bars in the evening or in every available holiday slot. Adam, it would appear, could get by freelancing for a Mossad that controlled him with a combination of mail and bribery. It was a novel approach to student financing, to say the least.

The letter-writing went quiet for a while as there was nothing to report during the exam period. The day Adam finished, he emerged from the examination hall to find Richard, who had finished the day before, waiting with a bottle of cheap champagne. The two of them were planning on spending the rest of the day in various pubs across London, joined by Lucy and some of her friends in the evening. (Eleanor doesn't have any of Adam's letters to Lucy during this period – or at least she claims not to have any of them. Personally, I think it is more likely that the relationship between Lucy and Adam had developed and she was reluctant to share these private letters with me. She also claims they have no bearing on the case of Adam in hand.)

However, Adam's celebratory plans were interrupted by Samuel Joseph who appeared outside the examination hall just after Richard had popped the cork on the first bottle of champagne. From conversations with Eleanor and an examination of his letters — which, in this case, need not be transcribed in full — the exchange appeared to go something like this:

'Congratulations,' said Joseph. 'I hope they went well.'

Adam looked at him warily. This was really not the moment to be congratulated by his handler. He wanted to go and get drunk with his best friend and his girlfriend. The freedom he had written about, longingly, in earlier letters to Lucy was tantalisingly close. And now this. He said as much to Joseph.

'I'd just like a quick word if that's OK,' said Joseph, choosing to ignore Adam's tone.

'In trouble with the big cheese, are we?' said Richard, laughing. 'They can't expel you now. You've finished.'

Richard, of course, had no idea just how big a 'cheese' Joseph was. Or how much trouble he could potentially get Adam into. Adam told Richard to go and wait for him in the pub. He would catch him up in a moment. He turned angrily to Joseph.

'Calm down, Adam,' said Joseph. 'I just want to talk to you about a little employment opportunity we've arranged for you in the summer holidays.'

At this point, Adam appears to have lost it with Joseph, pushing him up against a wall out of sight of his peers, raising a fist to his face and saying something along the lines of, 'You can stick your fucking "employment opportunity" up your fucking arse and you can fucking well leave me alone. I've just finished my fucking exams.'

Joseph, as Adam has hinted in his descriptions, is a

physically slight man. Faced with a raised fist from a tall, strong, young man, he quickly backed down.

'Fine, Adam, fine. Have it your way. We'll speak tomorrow. Here, go and have fun.'

Joseph handed Adam a ten-pound note, released himself from Adam's grip and disappeared from sight. Adam went out to celebrate. The next day, he got a call from his mother to say that their family dog had died, apparently run over. For a dog that never went as far as the road — Fleetwood House and its estate were so vast that there was no need — it seemed a curiously suspicious incident. Adam, who felt guilty that it was a punishment for him losing his cool, didn't mention the incident outside the examination halls until years later. But Eleanor had always suspected that there was more to it than met the eye.

Joseph never brought up the subject with Adam again. The message, however, was clear: you play by our rules or not at all. Cross us and we'll cross you back. Harder. And where it hurts. Killing a family dog might have been a relatively trivial matter, but it pointed to a wider, stronger power play: we know where you live and where your loved ones live and we have the capability and the willingness to harm them.

The incident marked something of a turning point in Adam's attitude. As we can discern from certain extracts in his letters at the beginning of 1991, he initially appeared to thrive on the novelty and the sense of excitement. But from this moment on, it was no longer a game to be played. He had left school and was about to join a world that was, if not exactly real, then at least extremely scary.

We rejoin his correspondence in the summer holidays during which he had sensibly accepted Joseph's offer of a 'little employment opportunity'.

London
3rd August 1991

Dear Mum,

Well, as I mentioned while home at the beginning of the holidays, Mr Joseph has got me a summer job working on the Daily Mirror. I thought he was joking when he first said it. Why would I want to go and be a journo hack? What possible use would that be to anyone? And surely I'd stick out like a sore thumb at a tabloid newspaper.

'That's exactly the point,' said Mr Joseph. 'Look upon this as a little test to see if you have any aptitude for espionage. If my hunch is right, you'll pass with flying colours.'

Mr Joseph's point is that spying and journalism aren't so very different. You have sources. You have to gain people's trust in unfamiliar circumstances. You have to persuade them to speak. You have to find out stuff about them. And often you have to betray them. At its most extreme, investigative, undercover reporting is exactly the same as spying under deep cover. Except that the reporter is ultimately looking to blow the story up as widely and sensationally as possible, while the spy has a number of different options available as to how he actually deploys the intelligence.

That was the spiel, in any case. The reality so far has been a little different. August is traditionally referred to as the 'silly season'. Parliament is in recess, the city bankers are all on holiday in Tuscany, as are newspaper executives and most of the senior journalists, leaving their juniors and work experience bods like me with next to nothing to write about.

So, what do we do? In age-old journalism tradition, we make it up. Well, not entirely. Most of what we write is based on truth, but you have to look pretty closely among the sensationalism to find that truth. So far this week, we've had full-scale investigations into a 'Killer swarm of British mosquitoes' and 'Scientists report amazing discovery' - that John Major's face can be drawn by playing join-the-dots with the stars. We are currently locked in something of a circulation war with our main rival which has led to both papers scraping the bottom of the barrel in a bid to secure new readers.

I'm not sure the other hacks think a great deal of me either. I can't blame them, really. Work experience kids are two a penny (if only they did pay us that much) and probably cause more trouble than they're worth. Also, the

Mirror is a crusading, left-wing tabloid which doesn't think a great deal of what the Thatcher government got up to over the last decade. A wet-behind-the-ears public schoolboy en route to Cambridge is probably the last person they wanted to have around here. They've all been to the school of hard knocks. I've been to the

Who does?

HP

school of St. Paul's. 'Daddy got you a job here, did he?' said the news editor on my first day, perhaps more perceptively than he realised. (Now that really would have been a story if I felt like sharing it.) 'Why don't you piss off and get a job in the City instead like the rest of your chums?'

It was not the friendliest of welcomes and the first week didn't get much better. The news editor – a particularly vicious sod called Rob Helen – has conspired to make my life as difficult as possible. I've been dispatched on the most spurious non-stories which mainly involve pestering innocent members of the public who should have been left well alone. When I am allowed in the office, Helen delights in bullying me in the most playground and childish manner conceivable. On one occasion, I was made to stand on my desk while he told everyone what I was doing there, which school I had gone to and which

107

university I was bound for. His favourite trick was to ask me to get him a cup of tea which he'd then pour on my trousers. 'Oh dear, Carter,' he'd say. 'I appear to have spilled it. Better get me another one.'

On the third day, I decided I'd had enough – it's difficult to know how to conduct yourself in a new office as the new boy, but if this was office life, I didn't want it – and confronted him. 'Rob,' I said. 'You're a silly twat with a silly girl's name for a surname. Now either give me something useful to do or I'll take my £3 per week travel allowance and go somewhere else.'

Helen seems to like someone who stands up for himself. He smiled, clapped me on the back and demoted me to data entry for the sports results pages. Maybe standing up for yourself is overrated.

Helen aside, the Mirror is not a happy ship at the moment. The rumour is that Robert Maxwell, the owner, is in all sorts of financial trouble and that the paper could even go under. 'Jump while you can' is the favourite mantra of James Martinson, the deputy editor, as he stomps around the newsroom. 'We're all doomed.' And then he likes to walk from desk to desk, counting them off triumphantly on his fingers. 'News desk, doomed. Sport, doomed. Business, doomed. Features, fucked beyond belief.'

The most notorious personality here, though, is a guy called Alastair Campbell, the political editor. Fortunately, we don't get to see much of him as he's in Westminster most of the time. He's got a fiery temper and is not one to cross, by all accounts, especially if you've got a bad word to say about Maxwell.

Maxwell – a Czech-born Jew – is an interesting one. According to Mr Joseph, he is a 'huge asset to Israel', although he was deliberately vague about what he meant by that. Certainly, there is a rumour that, in 1986, the *Sunday Mirror* was approached with the inside story of Israel's Dimona secret nuclear weapons facility by an Israeli, Mordecai Vanunu, who had worked there. Instead of printing it – and securing the scoop of the decade – Maxwell dobbed Vanunu in to the Israeli authorities in London. Vanunu was lured by a honey-trap, arrested by the Israelis and sentenced to solitary confinement. The *Sunday Times* got the story instead.

You wouldn't have thought that such behaviour – loyalty to a foreign power over and above journalistic integrity – would endear Maxwell to his employees very much.

> He remained in solitary for the best part of two decades
>
> HP

My hunch is that Mr Joseph managed to get me a job here – as a test combined with some sort of bizarre training programme – because Robert Maxwell, too, is a Mossad informer. That strange suspicion aside, I cannot see what benefit my kettle duties are to anyone, even if I have learned how to adapt in a hostile environment, spike Helen's tea with laxatives and drink beer and swear with the best of them.

Love from Adam

Note from Harry Pearce

Whether or not the newspaper tycoon Robert Maxwell worked for the Israeli secret service Mossad is one of the enduringly fascinating questions of international espionage – enduringly fascinating to both the media and the British Intelligence community alike, for the honest answer is that we simply don't know.

Robert Maxwell died in the early hours of 5 November 1991, a few months after Adam was working at one of the newspaper titles he owned, in the seas near the Canary Islands. Did he have a heart attack? Did he jump? Or was he pushed? Three separate autopsies were all inconclusive.

On the one hand, Maxwell was sixty-eight, weighed twenty-two stone, suffered from a weak heart and lungs and was generally in poor health. It is not unlikely that the time had come for someone in that condition.

The suicide theorists point to the fact that he had plundered his own company's pension fund to prop up his finances. The *Financial Times*, among other media outlets, were on to him. Bankers were rapidly selling shares in his companies.

Most lurid are the conspiracy theorists who believe he was assassinated in some way. One accusation is that Maxwell held damaging files linking the murder of Georgi Markov in London in 1978 to MI6. MI6, fearing that he was about to publish these in the *Mirror*, tracked him down and had him killed. This theory, at least, can be discounted. There is nothing in MI6's files to suggest any such operation.

More intriguing is the notion that Maxwell was assassinated by a Mossad *kidon* unit. There are a number of books which allege this although their evidence is shaky, to say the least. The allegation is that Maxwell, a Mossad informer and Mr Fix-it, was desperate for cash to prop up his ailing businesses and attempted to blackmail Mossad into helping him out. Fearful that he was about to print their secrets, they had him silenced.

It's an entertainingly ridiculous notion, but it doesn't tally with Mossad's normal *modus operandi*. Maxwell might well have worked for Mossad — we are certainly convinced that he did on an informal basis, as you might have expected from such a high-profile Jewish supporter of Israel — but it is highly unlikely that he was also assassinated by his one-time employer. The Israeli government gave him the next best thing to a state funeral, with President Chaim Herzog, Yitzhak Shamir, Ariel Sharon and Shimon Peres all in attendance at his graveside on the Mount of Olives. Herzog said of him that 'he scaled the heights. Kings and barons besieged his doorstep. He was a figure of almost mythological stature. An actor on the world stage, bestriding the globe, as Shakespeare says, like a colossus.'

A recipient of such hyperbole does not appear a likely target of an assassination attempt. Not for the first or last time — *viz*. the widespread belief in the Arab world that the 9/11 attacks were orchestrated by the Israelis — Mossad has been afforded more credit than it was due in the eventful life and death of Robert Maxwell.

London

10th September 1991

Dear Mum,

I'm not sure you can get hold of a copy of the *Daily Mirror* within a twenty-minute drive of Fleetwood House so it is unlikely you saw Monday's edition this week. I'm enclosing pages 1-5 of that edition. I thought you might be interested in the true story behind it.

It all started just after I finished writing the last letter to you. Helen called me into his office and said that if I was going to be 'loitering around like a posh git' I might as well put my education to some use for the paper. What did he mean by that? A Latin column for the *Mirror*?

'Don't get smart with me, Carter. I don't like you. But my boss seems to, so we've come up with something which might suit you. You should know that I was completely against it, as I'm sure you're going to mess it all up, but let's see what happens.'

After fifteen minutes of this morale-boosting pep chat, Helen disappeared into morning conference without actually revealing what his plan was.

As the lowest of the low, I'm never normally allowed to attend conference. They huddle in the editor's office – the one nearest the window of course – and have serious debates over the weighty issues of the day: which pop star is cheating on who; what their editorial line should be on a footballer's wife's breast implants. And so on. While they're in there, the rest of us can do as we please. Then they finally emerge to hand down the orders from on high – 'The ed's particularly keen this week on star constellations that resemble John Major's face' – and we underlings all scuttle around looking suitably impressed and fearful to do our masters' bidding.

However, this particular morning – about four weeks ago – Helen stuck his ugly face out of the office and yelled, 'Carter, get in here. Here's your moment.'

I walked into a room of twenty or so middle-aged executives.

'This is Adam Carter,' said Helen, sneeringly, by way of introduction. 'A bright young thing.'

The middle-aged executives eyed me warily.

'How would you fancy a spot of undercover work?' said Helen.

'I'd like that very much,' I said.

'Excellent. It's high time we pulled off an investigative scoop for our readers. We've been a bit short of them lately. And as you know, security is all the rage. So we'd like to see how easy it would be for someone like you to infiltrate a high-profile target in the capital. You've got a choice: Buckingham Palace or Downing Street.'

'It would have to be Downing Street,' I said.

'Quick as a flash, Carter. Why not Buckingham Palace?'

'Well, it's been done before, hasn't it? Michael Flangan, wasn't it? Got into the Queen's bedroom in 1982. Not exactly a journalist, I know, but I think it would be more topical to go for Downing Street. Plus I think it would appeal more to the Mirror's left-wing target audience to have a pop at John Major's lackadaisical security than having yet another go at the royal family. As you will remember, there was also an IRA mortar attack on Downing Street earlier this year, raising obvious concerns about the degree of security protecting the Prime Minister and the cabinet.'

Actually Michael Fagan, a 31-year-old unemployed Irish father of four

HP

Did I imagine it or did Helen look momentarily impressed?

'Good, Carter, good. Well, don't just stand there. Go and start your research.'

Just as I turned to leave the office, I heard another, deeper voice behind me. It was Alastair Campbell: 'Just make sure you get a picture of Major with his bloody shirt tucked into his y-fronts.'

What a strange man.

My remit was to see how easy it would be to get a menial job in Downing Street. Once inside, I would also act as a lookout and liaison man for a second reporter – a former military man called Jeremy Lyell - who would attempt to break into Downing Street through the gardens at the back. The idea was to show that Downing Street is uniquely vulnerable to both attack and infiltration, especially in comparison to the residences of other world leaders. The contrast with the United States is particularly instructive. The White House might have an address - 1600 Pennsylvania Avenue - but it's pretty difficult to get close to it. Downing Street, on the other hand, doesn't even have gates. It's not a normal street, but it could easily be mistaken for one. Certainly, a tourist walking down Whitehall could be forgiven for not believing that the most powerful person in Britain lived at Number Ten.

The initial process was childishly simple. I signed on to a temping agency, submitted a convincing CV, complete with false references, and had an interview at Number Ten within three days. They've been very short of well-presented young tea boys recently, apparently.

My interview was conducted by a terrifying, matronly woman called Genevieve - she did not appear to have a surname - who later turned out to be my boss as well. My job would be very basic and entirely suited to a school leaver in need of some extra pocket money, according to Genevieve. In the mornings, I would be expected to be in Downing Street by 7 a.m. in time to take John Major his morning cup of tea and porridge (without sugar). The day would then be taken up with cleaning, polishing, brewing, wiping, mopping, etc. Biscuits were to be arranged in a clockwise fan on the specially branded plates and wheeled into cabinet meetings within five minutes of them starting. Any later than that and an irate, hungry Prime Minister would press the nuclear red button. Armageddon would ensue and, far worse, I would be sacked.

In the afternoon, the Prime Minister liked to have at least three cups of tea, spread at fairly regular intervals. If his door was open, I could just walk straight in and put down the tray. No one stood on ceremony in Downing Street. Mrs Major had quickly grown used to the sight of her husband being briefed in their marital bedroom, both in the morning and the evening. If, however, the door to Mr Major's study had only been left ajar, I should knock twice, pause, knock twice again, wait for an acknowledgement from within and then proceed into the room. If, on the other hand, the door was entirely shut, under no circumstances was I to attempt entry. The tea could wait until later.

In the late afternoon, I would have a break of at least, but no more than, fifteen minutes, during which I was not to leave the staffroom. Duties in the evening would obviously depend on the prime ministerial schedule. Often, he would be expected to attend some function or other outside Downing Street. On other evenings, they would entertain guests at home and I would be enrolled as an additional waiter. On the rare occasions that they had neither external nor internal duties to attend to, I could have the evening off.

Did I have any questions? No?

'Excellent, Mr Baxter, you can start on Monday.'

The routine proved to be every bit as predictable, although somewhat less tedious, as Genevieve described. It was August, Parliament was in recess and most MPs, along with newspaper owners, had already absconded to Tuscany. John Major, however, was as hard-working and conscientious as you'd imagine. He was also a very charming man and far less grey and bland than his public image would have you believe.

On my first Monday morning, I walked somewhat nervously - not only was I undercover, I was undercover in Downing Street - into his office for the first time. Major was scribbling away on something or other, his impressively red phone arranged on the desk in front of him.

'Hello, Tom,' he said, his eyes never lifting from the document-scanning. 'Thanks very much for that.' I must have hesitated a moment longer than usual for Major looked up from his scribblings and caught sight of the new boy. He put down his pen, jumped to his feet and proffered a right hand.

'I'm so sorry,' he said, smiling engagingly. 'I had

forgotten that Tom was moving on and being replaced. I wouldn't like you to think that I don't take an interest in what goes on around me. My name is John Major. What's yours?'

'Johnny Baxter,' I stuttered. 'It's a pleasure to serve you, sir.'

'Nonsense, Johnny. I'd wager you've never done anything less pleasurable in your life.' Major laughed. I looked him in the eye – there was humour there, humanity too – and smiled.

'What about you, Prime Minister?' I asked. 'Have you ever done anything less pleasurable in your life?'

Major laughed again, louder this time. 'You know, I think you've pretty much hit the nail on the head there, Johnny.' He gesticulated at the room around him and picked up the papers on his desk, letting them fall through his fingers. 'Yep, nail on the head. It's August, the sun is shining outside and I'm sitting here wading through this crap. And where are my cabinet colleagues, you might ask? Ably and honourably helping me in the noble and difficult task of running the country? No. They're all on holiday. Do you know what they are, Johnny? Bastards. Absolute bastards. The lot of them. In it for themselves. Bastards.' Major slumped back down in his chair, seemingly defeated by the invisible bastards. 'You won't tell anyone I said that, will you, Johnny? It was probably a little indiscreet of me.'

I assured him that his secrets were safe with me.

'Good, Johnny. Good. You have a trustworthy face. I think we'll get along very well in our teatime chats.'

As I closed the door to the Prime Minister's study, I've rarely felt so guilty in my life. This article was going to be like kicking a puppy. He was a nice man. His privacy was invaded enough as it was. Why did we have to make everything worse? I rang Helen and told him my concerns, but he was having none of it. 'This is fucking gold dust, Carter. You're on the inside, you've got his trust and he's leaking like the *Titanic*. Lyell is in place, you're in place, everything is in place. This is going to be the scoop of the century. Don't go soft on me now, Adam, just as you're finally becoming some use.'

If I'd hoped the situation was going to get any easier, I was wrong. By the end of my second week in Downing Street, I appeared to have become John Major's best friend. Maybe he was lonely. Maybe he genuinely liked me. Certainly, I genuinely liked him. He was witty, self-deprecating and good company. Helen was right: I was sitting on a tabloid gold mine. Much of what I heard was merely scurrilous tittle-tattle but some of what I discovered would genuinely endanger the security, not only of the Prime Minister, but of the country itself. Could I really let this be published? Could I trust it in Helen's hands? Feeling deeply uncomfortable, I decided to ring Mr Joseph. Most of all, I needed a way out. Perhaps he was the man to provide it.

Mr Joseph was delighted to hear from me. 'Adam, congratulations,' he said. 'My sources tell me you're doing the most amazing job. Bob himself is delighted. You're a natural undercover – not that I ever doubted it, of course.'

I started to shout at him. 'If this is your idea of a test or some sort of bizarre training role play, then you're more fucked up than I thought. I'm not doing this a moment longer –'

'Adam,' interrupted Mr Joseph very quietly. 'I don't think you need to be reminded of the consequences of speaking your mind too openly.'

I stopped shouting at him.

'Good, Adam. Now, be a good boy and do as you've been told.'

Over the next three weeks, I was a model undercover tabloid journalist. I made friends with everyone from the Prime Minister down to the postroom boys. I listened carefully, took notes in private and prepared myself to betray them all. Having noticed that mid-afternoon was the most likely time to find Major at his most chatty, I started hiding a Dictaphone in my trousers when I took Major his afternoon tea. According to Helen, this was very important. If the government attempted to sue following publication – which they almost certainly would – we would

require as much proof as possible of the allegations we'd
printed. By the end of the third week, I had so much
material that Helen could have pulled me out there
and then and run the story as it stood. His greedy and
costly error – and my saving grace – was to attempt
the double whammy with Jeremy Lyell performing his
commando infiltration of Downing Street by the
back wall.

'It's all very well getting you into Downing Street
as a tea jockey, Carter,' said Helen. 'Any old monkey could
do that. What our readers really want is a bit of
excitement, a bit of glamour, a bit of adventure. Jeremy
will give that to them.'

Fine, I thought, hanging up the phone. If that's
the way Helen wants to play it, I can bloody well give it
to him as well. Ironically, Lyell's infiltration would be
my escape route. My job on the evening he attempted to
scale the walls was twofold. On the one hand, I was
expected to act as lookout duty, informing Lyell by means
of two-way radio when it was safe to hide, jump or make a
run for it. I would also act as official photographer,
capturing the precise moment at which Lyell impregnated
the supposed fortress security of Downing Street. Somehow,
I had to get ourselves found out.

This was not my game, the rules had not been drawn
up by me, but there was no one saying that I could not
rewrite the rules a little.

The trick, of course would be doing this in such a way that Lyell suspected nothing. It would not be easy. He was, as I have said, a former military man. Any blatant attempt to attract attention would be swiftly noted. I didn't like the idea of getting a former military man into trouble. On the other hand, I rather felt that former military men should find better use for their talents than breaking into Downing Street's gardens on behalf of tabloid newspapers.

The most convincing ruse I could devise was to feign a misunderstanding concerning the radio frequencies. I had already met Lyell briefly before starting my job in Downing Street. At the meeting, we had agreed to set our radios to 66 Khz. In emergencies, we would use, in descending order of preference, 58 Khz, 74 Khz and 68 Khz.

During my month in Downing Street, I inevitably made friends with some of the security guys, as well as people in the communications room. One of them told me, perhaps somewhat indiscreetly, about the way the security team communicated with each other. As you might imagine, they had their own secure frequencies, which changed on a weekly basis. This, I was pretty sure, was something Lyell did not know. When I first met him, he told me that our frequencies were selected on the basis that they were the least likely to be used by professionals. The reasoning behind having so many alternatives was that

these amateur frequencies were the most prone to weak
and fluctuating signals. It was therefore thought very
unlikely that they would be monitored. All I had to do
was to make sure Lyell switched to the official frequency
at the most opportune moment and make the mistake look
as innocent as possible.

I was lucky in that the chosen night was far from
ideal for Lyell. The daytime weather had been warm and
balmy, the night itself was starry and clear and Major
decided to hold an impromptu garden party. Although I
had known nothing about this last-minute change of
plan, it had the advantage of giving me the perfect excuse
to be in the garden, performing my loyal duties as a
waiter.

As expected, my radio fizzled into life on frequency
66 Khz at 10:45 p.m.

'Lima, this is Bravo, over.'

'Reading you, Bravo. Just. But what the fuck is all
that noise in the garden? Over.'

'You're going to have to wait. There is a party going
on. Over.'

'I'm not sure I copied that, Bravo. Please confirm
message as heard: get skates on and ignore party? Over.'

'Lima, that is not the message. Repeat, that is not
the message. Over.'

By this stage, the radios had become almost
unintelligible. Subsequently, it came to light that Lyell

alternated frantically between frequencies, hitting some of the chosen amateur ones while simultaneously stumbling upon the one being used by the Downing Street team that night. In the aftermath of the fiasco, Downing Street's lawyers presented the Mirror with a transcript which went something along the lines of: 'Bravo, this is Lima, I'm switching to back-up channels. I cannot wait any longer. I hope the camera is ready. Rendezvous, as planned, in Prime Minister's bedroom. Out.'

I have no idea what Lyell was like as a professional soldier. But as a tabloid agent provocateur, he was pretty bloody useless. There was no need for any elaborate cleverness involving radio frequencies. Lyell was perfectly capable of shooting himself in the foot. Farcically, he attempted to jump over the wall just as the band were striking up the final number and their swivelling spotlight came to rest on the wall behind them, illuminating a man who was theatrically dressed in full combat fatigues and camouflage face paint.

Who knows what Lyell was thinking at this point? The original plan, as conceived by Helen, was for him to gain access to Downing Street by its gardens and penetrate as deeply as possible into the house, where I would be on hand with the camera to record the event for our readers and for posterity. On seeing the amassed gathering of party-goers, one might have expected Lyell to turn and run. However, he seems to have thought that the party was all part of some sort of elaborate set-up. Jumping from the wall, all eyes on him now, he landed and rolled as deftly as a parachutist. The band stopped playing. Guests gasped. Security, who had heard Lyell's curious battle cry on their radio frequencies, came running round the side of the house. Everyone looked back at the top of the wall to see if there were more to follow. The remaining two brain cells in Lyell's head rubbed together to produce something resembling a coherent thought: he was in a trap of his own making. The wall he had just leapt from was at least fifteen feet high. He could not get out the way he had come in. The only way out, therefore, was through the guests, the house and out into Downing Street itself.

Genevieve, stout, house-proud matron that she was, decided that enough was enough and moved to try to restrain Lyell. Lyell might been stupid but he was not about to be taken down by a housekeeper. Pushing brusquely past her, he sidestepped the first two security guards and started to run at full pelt towards the house. His direct route would take him within ten feet of me and the Prime Minister, whose glass I was in the process of refilling.

'Do something, Johnny,' hissed Major.

Do what? The man I was meant to be working with was running towards me. The man I was meant to be working for was standing behind me. One was the freelance employee of a tabloid newspaper; the other was the Prime Minister. Put like that, there really was no choice. Major was right, I had to do something. And I had to do it straight away.

Lyell was bearing down on me fast and there was a glimmer of recognition in those stupid eyes. His jaw moved wordlessly and it looked for a horrible moment as if he might be about to shout out my call sign – Bravo – or, even worse, my real name. It was a risk I could not afford to take. It was also my way out of this mess. Handing Major the jug of Pimms and my tray, I squared my shoulders and took Lyell down in a crunching, straight-on rugby tackle. The security guards quickly ran over and restrained him, Major clapped me on the back and the party continued as if nothing had happened. As Lyell was led away, I heard one of the security guards remark to his boss that the intruder must have someone on the inside. 'There were two radios,' he said. 'And they were using call signs.'

The boss turned to his underling. 'Find me that insider.'

Five minutes later, after having my hand shaken and my back patted by almost every guest at the party, I made my excuses and quietly slipped away in a taxi to the Mirror's offices.

This strange turn of events obviously posed something

of a dilemma as far as Rob Helen was concerned. On the one hand, I had an absolute wealth of material, both photographic and anecdotal. We knew every detail of Major's timetable and personal habits – where and when and how he ate his breakfast, what he thought of his colleagues and which sock he put on first in the morning. It was all far too good not to publish. On the other hand, the Downing Street authorities held our man, Lyell, who had quickly spilled all the beans under questioning. Lyell was so stupid that, when searched, they even found his canteen swipe card for the Mirror.

I would like to say that Helen's dilemma was an ethical one, but that would imply that the man had some sense of what ethics were. The original justification, tenuous though it was, for the story was that the Mirror would be valiantly exposing security weaknesses in Downing Street's set-up. As it was, we had actually exposed very little at all. True, my references might not have been checked very well but my presence was merely a nuisance and not exactly a terrorist risk. Lyell's attempt to storm the barricades had drastically misfired.

'So what's the bloody story then?' shouted Helen in conference next morning – a conference in which I was very much the centre of attention for once. 'Where do we go with this now?'

All the middle-aged men in the room started to shout at once. Burn Lyell and print Carter's story. Publish and be damned. Tell them it's in the public interest. Where's our lawyer got to?

'There's another problem,' said Helen's deputy. 'Captain Bob is so impressed by young Adam here that he wants to use him again for undercover, investigative stuff. So we're not allowed to use his picture or his real name in this story. He doesn't reckon it's worth exposing him at this young age. Would make any future stories much harder. Save him up for a really big one.'

'That's it!' I exclaimed.

'That's what?' said Helen, sneeringly.

'I've found your compromise. Let's look at the facts. On the one hand, Downing Street have got us over a barrel. They've got Lyell, they know who I am and they could do both of us for breaking and entering. If the true story came out it would be very embarrassing for us. Our rivals would have a field day and we would look very amateur. It would forever be remembered as the almost scoop which went horribly wrong. But that's not to say that we don't hold any cards of our own. We're sitting on a sensational story which would boost sales, establish our reputation as an agenda-setting, serious newspaper and cause huge embarrassment to Downing Street. If written in the right way, the story could even bring about Major's downfall. Would he ever be taken seriously again?

'Neither of the two parties involved is going to be able

to have their own way entirely. Downing Street cannot suppress any publication; we will not be able to publish exactly what we want. So we broker a compromise. We write something that makes us both look good. And it goes something like this: the Mirror infiltrated Downing Street in an attempt to expose flaws in the Prime Minister's security. However, we found the security procedures to be pretty much faultless. We then go on to publish some of the more gossipy titbits about the Prime Minister's routine but we stay clear of anything too controversial. We write enough to draw the reader in and get people talking in pubs but we don't go so far as to embarrass the Prime Minister or endanger his security. The more damaging information we obviously keep on file for future, unattributable background use. I'm sure Alastair will think of some inventive way to use it. The crux of the piece will focus on the night on which Jeremy Lyell – a troubled, former soldier with absolutely no links to the Daily Mirror – attempted a mad, drunken entry to Downing Street. Maybe he could be a victim of Gulf War syndrome. In return for cooperating with the story, all charges against Lyell will be dropped and we will pretend to pay for his psychiatric treatment. Whether or not you use him again is obviously up to you. The article will praise John Major for the calm way in which he reacted to the intruder and will highlight the valiant, brave behaviour of the undercover Mirror reporter. Downing Street saves face, we get our scoop, Lyell gets off, our sales rocket sky high and everyone goes home happy.'

Helen's cynical features broke into the first proper smile I'd ever seen from him. 'Adam, you are not half as stupid as you look.'

The editor smiled too. 'And Adam, you're really happy not to be involved in this in any way at all?'

'That's absolutely fine by me,' I said. 'I'd like to write it of course. But why don't you give the byline to someone else. And the picture credit.' I broke off and smiled across the room. 'Why not Helen? He hasn't had much in the paper recently.'

That, then, is the true story of what happened during my time in Downing Street. God only knows what it was all about as far as Mr Joseph and the rest of them were concerned. Was it about Maxwell? Or my father? Or just another training test, one more hoop for me to jump through on behalf of Mossad in order to prove myself? I just don't know at the moment. But for myself, I can certainly say that I've grown up a lot over the last month. I've learned the difference between loyalty and betrayal and between doing what is easy and doing what is right.

I only have a couple more weeks left here now, which will probably be spent back on the sports pages doing data entry. Hopefully then I will be left in peace for a while.

I can't wait to come back home and see you before starting at Cambridge.

    Love, Adam

Note from Harry Pearce

In Section D, Adam Carter was always one of our most effective undercover operatives. In the extract reproduced above, it is clear that he had developed all the necessary attributes and characteristics at a very early age.

It is worth pointing out that Adam was far more than a simple undercover tabloid journalist during this exercise. In many respects, he was actually a triple agent, acting not only on behalf of the *Mirror*, but also his blackmailers in Mossad and, of course, his own interests as well. That he was able to serve so many masters — keeping them all happy while never jeopardising his own set of morals — was a truly remarkable feat for a young man.

To a certain extent, Adam was also serving the Prime Minister, John Major. As an aside, it is interesting to note that almost everyone who met Major in private sings his praises. Adam was not the only person to be won over by his quiet charm. I recall being similarly impressed when meeting him around the same time.

There is an interesting postscript to this episode which is worth recording here. As he described, Adam told a conference of senior *Mirror* journalists that he had kept all the more risqué photographic and recording evidence which, while not publishable at the time, could be kept on file for future use as they saw fit. In reality, Adam actually handed the likes of Campbell blank tapes and empty photographic files. It was not until years later, when Major was under almost unbearable pressure from his cabinet colleagues, that the journalists tried to heap more on him and discovered Adam's deception.

Meanwhile, Adam bundled up all the incriminating evidence and sent it in one large recorded package to Downing Street, including the small secret mark under the postcode used by recognised correspondents to ensure that the parcel would eventually be opened by the Prime Minister himself. Inside, Adam enclosed a short note: 'Dear Prime Minister, I thought these might be safest in your hands. I'm sorry for what happened. I hope it might be some small mitigation that it could have been a whole lot worse.'

Major wrote a handwritten letter by return of post: 'Dear Johnny, thank you. Now get a proper job.'

As far as Samuel Joseph was concerned, Adam already had a proper job and he was doing it excellently. His handler was so pleased with how Adam had kept his cool while undercover that he gave him an additional cash handout of £1,000.

As I hinted earlier, we cannot be sure of the extent to which, if anything, Robert Maxwell himself was involved in the training and monitoring of Joseph's young protégé. However, it was certainly instructive that the senior journalists at the *Mirror* seemed so willing to pull Adam's byline. As far as they were concerned, Adam was a valuable investigative asset who should be kept under wraps as long as possible until he was mature enough to pull off a really big scoop. When he left the *Mirror* at the end of the summer holidays, it was on the understanding that he could work there as many university holidays as he liked. He was also offered an open-ended place on their graduate scheme as soon as he left university.

Mossad, of course, had bigger plans for Adam which could not be realised if his name and picture were splashed all over a best-selling tabloid newspaper. But as far as they were concerned, he had just passed his first test with flying colours.

For the time being, however, further excitement with Mossad lay in the future. On finishing his eventful work experience at the *Mirror*, Adam took a much-needed, enjoyable and, best of all, uninterrupted holiday with Richard Dempsey, inter-railing around Europe. Waking up one hungover morning in Budapest, Richard had a message from the youth hostel manager to phone home. Someone had dropped out from their place to read history at Trinity College, Cambridge, at the last minute. Would Richard, who received straight As at A level as well as a smattering of commendations and excellent references from his teachers, like to take up the vacancy? Richard accepted in a flash and they went out to celebrate with another drunken night in the Hungarian capital. The two boys, who had been almost inseparable since birth, would be continuing their education together.

We rejoin Adam's correspondence — to Lucy this time — in his first term reading Arabic at Cambridge.

Trinity Hall, Cambridge
15th October 1991

Hi Lucy,

Freshers week was so much fun, although I wish you'd been here too to enjoy it with me. I think the idea was to ease us gently into university life. In reality, this has meant doing absolutely no work at all and drinking a huge amount. I thought I had encountered some pretty major alcoholics in the rugby team at St. Paul's, and among the journalists at the Mirror, but they were nothing in comparison to the older, seasoned students in my college. Perhaps it's the horrible weather, or the sense of freedom among a bunch of young people living together, many of them away from home for the first time. Whatever it is, I've been drunk pretty much non-stop since arriving here seven days ago. There have been toga parties, boat club parties, football team parties, parties on the roofs, parties in our rooms, parties in seedy nightclubs and underground cellars that pass for bars, parties which everyone calls bops or 'squashes' at which squash is pretty much the only drink not on offer. So many parties . . . I wish you'd been here.

One of the upsides of being drunk the whole time is that you don't mind so much having exactly the same conversation with everyone you meet. Which A levels did you do? Which school did you go to? Have you had a gap year? The first night I got so bored of this that I started making up more entertaining responses. I was an outlaw from Peru, a 14-year-old from Bavaria who had passed his international baccalaureate four years early, a prisoner who had taken the first year of his degree in jail etc. It made the evening go a whole lot more quickly, especially as everyone seemed inordinately interested in the fact I was doing Arabic, which got very tedious after a while. I suppose it is more interesting than studying English or engineering like everyone else.

However, there are lots of nice people here and I've made some really good friends already. In particular, there is an awesome guy called Bilal, a Palestinian from a really old aristocratic family who's studying Arabic. Wasn't that a bit lazy, I asked, given that he was already fluent in the language and probably more familiar with the culture and history than most of the professors who will be teaching him. 'Of course it's lazy,' he said. 'That's the whole point of university.' I think I'm going to get on very well with Bilal.

The first week has been so manic that I haven't seen much of your brother at all. He's next

This was symbolic of a more general trend. Adam and Richard saw a lot less of each other once they moved to university and made new friends

HP

door, in Trinity which, despite being newer than Trinity Hall, is bigger, richer and significantly more smug. They like to joke – in as far as anyone from Trinity tells jokes – that the college has produced more Nobel Prize winners than France. Richard came round to my rooms on the third day. 'Ah yes,' he said. 'Trinity Hall, the place where the students from Trinity go to eat.' Even if you're familiar with the Cambridge lingo – 'hall' is the name we give to the dining room – this joke is not particularly funny.

London feels like such a long way away, even though I know it's under an hour by train. You have to come and visit me soon. I miss you so much. My new friends are giving me enough stick as it is about going out with a sixth-former. Now they're beginning to wonder whether you actually exist.

Love Adam

Trinity Hall, Cambridge
15th October 1991

Dear Mum,

Thanks very much for your letter; I am glad everything is going well at home. Cambridge is fun. I'll write again properly when I have a bit more time. I'm working so hard at the moment.

Love Adam

Note from Harry Pearce

When I first read the above note from Adam — as collated and presented in the file handed to me by Eleanor — I assumed it was one of his decoy notes. It was certainly very similar to the many lifeless, detail-free letters sent by Adam during his final year at school, which I did not deem necessary for inclusion in this file. I was somewhat surprised, therefore, to discover that it was sent by the same elaborate, secret method that Adam and Eleanor had first struck upon at the beginning of 1991.

Eleanor, of course, was not born yesterday, as she put it with a wry smile. She had enjoyed herself at university — she had admitted as much in her confessional letter to her son — and she fully expected that Adam would be doing likewise, whatever the strange nature of the background threat.

For Adam, his first term at university offered the chance to embrace some semblance of normality. He made new friends and threw himself into every aspect of university life. That December, he was the youngest person in thirty years to start in the Varsity rugby match against Oxford at Twickenham. According to the report in *The Times*, 'Adam Carter acquitted himself well on his debut, passing expertly out of hand, kicking intelligently and possessing an uncanny eye for a gap.' Cambridge, I'm afraid to say, beat Oxford 15-12.

As a member of the Blues rugby team, Adam was expected to train daily, with the inevitable result that his studies suffered. He also 'discovered' — although I would be surprised if this discovery hadn't surfaced earlier in his teens — a natural inclination towards partying. Women threw themselves at him — even the stuffiest Oxbridge colleges had become co-educational by this stage — and Adam was not always able to resist. For all his protestations of love and longing in his letters to Lucy Dempsey, she was a very long way away, at school in London. Other, more worldly girls were willing, available and lived on the same corridor. Their relationship slid, unacknowledged at first.

The bacchanalian fun and games of Freshers week were also a misleading indication as to what to expect for the rest of the term. Learning Arabic from scratch at Cambridge was no walk in the park, especially when the rest of the small class was made up of either Arabs, such as the friend, Bilal, Adam mentioned in his letter, or students who were a great deal more keen, or had a lot more time on their hands, than Adam. At the end of 'sixth week', Adam had his first serious run-in with trendy don Dr Mark Roupell, an encounter that he recorded somewhat shamefacedly in a long, apologetic letter to his mother at the end of his first term.

'I've come across plenty of students like you in the past, Adam,' said Roupell. 'Don't think I haven't been around here long enough not to. All you care about is the short-term, the immediate challenge. So you turn up to my interviews, all bright-eyed and bushy-tailed, your schoolboy faces scrubbed, your shoes polished, your ties tied properly for once and you convince me that you've wanted to study Arabic since the day you drew your first breath. Then the moment you arrive at the university, you get bored and I don't see you for months. Don't try and pretend that's not the case. Graduation seems years away. It *is* years away. Four years. So why not have a bit of fun in the meantime, eh? Chase some girls. Drink some pints. Score some tries. After all, you can always cram it at the last minute, can't you? Learn an ancient, nigh-on impossible language in a month or so at the end of the four years? Can't be that difficult. After all, you got into Cambridge, didn't you? You must be some sort of genius. And that's what other students do in history or English or geography. Well, Adam, I have news for you. Arabic isn't history or English or geography. You can't rely on your happy-go-lucky charm to get you through. Either you know the part seven past participle of the verb "to eat" or you don't. You can't *convince* me that you know it if you don't. It's that simple. There's one correct answer. And it requires learning. And application. So, what's it to be? My way or the highway?'

Adam chose Roupell's way. By the end of his first term, he had succeeded in finding a happy medium between keeping his tutor content and having a good time. In retrospect, though, these growing pains were probably a good thing, for they gave Adam much-needed time and space to grow into himself. Mossad wisely left him to his own devices during this period. Adam heard nothing at all from Mr Joseph or anyone else for that matter. If MI6 recruiter Roupell had ever thought him a good bet he would probably have changed his mind on the basis of

Adam's behaviour that term. Adam at that stage was the very model of the kind of person they used to select, the kind of twit who so regularly ballsed up Six's operations abroad.

By the end of the year, it was fortunate that Adam had got whatever it was out of his system, for at the beginning of 1992 events unfolded which required a maturity way beyond his limited years.

4
David Horovitz

Trinity Hall
Cambridge
8th January 1992

Dear Mum,

Thank you for giving us all such a wonderful time over Christmas and for your letter which arrived this morning. I think you're worrying unnecessarily about Simon Dempsey's health. Sure, he's not as young as he used to be but I think he's still in pretty fine fettle for a man of his age. I got a Christmas thank-you letter from him today as well, and he certainly made no reference to any health worries.

A more pressing concern at this end is that Mr Joseph has been in touch again. His son, Ben, is studying medicine a few doors down at St. Catharine's College, so he has the perfect excuse to be in Cambridge. As I'd suspected - but secretly hoped wasn't the case - Mossad had not really lost interest in me. Last term was, according to Mr Joseph, a 'period of grace' in order for me to find my feet at university. Now it is time for me to 'earn my way' again.

As he mentioned at our first-ever meeting, Mr Joseph is still concerned about the potential for radicalisation among the young Muslims in Cambridge. I'm not entirely sure I see what he means by this. Most of the British Muslims in my college are as integrated and as emancipated as you could imagine. The majority of them drink; those who choose not to are still very much involved in college life. In the university at large, there is, of course, a vast range, from those who take their faith very seriously to those who don't take it seriously at all. There are a few girls who wear veils, mainly in the remaining all-women colleges, Newnham and New Hall. As you would expect, there are a number of mosques and a smattering of Muslim-dominated student societies. But I can see absolutely no evidence of radicalisation, and I said as much to Mr Joseph. If any student body in the university was to be feared, it was the all-powerful J Soc (Jewish Society), who successfully lobby the union every time they hold a controversial debate on Israel or invite speakers who are not to the society's liking.

'That is where you are wrong, Adam,' said Mr Joseph. 'Wrong, yet again. There is sedition and unhappiness and uprising everywhere. You only have to keep your eyes open to notice it. And it is your job to notice it first and to warn me.'

It had been pleasant to be able to forget about Mr Joseph for a while. Now that he is very much back in my thoughts, I had forgotten how unsettling he is as a character. Either – as seems likely – he is mad. He sees enemies everywhere. Or he knows much more than the rest of us know and much more than he lets on. I'm not sure which of the two alternatives is scarier: having a mad handler or an omniscient one.

Anyway, I'm doing my best to keep Mr Joseph happy, providing him with fairly spurious reports and details on who's who in the Cambridge Arab and Muslim community. I suppose he has something of a point. I am uniquely placed to be able to observe what is going on without arousing suspicions. As an Arabist, it is only natural that I should take an interest in people of that background. Still, none of it makes any sense to me.

Love Adam

Trinity Hall
Cambridge
20th January 1992

Mum – oh my God: it's happened. My father has made contact, and in such a way that suggests they know more about us than we had ever imagined.

I don't know if I mentioned in my last letter that I have started rowing for the college. Now that the rugby season is pretty much over, I thought it would be good to stay fit by doing something different. Also, I've spent a lot of time outside Trinity Hall and thought it would be a nice thing to do something a bit more college-based. So I started training for the third boat, which is good fun and a bit of a joke. In theory, we're meant to go for an early morning run and training at least three times a week. But in reality we're all far too lazy. So, as a compromise, we go every Monday and Thursday.

This morning, a Thursday, I got up at 6:30 a.m., pulled on my tracksuit and checked my pigeon-hole in the porter's lodge to see if I had any post. It was empty. When I returned from training an hour later, I was, as usual, the first back into the porter's lodge after our final run. There, in my pigeon-hole, was the letter I have transcribed below. Although headed 'via Tel Aviv', there was no stamp or address on the envelope. It had clearly been placed there by hand by someone who knew my routine. The envelope itself was marked: 'Adam Horovitz'.

I'm afraid some of this might make for harrowing reading. But I cannot think of anything else to do apart from to send you a copy.

Via Tel Aviv
Israel
January 1992

Dear Adam,

You must forgive me for writing to you. In fact, there are many things you must forgive me for, but we shall come on to that later. Let me start by saying that I never imagined it to be like this; I never wanted it to be like this. I did not want to pick up a pen and write to a 19-year-old son I have never seen to tell him that I am his father. But there is, unfortunately, no other way. Circumstances dictate; we must follow them.

There are a number of reasons, Adam, why we cannot currently meet face to face. The first is a question of simple practicality: you are at university in England, a country which I'm currently banned from visiting. At the moment, I am based abroad, involved in a situation from which I cannot easily extricate myself. A good friend of mine has consented to deliver this letter to you.

Also, and there is no delicate way of saying this, it is perhaps not unfair to say that we both have equal grounds to fear the other. I have no doubt that your mother, Eleanor, has told you about me. You know the kind of man I am — although I would like to change that impression — and you're probably aware of what I'm capable of. On the other hand, Adam, I also have very good grounds to fear you. If you believe the biased version of events that your mother has no doubt told you, you probably think me a monster. I would like to set that record straight. But first, let me remind you that we are colleagues as well as family. We serve the same cause; we want the same thing: peace and security for the great country of Israel.

You see, you're Jewish, Adam. And what a great Jew you're turning out to be! I've heard wonderful things about you from my old friend, Sam Joseph. From what he says, you were just like I was at your age: slightly brash, a little arrogant perhaps, but full of zest and enthusiasm and a lust for life. My sources are everywhere and they report back on you very favourably. What you did while at the newspaper and at Downing Street was remarkable for someone your age. Did you enjoy it, I wonder. That's one of our favourite training exercises and you passed with flying colours. It's a shame in some ways, for you would have made an excellent journalist. But we have bigger and better things for you in mind.

Adam, I want you, in time, to know everything about me. It's very important that you have the full picture before we meet. I want you to know about my childhood and my arrival in Israel, the things I did before I met your mother and the things I have done afterwards. A life is more complex and more beautiful than a simple chain of events. Take one event in isolation, freeze the camera on that snapshot and it makes no sense. View the entire picture in perspective and you'll start to understand.

There is no time now for me to tell you the story of my life. I shall write again when I promise to give you all the details. For now, though, I just want to write about your mother and how we met, as well as the background to the series of events which led to you sitting in an interrogation room in Tel Aviv airport and working for the Mossad.

Of course, I have no idea what your mother has told you about me. But from what Sam Joseph tells me, it appears clear to me that you are aware of my existence and that your opinion is not favourable. No, don't look so surprised. You may not have said anything directly to Sam but he is a much more perceptive man that he appears. He is an excellent handler and you're very lucky to be working with him. He knows the whole story.

I don't blame your mother for speaking badly of me, if that is what she has done. What incentive would she have to speak well of me? She is the doting mother who has looked after you for nineteen years, fed you, clothed you, bathed you, loved you. And what am I? An absent father, a foreign, threatening spy, a man who works for an intelligence service that now controls and blackmails you. Who could blame you for choosing one parent over the other? Or is the situation actually a little bit more complex than that?

This, Adam, is what really happened. The truth is a disconcerting one – the truth often is – but you are a man now, and a man of the world at that.

I met your mother in August 1971 in a beach bar in Tel Aviv.

I loved her at first sight. She was pretty, vivacious and irreverent. We became boyfriend and girlfriend. We saw a lot of each other. She fell in love with me and I fell in love with her.

At that time, she was working in a kibbutz in the Galilee in the north of Israel and I would visit her there as often as I could. Your mother shared a room with a friend from England called Hannah who took an instant dislike to me. Maybe she was jealous of your mother. Or maybe she just disliked me. I don't know. But I do know that she did her absolute poisonous best to turn your mother against me. I would often see her rolling her eyes when I entered the room or would overhear her saying rude things about me afterwards. Your mother and I would often joke about it. 'What she needs is a good man,' your mother would say. Well, she found a man – some guy called Daniel – but I'm not sure he could be classified as a good one. The feeling was mutual. He didn't seem to think much of me either.

None of this mattered, as far as your mother and I were concerned. Or at least I didn't think it mattered. We were happy, we were in love and we didn't need anyone else's approval. But as the year drew to a close your mother seemed to lose her sparkle. Perhaps she was homesick, or maybe she had simply fallen out of love with me. One day, she just vanished. I turned up at the kibbutz to collect her for our planned weekend away and there was no one in her room. Letting myself in, I could see a pregnancy testing kit. The result was positive.

I did everything I could to find your mother before she left the country. I admit that I abused my powers slightly by putting out alerts at the ports, the border crossings and the airports. But there was no malicious, ulterior motive. I wanted to check she was OK. I wanted to find her because I loved her. And I wanted to know what was going to become of our baby.

For several years I searched relentlessly for Eleanor. I tapped up all our sayannim in the UK but she proved impossible to find. There was very little to go on – her parents were dead, she had no siblings and she had appeared to change her surname. She had successfully vanished below the radar. My search became increasingly desperate. I got hold of birth records for the UK and scanned them but it was a fruitless, Herculean task. She had often mentioned that she would like to live in Australia for a while, so I ensured that my next overseas posting would take me near there. But still no joy.

After five years of this it was time to give up. I had to get on with my life and my career. I married and got divorced before we'd had any children, I lived abroad, I had affairs – I led a fairly typical life of an Israeli intelligence officer – and I did my best to put your mother, the love of my life, out of my mind. I was fairly happy, I suppose, in as far as anyone is happy. My career is interesting, my calling noble. I long to tell you all about it some day.

I don't want you to think that I forgot about your mother entirely. Every so often, I would awake, nauseous with pleasure, in the middle of the night because I had seen her in

151

my dreams. On waking, the experience was so real, so tangible, that it would take several minutes for me to remember with horror that it was only a dream – nothing more.

And I would often think about you as well, even though I had absolutely no details to go on. Had you even been born? And in which country? Were you a boy or a girl? Was I father to a proper little English gentleman or a surfing Australian tomboy? It was a pleasant fantasy to indulge. I would often try to imagine you, in all your different incarnations, to take my mind off a particularly dull or dangerous operation abroad. What would you be doing right now? What were your hobbies? Were you good at school like your mother or lazy and badly behaved like me? Were you even aware of my existence? Did you have my nose? Or your mother's hair? And would we get on were we ever to meet?

All these unanswerable questions drove me mad after a while. You might think that Mossad has unlimited resources but even we cannot find someone with no name, no registered place of birth and no description. It made me very upset.

Imagine, then, my excitement when I was phoned out of the blue by my old friend Samuel Joseph. Sam was the Israeli equivalent of what you Brits would call 'the best man' when I got married. We met at the University of Haifa which he attended for one year as part of the Erasmus exchange programme. We shared digs together and became close friends. The following year, I visited him in Bristol and was present at his graduation ceremony when he was presented with a First in engineering and the prize for the most successful undergraduate in his year. As you may know, he went on to have an extremely successful career in business. He has been a loyal servant to both his British homeland and his Jewish-Israeli roots.

Sam called me in the autumn of 1990 as he had just been made a governor of St Paul's School in London and was planning on accompanying a school trip to Israel in the Christmas holidays. He wanted to know whether I was in the country and fancied meeting up. Adam, as you will find when you yourself grow older, you inevitably lose touch with even your oldest and best friends. On the other hand, male friendship is such that it can always be picked up exactly where it was left off. It was wonderful to hear from Sam. We talked for hours on the phone and I was distraught that I would be outside the country for the entire duration of his visit, on yet another tedious official trip to Washington for interminable meetings with our patronising cousins in the CIA.

'Any people on the trip we should think about recruiting?' I asked Sam. 'You know our mantra: "Get them young".'

Sam laughed. For decades, he had been Mossad's main recruiter among young British people in the UK, combing the better universities and even some of the schools for the next generation of sayannim. 'Give me a chance, David. I've only just arrived. But I have a feeling it's not that sort of school.'

'Any sign of my child, then?' I asked.

Sam laughed again. It was an old, well-worn joke between the two of us. He was the only person who knew the entire story about Eleanor. It was he who had obtained the UK birth records for me.

'Not in this school,' he laughed. 'Although I promise to keep my eyes peeled for you.'

A few weeks later, Sam rang me again. 'I don't want to get your hopes up,' he said. 'But the most extraordinary thing has happened. I wouldn't even have noticed, were it not for a curious business concerning consent forms. All the children coming on the trip need to ask their parents to sign, confirming that they give their permission for their child to go to Israel – something to do with health and safety legislation. Obviously, this involves a huge amount of tedious paperwork for Geoffrey Hewson, the poor teacher in charge of organising the trip, so I offered to help him out. After all, my son was also coming on the trip and I was a newly appointed governor eager to make a good impression.

'Well, anyway, we'd just finished wading through the tickets and the cheques and were so tired by this point that we could barely be bothered to check the consent forms properly. However, by chance, the form at the top of the pile belonged to someone called Adam Carter. As I scanned my eye briefly over it, I noticed that the requisite signature had been forged in the most amateur way possible. The ink used was exactly the same as that used to fill in the rest of the form, and the handwriting, although slightly disguised – it looked as though a right-handed person had written with his left hand, or vice versa – was clearly the same.'

'So I turned to Hewson,' Sam went on, 'and asked him about Adam Carter. Was he a lazy or dishonest sort who often went in for forging his parents' signature? "No," said Hewson. "Adam Carter's an interesting one actually. His father died before he was born and he lives with his mother, Eleanor, and the Dempsey family, the parents of Richard, who act as his patrons. If he's forging a signature, I can only imagine that they have denied him permission to go —"'

I interrupted Sam. I was too excited. 'And this Eleanor? What does she do for a living?'

'She's a housekeeper for the Dempseys,' said Sam. 'But she is also a teacher.'

Well, you can imagine my excitement!

I instructed Sam to do everything he could to find out more about Adam Carter before going to Israel. Under no circumstances was the fact that your consent form had not been signed off properly to stop you going. Hewson should be bribed if needs be. In the meantime, I devoted all my energies to attempting to extricate myself from my planned trip to Washington. My boss, however, was having none of it. He is on the verge of retirement and I am expected to take over the job from him when he goes. This trip to Washington was vital as far as the Americans were concerned to convince them that I was the right person to fill his shoes. Short of actually admitting my hunch about your existence – which would

have amounted to career suicide – there was nothing I could
do to make sure I would be in the country at the same time as
you.

As it was, then, I instructed Sam Joseph to keep a very
close eye on you, a much closer eye than you may have
realised. When you and your friend Richard went to Gaza,
you were not alone. Neither were you alone when you visited
Hebron and other parts of the West Bank.

One of the advantages of working for Mossad, or Shin
Bet, or any of the myriad intelligence agencies which serve
Israel, is that Jewish people look so similar to Arabs. We are
all Semites, after all. We are all brothers. That burly
man in the shack on the beach in Gaza? Yes, he was one of
ours. That friendly person with blue eyes who encouraged
you to sit down in the small village in the West Bank
and smoke his shisha water pipe? Yes, he was also an
informer of ours.

There is a whole department in Mossad which works on
psychological warfare. One of its goals is to persuade Arabs
that we are all-powerful, all-encompassing, all-seeing. Fear
is a powerful weapon in its own right. But the truth is that
we often are all-powerful, all-encompassing and all-seeing.
Our enemies are right to be afraid.

The first time Sam and I spoke on the phone we discussed
ways in which I might make contact with you. But how
could I be sure it really was you? I was out of the country
and I was banned from visiting yours. I couldn't just appear

out of the blue and make contact. You probably hated me, even if you were aware of my existence. Neither could I be sure that any letter I wrote would be delivered to the right person. If I couldn't speak to you myself, I needed to find someone I trusted who could. I needed to engineer a situation in which we could find out more about you.

But how was I meant to do this? Have you kidnapped? Set you up for a crime you hadn't committed? Get the police involved so they would have a chance to interrogate you?

Fortunately for us – fortunately for me – by going to Gaza and the West Bank you played straight into our hands. Sam rang me in America with more information. Who was this plucky young man who had snuck away from his school trip to go and have adventures? Was he my son? And, if so, what a fantastic asset he would make for Israeli Intelligence. Sam and I articulated exactly the same idea at the same time: if I couldn't meet you normally, I would recruit you.

Our officers and agents at Ben Gurion airport have seen and done it all before. You would not believe how many secrets they are privy to doing that job. Neither could you grasp the sheer number of plots they have foiled in their airport. Getting them to talk to you would be child's play compared to some of the tasks they had been called upon to perform in the past.

The intention was to plant something compromising and suspicious in your bag. So imagine Sam's surprise when he opened it with this express intention – yes, he too has been trained as an active Mossad field agent – and saw that it was already littered with Palestinian artefacts. It seems that your friend, Richard Dempsey, has a sense of humour that is as imaginative as our blackmailing abilities.

The rest, of course, you know. Everything that has happened since then is as exactly as it seemed. Further checks were carried out to ascertain the veracity of your story. Once we had established that Eleanor was the person we thought she was, the strange phone calls stopped and we withdrew the people who had been spying on her. You returned to England and were approached formally by Sam Joseph in his official capacity as your handler. You have carried out a number of tasks with a high level of competence, especially during your time as an employee of the *Daily Mirror*. Your intelligence on the Muslim community in Cambridge, while low-grade, is proving very useful. On a couple of occasions, you have stepped over the line and have been duly warned and punished. It appears to me that you and the service have come to a degree of understanding.

That takes us up to today; the present. So, what next? What do we want from you? What can you expect from us? And from me?

Let me answer the second question first because you need, and deserve, assurances from our part. Mossad is the most loyal employer you could ever hope to work for. We demand and receive high standards but in return we look after each of our officers as if they were our own sons and daughters. Some intelligence agencies burn their undercover agents when they are discovered. That never happens in Mossad. We leave no stone unturned, no pressure point unexploited until we get our own people back. 'No one left behind' – that is the motto we live by.

Adam, in December 1990, you joined a new family: the family of Mossad.

But what of your own family? Adam, I am also your family, your father. I want to meet you. I want to know you, to love you. In good time, it will happen. Don't let your mother turn you against me. She is a wonderful woman, whom I loved dearly, but you have to ask yourself: is she really all that she seems? This, after all, is someone who kept the truth about your own father from you for eighteen years. This is a mother who told her only son about a fictional father who never existed (yes, Sam has passed on the tall stories you've told him), a mother who waited until she felt her own life was in danger before bothering to share the details with you.

I don't want to turn you against your mother either. She has brought you up well. But can you really trust anything she's told you, especially when it comes to me? Adam, as you know, women are emotional creatures, not often given to logic and reason. Why is her account any more believable than mine?

The truth is simple and the truth is this: I loved your

mother and she loved me but these things do not always work out. I would have liked to have been a good father to you, a proper father. Perhaps it is not too late. The nature of my job does not help but at least it is now your job too. We have something in common. You might think that it was strange to recruit you but it was the only option available as the circumstances unfolded. It was for my own protection as well as yours. Only in this way can we truly understand each other.

Look after yourself. I shall write again soon once you have had time to read and digest this.

Your Father (David Horovitz)

It was probably fortunate that David Horovitz concluded his extraordinary letter without giving any way of getting in touch as its contents appeared to drive Adam into a furious rage. The postscript that follows was clearly written in the throes of an emotional outburst. Adam was also motivated by a desire to reassure his mother that he had not been swayed in any way by these new developments. A sensitive son, he was obviously aware of the potential impact of his father's insinuations and accusations. He wanted to show whose side he was on. Perhaps most of all he wanted the cathartic opportunity to vent some spleen.

HP

PS Mum, this is how I would reply given the chance.

Dear Mr Horovitz,

Throughout your unwelcome letter you refer to me – annoyingly, repeatedly and ingratiatingly – as Adam. I refer to you as Mr Horovitz as I neither know nor like you. What little I know I do not like. You are not my father.

'Adam,' you write. 'I want you, in time, to know everything about me.' I believe I know enough already. I believe I have the measure of you, as a failed man, a failed husband and a failed father. In your entire lengthy letter, I believe you only write one partially accurate sentence: 'There are many things you must forgive me for.' Well, you're right: almost everything you have done in your life you have done badly. Many of your actions require forgiveness. Whether they merit forgiveness is another question altogether.

I don't think I shall ever be able to forgive you for the way you've treated my mother. Even if your version of events in Israel is true, why would she run away just because she was pregnant? Why would she vanish?

Those are the actions of someone who is scared – with good reason, I believe – not someone who has merely fallen out of love. And if she really had fallen out of love, why would you be so paranoid about her 'speaking badly' of you? Surely she would have told fond stories of my dashing, long-lost Israeli father with whom she conducted a brief, but unsustainable, fling, and not waited nineteen years to tell me, fearfully, about the man who abused and terrorised her. I believe I detect a guilty conscience in your suspicions.

Worse still, you cannot content yourself with merely pointing out that her account might be slightly biased. That I could have accepted. But you go on to attempt, with weasel words, to sow doubts in my mind about the very nature of my mother's character. On the one hand, you don't blame her for speaking badly of you. How very big of you! Then you go on to question whether my mother is really 'all that she seems'. Well, I don't know what she seemed to you, Mr Horovitz. You only knew her for a couple of months, when she was very young. I have known her all my life. I, too, don't know how she seems, but I do know how she is. She is indeed an 'emotional creature', much given to love, compassion and understanding and yes, logic and reason too.

Mr Horovitz, I do not blame you for falling in love with my mother – if, indeed, that was what it was. I would rather not know that you regularly awake, 'nauseous with pleasure', in the middle of the night because she has appeared in your dreams. I question your judgement in deciding to share this with me. But I am old enough and wise enough to understand that life is complicated and some things happen which not all of us can understand.

Yet there is one thing I do understand. There's one thing that I will not let pass. Whatever the truths and untruths of your competing accounts, one thing is very clear: my mother does not like you and she does not want to see you. So I ask you to leave her out of this, whatever 'this' ends up being. Stop watching her house. Stop using her as blackmail bait. Your argument – your attempt at reconciliation, if you like – is with me; me alone and not her.

But then, I'm not sure I shall ever be able to forgive you either for the way you have treated me. I suggest you read your letter again, particularly the bit in which you muse about how you might 'engineer a situation' by which you might find out more about me. Should I be kidnapped? Set up for a crime I haven't committed? Or interrogated by the police? Later in the letter, you appraise my work over the last year and a half: 'On a couple of occasions, you have stepped over the line and have been duly warned and punished.'

I ask you: are these the words of a contrite and loving father?

Why am I 'career suicide'? If you'd really cared about making contact with me, you would have cancelled your trip to Washington. Why spy on me? Set me up? Recruit me? Clearly your career is far more important to you than I am.

And do we really 'serve the same cause'? You work for

Mossad because you love your country. I work for Mossad because I was compromised, set up and blackmailed by foreigners who work for my psychopath of a father. I work for Mossad because I have to, because if I didn't you'd threaten my mother, the only family I have left in the world.

So forgive me if I decline your invitation to 'join a new family, the family of Mossad'. I have my own family already and I will stop at nothing to protect it.

You open your letter by stating that there are a number of reasons why we cannot meet face to face. I can think of only one. If I saw you at the moment, in my current state, I would kill you. And then you would discover that you are not the father to a 'proper little English gentleman'.

Adam Carter

Note from Harry Pearce

These two letters — one delivered by hand by the best friend of her former boyfriend; the other written, but not sent, by her only son — understandably caused Eleanor no small degree of consternation when they arrived at Fleetwood House in the usual secret way.

Here was a man she hadn't heard from in over eighteen years attempting to drive a wedge between her and her son. On the one hand, he declared that he had never fallen out of love with her — an unsettling notion for someone who had never entirely got over him either. And yet these declarations of unrequited love were accompanied by a manipulative attempt to win Adam over to Horovitz's point of view. This was all rounded off a with a fiery postscript which, while eloquently and passionately written, was troubling in the extreme. Had Adam really meant everything he had written? If so, he was in a dangerous, borderline criminal, mood. Or what if — perhaps worse still — he hadn't meant any of what he had written? What if his father had successfully won him over and turned him against his mother? Maybe this was all an elaborate ploy, a boys' front to keep Eleanor out of the loop and isolate her still further. She had already lost one man she loved. She couldn't bear to lose another.

Wracked with paranoia and guilt, and throwing caution to the wind, Eleanor immediately jumped in her car and set off for Cambridge. Arriving around lunchtime, she was just too late to catch Adam before he set off for afternoon rugby practice. When he came back to his rooms around 5 p.m., he found his mother making tea and cake for — and thereby friends with — the entire corridor. If anyone could be said to embody the British ideal of a calm head under pressure it was Eleanor Carter.

As it was, her fears were quickly allayed by Adam. They had a full, open and frank conversation. Of course he was intrigued to know more about his father. Of course he would be interested in meeting him if a safe opportunity arose. If so, he would put all violent thoughts to one side; it had just been good for him to get that out of his system. But did he believe David Horovitz's side of the story? Did he trust him? Of course he didn't. He wasn't naive, nor was he disloyal.

Likewise, Eleanor assured her son that she had no more feelings for David. Of course, she was flattered, even somewhat touched, that he still appeared to hold her in such high regard. Of course, it had reawakened memories of some of their happier times together. But she was not stupid. She was not in her twenties any longer. David was, and always would be, a flawed, manipulative man. Leopards did not change their spots, especially leopards who happened to be Israeli intelligence officers. She, too, knew where her loyalties lay.

However, I must admit that my personal impression is that they were both lying to each other at this stage. Adam had been through a turbulent two years. If he met his father – and I believe he really wanted to – he might well have struck him in anger. But it is equally likely that he would have hugged him in forgiveness. Adam had started to display some of the signs of Stockholm syndrome in his relationship with his Mossad handlers. They might not have 'kidnapped' him as such but the effect on his lifestyle and freedom to choose was similar.

More importantly, Adam was driven by a simple curiosity. 'Nothing is to be feared, it is only to be understood.' I remember Adam saying that to Jo once on the grid when she asked if he ever got scared on operations. He did not want to fear his father, he wanted to understand him. Having spent his entire life so far believing in a dead, fictional father he would never meet, the idea of meeting his real one — however unsavoury or unsafe a character he might be — was intoxicating. Moreover, it is difficult to hate entirely someone you have never met, especially if that someone shares half your genes.

Similarly, I believe Eleanor was more affected by Horovitz's declarations than she let on to Adam in a January afternoon and evening in his small digs in Trinity Hall. Eleanor is a tough woman, a survivor, but at heart she is also a romantic. Horovitz was her first love, her only true love. However damaging that love might have turned out to be, you couldn't take that fact away from her. Like many formidable women, she found other men weak by comparison. Horovitz appeared a deeply flawed man but he was still a real man at that. Love makes choices based on love, not on reason.

It is my belief that Horovitz was fully aware of the effect his letter would have on Adam. As he knew from his conversations with his friend, Samuel Joseph, Adam was an ambitious, talented young man in search of a father figure. Well, he could do better than that. He wasn't merely a father figure; he was his father. So Horovitz knew that he could write pretty much anything he liked and Adam would at least read, and potentially even be swayed by, his words.

It appeared, then, that Horovitz had secured his bait. But to what ends did he plan to deploy it? Is 'deploy' even the right word? Or did he simply want reconciliation, only on his own terms?

A week later, a second letter arrived in Adam's pigeon-hole, delivered and written in exactly the same way and at the same time as the first. It is too long to include in full in this file, but it was deeply affecting, deeply moving and deeply personal. While the first letter cajoled, the second charmed. Clearly as much thought had gone into it as went into Eleanor's first letter to Adam. In particular, it filled in the missing biographical details on Horovitz's life, as promised. It is worth highlighting the salient points here.

Born a Jew in 1937 in the north part of Berlin, Horovitz had had to deal with hardship early in life. His family were moved from concentration camp to concentration camp, bribing their way to survival, mainly by offering the services of Horovitz's father — a skilled paediatrician — for free. By 1943, the Nazi regime had become so murderous that they did not care for any Jewish skills, doctor or not. The Horovitz family were put on a train to Auschwitz where David's two brothers, one sister and mother were all killed in the gas chambers. David's father survived because one day, while almost certainly en route to the gas chambers himself, he noticed a strange rash on the only child of the camp's commander. Dr Horovitz diagnosed meningitis and treated the child, who survived. In return, the commander spared his life and the life of his only remaining son, David.

Dr Horovitz died, of exhaustion and a broken heart, on the same day as the death camp was finally liberated. David Horovitz, now a child of nine, went to live with an aunt in Tel Aviv and was present at the birth pains of the new nation of Israel. Closer to home, there was also pain at the hands of a brutal aunt who had always resented David's mother. Horovitz escaped her clutches as quickly as he was able, leaving school a year early and lying about his age in order to take up military service.

He thrived in the army and decided to stay on after the end of his allotted three years. In 1967, aged thirty-one, he excelled during the Six Day War and was promoted to full colonel. However, a desk job was the last thing Colonel Horovitz wanted. Horovitz was a soldier, a man of action; he was not really colonel material at all. So when one of his few school friends approached him about a job in military intelligence, he leapt at the opportunity.

After six months working for army intelligence, Horovitz joined Mossad on secondment and enjoyed himself so much that he decided to stay there. Mossad also enjoyed having him as an employee. He was wiser and tougher than their more naive recruits who had joined straight from university, while still retaining some of the youthful enthusiasm and ability to learn that most of the older secondees from the army lacked. Horovitz rose quickly through the ranks.

It was around this time, in 1971, at the height of his powers and arrogance, that Horovitz met Eleanor. Most of the rest of the story is already familiar to us. We either know it from Horovitz's first letter or from Eleanor's own account. Horovitz does not add much to either in his second letter; he glosses over most of the potentially more interesting details for understandable reasons of security.

But by reading between the lines, a clear picture emerges of a talented man who was continuing to 'go places' with Mossad. I spent an interesting few hours in Vauxhall comparing Horovitz's letter with the files MI6 have kept on suspected Mossad operations over the last four decades. It was instructive to note that almost every place and every date which Horovitz alluded to, however obliquely, tallied with suspected Mossad activity. In particular, he appears to have been intimately involved with 'Operation Wrath of God', Mossad's response to the massacre at the 1972 Olympic Games.

In 1992, aged fifty-six, Horovitz was clearly in the top tier of Mossad's hierarchy. There was even a hint — and it was no more than that — that he might have been in line for the top job itself. His opaque reference to a visit to Washington to secure CIA approval for his new promotion certainly indicates he was a serious player. It is also worth remembering that Israel, in comparison to many other Western countries at least, is something of a gerontocracy. Ariel Sharon, for example, was well into his seventies when he became Prime Minister. There was no need for Horovitz to be in any rush.

As expected, Adam also showed the second letter to his

mother who was able to verify some of the early background biographical detail. What Adam didn't mention, however, was the concluding paragraphs. They went like this:

'So, Adam, that, as far as I am at liberty to do so, is the full story of my life. Perhaps it is too much to ask that you will now see me in a good light but I hope, at least, that it helps you see me in a better light.

'I regret now some of the things I wrote in my first letter. Parts were too hasty, too direct. This is the letter I should have sent first; it is, after all, the letter I wrote first. Adam, I respect and care for you very much. Even though I have never met you I feel like I know you. I know you through what Sam has told me, but I also know you because you are my dear son.

'Once you have had time to read and digest my letters, perhaps you would consider writing back. It would mean a lot to me to hear from you. Please leave any correspondence in your pigeon-hole en route to rowing on any Monday morning you choose. It will be checked regularly. Mark the envelope "Adam Carter, Secretary, Trinity Hall Tennis Club" and I shall know that it is intended for me.'

Two weeks later, Adam duly left the following letter to be picked up by the unknown messenger.

Trinity Hall
1st March 1992

Dear David Horovitz,

Thank you for your letters. I'm sorry for the delay in replying but I've been very busy with various things recently. I also wanted time to mull things over properly in my own mind before writing back to you. I wanted to make sure that I put down my thoughts in the right way. I'm sure you understand.

You will probably not be surprised to hear that I was livid when I first read your letter. I was angry that you could contact me in such a presumptuous way; angry at your insinuations regarding my mother; angry at your invasion into my privacy. I thought about never contacting you. I considered showing your letter to the British authorities.

But I think that, most of all, I was angry with the situation, the circumstances in which we find ourselves. Maybe 'anger' is too strong a word. Perhaps I mean disappointed, or merely sad. It is sad that I never knew you earlier, sad that I have spent my entire life thinking you were someone else.

Your first letter gave little context. I thought you were manipulative, self-centred, threatening. But now that I know the context – the background – to your life, it begins to make more sense. How would I live the second part of my life if the first had been like that? How would

I think of my own country if it was a safe haven after the systematic destruction of three-quarters of my family, or if I had spent all of my adult life fighting tooth and nail to defend it?

And as for my mother, well, I know that there are two sides to every story. I don't mean by that that I fully accept your side, but I am prepared to acknowledge that the situation might be more complex than it appeared at first glance. That's not to say that I forgive you - if forgiveness is what you are requesting - but let us just say that I'm growing to understand you. The path to understanding you entirely will no doubt be a long one, but it is a journey that I am prepared to go down.

You still haven't told me why you're banned from visiting England. Does it have anything to do with the cartoonist Mr Joseph told me about? It would be really good to meet you. Perhaps I could make another trip to Israel when you're next back in the country.

In the meantime, please keep on telling me more about your life.

Adam Carter

Tel Aviv
Israel
30th March

Dear Adam,

I cannot tell you how much pleasure it gave me to read my first letter from my son. You write well – honestly, directly, perhaps even a little bit brutally – but it is a style that pleases me. Your words clearly come from the heart. I'm glad you tell me that my contact and my behaviour have made you angry. Although I apologise for that, I would have been worried if they hadn't. And now that you have been honest with me regarding things that cause you no pleasure I am far more likely to believe you when you tell me that you are pleased with something.

As you can see from the address at the top of this letter I'm now back in the country: my country, the best country in the world. Unfortunately, I cannot tell you where I have been this time. Hopefully, one day, I'll be able to.

You ask why I am banned from visiting the UK and you hit the nail, how do you say it, straight on the head. In 1987, I was the Mossad station head in London. It was one of the best jobs abroad in the service – less political than Washington, less scary than Moscow, more important than Paris. One of the best things about working in a friendly nation is that no one cares too much about your cover story. You can let your security grow very lax. In one week alone, I found myself being introduced by the Ambassador as the

Cultural Attaché, Financial Adviser and Third Undersecretary to the same person at three separate cocktail parties. But this was the 1980s and no one seemed to care too much. The general assumption was that all Israelis were spies in any case.

Only the climate and the food let down your great capital. I used to love strolling into Kensington Palace Gardens, around the lake and into Hyde Park. Sometimes I even did the entire circuit without being rained on. Yet still, it is one of the most beautiful corners of one of the most beautiful cities in the world.

One of my other favourite cities in the UK – in the world, even – is Cambridge. I used to visit it often during quiet weekends. We had a lot of informers there, of course, but it wasn't the work I went for. Cambridge has a quiet, romantic charm which busier, more cosmopolitan Oxford lacks, in my opinion. I'm glad you've decided to go there. It means I can imagine the places where you are, the backdrops to your life, even if I cannot actually meet you yet.

So anyway, I spent an idyllic year in the UK and then the whole cartoonist saga blew up. We don't need to go into the details; it is enough to say that the British government was furious. Margaret Thatcher actually took the unprecedented step of inviting me to Downing Street for a personal audience. It was, according to her private secretary who showed me out afterwards, one of the rare occasions on which she violently swore at anyone.

I hope that answers your first question. As regards your other question as to when you might manage to meet me, can I suggest that we try to arrange something for the summer holidays? I believe you have a very long break in July and August with not much work to do if British students are anything like as lazy as their Israeli counterparts. Why don't you come out and visit me then? Give me plenty of warning and I'll book the flights and make sure I'm around. If you come in August, I could even secure you a place at 'The Factory', Mossad's elite training facility. You might not be a fully fledged member but I could at least get you sufficient clearance to see what kind of career might be available to you were you to stay with us.

In the meantime, Adam, there is a small something I'd like you to do for me. Sam Joseph will be in touch with the full details but I wanted you to hear it from me as well. You should trust this man; he is one of my oldest and best friends. The mission he will give you is vital to the security of both my nation and yours, my personal security as well as your own.

Your father, David

Trinity Hall
Cambridge
3rd April 1992

Dear Mum,

I hope you're well and not worrying too much. In fact, I do believe that, very soon, there should be no more need to worry at all. You see, I've just received another letter from David in which he has promised to leave us alone entirely. He cites work pressures mainly, also a recognition that he has done wrong by us and we deserve to live in peace.

I shall let you know if anything else happens but it looks, at last, as if we might be able to return to some degree of normality.

I hope so.

I love you.

Adam

5

Operation Bilal

Note from Harry Pearce

Midway through 1992, the correspondence between Adam and his mother entirely dried up. Adam no longer wanted to share developments with his mother — this was now something personal between him and his father — and tried to convince her that there was nothing more to report. Eleanor, of course, was not so naive as to think events could come to such an abrupt end. If Horovitz really had been trying for almost two decades to effect some sort of reunion, why would he give up so suddenly just as his end goal appeared to be in sight? Quite simply, Eleanor did not believe Adam. It created a sad rift between the two.

In the absence of any further correspondence at this stage, we are fortunate to have a complete record of the extraordinary events that followed in the form of an MI5 report which a youthful Adam was asked to compile. As you will see, it is considerably more emotive and far-ranging than a standard report written by a professional officer in the employ of the Security Services. This, of course, was exactly what MI5 instructed Adam to do: 'Write down everything, as it happened, as you experienced it and as you felt it. Leave nothing out, however irrelevant you might think it is. We will judge the relevancy.'

It took no small amount of digging for me to uncover the original. The document that Adam wrote in the summer of 1992 was 'Eyes Only' and destroyed by the relevant case officer as soon as he had noted down the salient facts and typed up his own, more professional report (which was much abridged and subsequently destroyed).

However, bureaucracy always leaves a slime trail. Another, more senior, officer told Adam that it would be a good idea to keep a record somewhere of his own, original first-hand report as a security in case MI5 ever turned on him. As Adam would already know from his brief stint as a journalist, no one is ever happy with how they are reported. You can't beat a first-person account.

This senior officer helped Adam to transpose his report on to micro dots — text so small that you can fit tens of thousands of words into the size of a single full stop. I eventually discovered the original — we shall come on to how later — in the *Hans Wehr Dictionary of Modern Written Arabic* (edited by J. Milton Cowan) on the second floor of the Trinity Hall library.

The second half of Adam Carter's report follows below (the first half dealt with events between 1990 and March 1992, with which we are already familiar). The reason the report was written up for MI5 will become clear during its reading.

OPERATION BILAL

Initial report by Adam Carter for MI5
June 1992

David Horovitz's letters

With the benefit of hindsight – if three months counts as sufficient distance to be considered hindsight – I can see that my father's early letters aroused a number of different emotions in me. There was anger, of course. Fear, too. But most of all I was curious – the best of emotions. It was the same curiosity that took me to Israel in the first place.

My curiosity has got me into a great deal of trouble as well, but it also stopped me from ever being entirely closed off to the idea of meeting my father. I wanted to know what he was like more than I wanted to indulge myself with the luxury of hating him at a distance.

And by this stage, I'm not even sure that 'hate' is the right word to describe my feelings towards him. You've seen that powerful second letter he sent me. He was an admirable man in many ways – ambitious, cultured and plain speaking. I also felt he was a very troubled man, however much he tried to hide it. I believe I respected and sympathised with him in fairly equal measure.

It's certainly difficult not to sympathise with my father. Imagine the pain of losing someone you truly loved. Imagine the even worse pain of knowing that there is someone out there who probably has half your genes and you have no way of contacting them. Maybe you've walked past them in the street without even noticing. Perhaps they're a public figure, a genius, a politician, a writer or a professional sportsman. Or maybe they're a murderer. The worst thing is that you'll never know.

I can also empathise with this sense of impotence because I believe that children who do not know their parents experience a similar emotion. I know many people go through their lives without the luxury of two parents. Some are orphaned or neglected, cheated by death or abandoned in a divorce. I grew up thinking that my father had died before I was born. I grew up imagining him looking down on me, looking out for me as I tried to make this invisible presence proud.

I grew up on a lie.

So when I found out the truth – or, at least, what I thought was the truth – can you blame me for wanting to find out more? I know of some adopted children who spend half their lives trying to track down their real parents, torturing themselves in the process. They make it their life's mission. So when everything apparently fell on my lap, I simply could not resist the bait.

I think I would have done almost anything if it involved meeting David Horovitz at the end of the process.

Bilal Tarikh

David Horovitz had indicated in his third letter to me that I should expect another visit from Mr Joseph very soon. During my time at school, Mr Joseph had made something of a habit of appearing, unannounced and uninvited, on the touchlines at the end of a rugby match. He didn't disappoint this time either.

It was the final match of the season and I was in a pretty bad mood. I'm not normally much of a worrier – generally, I just like to sit back and let things crinkle out – but plenty had been preying on my mind recently. Off the pitch, I had been worrying about work and, of course, about my father's letters. Also, I don't know whether you will judge this relevant (but you did ask for all the facts) I had been worrying about my ex-girlfriend, Lucy. We'd broken up at the beginning of that term and I would be seeing her for the first time, along with the rest of the Dempsey family, at Easter. How would they react? Would Simon and Sarah Dempsey be angry with me?

I had a few worries on the pitch as well. The Varsity match last December had been one of the highlights of my life but it also seemed to mark the pinnacle of my rugby-playing career. Ever since, I had been plagued by regular injuries. Whereas I was once the natural, maybe even the only, choice to start the match at fly half, I was increasingly finding myself on the bench. My rival was off sick for this match. If I didn't put in a decent performance I could probably wave goodbye to my chances of being guaranteed a place in the squad next season.

At half-time, the score was 10–9 to us. Then Loughborough University scored two more penalties straight after half-time. With five minutes to go, they were still leading 15-10. In the final minute, our inside centre danced through their three-quarter line and put the ball down right in front of the posts. The score was 14–15. All I had to do was slot the simplest of conversions and we would win 16–15, rounding off a glorious unbeaten season in style.

I don't know what happened as I lined up that kick. Normally, I am capable of emptying my mind entirely. It can be the noisiest pitch in the world but all I see is myself, the ball and the posts. I close my eyes and play the successful kick three times in my imagination before running up and taking it. If I have already imagined the successful outcome it helps it actually come about in reality.

But this time, I just couldn't empty my mind of thoughts. All I could see was my mother and the shapeless form I associated with my father. I knew for absolute certain I was going to miss the kick. I should have stopped, reset and started again. But I didn't. I couldn't. I ran up, slipped and sliced the ball wide of the right post. The whistle blew. We had lost by one point.

It was an inauspicious moment for Mr Joseph to try to strike up a conversation. Yet in some ways, his presence there was welcome. After all, there were more important things than rugby now. He was easier to deal with – more straightforward even – than the faux sympathy and condolences of my teammates which did little to hide their true disappointment and disgust. I didn't blame them; I felt pretty disappointed and disgusted with myself at that moment.

Mr Joseph give me time to shower and change while he sat in the car park and waited. Fifteen minutes later, I emerged and climbed into the passenger seat of his expensive German saloon. The engine, I noticed, was still running.

'I don't want anyone to overhear us,' he said, revving the engine slightly.

'Of course.' I nodded, as if this sort of thing happened to me every day.

'Now,' said Mr Joseph. 'Tell me everything you know about your friend . . .'

He gave another little rev of the engine to disguise the name.

'. . . your friend Bilal Tarikh.'

Mr Joseph took his foot off the accelerator. The rev counter returned slowly to idling and I started to tell him everything I knew.

Bilal was the same age as me, the same height as me and had a very similar outlook on life to me, but our respective upbringings could not have been more different. His father was Jamal Tarikh, the head of the wealthy and vastly influential

Tarikh family which had held sway in Palestine for the best part of the last four centuries. Jamal, an intellectual moderate and a doctor by trade, had decided to stay out of politics and was respected by, and had friends among, Palestinians and Israelis alike. He spoke five languages, had degrees from three different universities, including Harvard and the Sorbonne, and had married a beautiful English girl who was the daughter of an English aristocrat: Bilal's mother, Vanessa.

Tarikh was adamant that all his children should be educated in the area he liked to call Palestine until at least the age of sixteen. Thereafter, he sent them all to English boarding school from where five of his six children proceeded to Oxbridge.

Bilal was the youngest of the siblings and always thought the most likely to turn out to be a black sheep. He certainly had all the attributes of a likeable roguish failure: a charming, easy-going manner; a rakish glint in his eye which made him attractive to a certain type of woman; a laissez-faire approach to academic study; not to mention a mean eye for any sort of spherical sporting object, particularly a polo ball.

Yet he was also fortunate that not all the brains had been watered down by the elder members of his family. Bilal was far from stupid. Trinity Hall might have given him a place in the hope and expectation that his rich father would help to

He never did, as it turned out

HP

refurbish the library but he would almost certainly have got in on his own merits as well.

And yet his choice of subject, Arabic, was a curious one which said much about his character. Bilal was widely read and widely educated. He was the only person I knew in my college who actually read outside the subject. His interests included history, politics and Persian literature. So why study Arabic if he already spoke it, already wrote it and had already read ninety per cent of its literature? 'Because I don't like being told what to do,' he said to me on one occasion. 'I like to study because I want to, not because I have to.'

As I say, this attitude towards his work was typical of Bilal's attitude towards life in general. The fact that he was very much his own boss made him a lot of fun to be around. The first year of university is, I think, a strange time in a young person's life. Some people arrive there knowing everyone already; others know no one at all. But everyone is trying to prove themselves, reinvent themselves and make a fresh start. It is the transition phase – a long transition phase – from childhood to adulthood.

Yet none of this seemed to matter to Bilal. He was already light years ahead of us in maturity. He related tales of friends back in Palestine who had been arrested by the Israeli police, interrogated and beaten up. He spoke of riots and demonstrations, bitter feuds and ancient politics. The rest of us had tales of the Home Counties and 1980s London. It was difficult to compete. It was difficult not to feel very young next to him.

Bilal, however, combined this worldly maturity with a gloriously juvenile approach to life in general. He was always the last to leave a party and the first to suggest any number of ridiculous schemes. I remember one Tuesday evening in the middle of our first term when someone remarked over dinner that the excitement and novelty of freshers week had worn off. Bilal's bright eyes suddenly lit up behind his soup spoon. 'Well, let's do something about it then,' he said.

'Do what?'

'Let's go to Paris,' said Bilal. 'No point being a student with no work to do if you can't up sticks and go to Paris midweek.'

So we did. Four of us, for forty-eight hours during which we didn't sleep at all. Bilal footed the bill for the entire party.

Bilal had a huge number of friends but I think it's fair to say that I was one of his closest. We were the only two people in our year in college studying Arabic so we inevitably spent quite a bit of time together (not that Bilal bothered to attend lectures very often). He was always generous with his time and his expertise, regularly helping me with any Arabic assignment I hadn't fully grasped.

But I think we would have been firm friends even if we had been in entirely different colleges studying entirely different subjects. Bilal was a very easy person to get on with. Despite possessing all the attributes of a playboy, he was also loyal and generous to a fault. You wouldn't want to cross him but he was a wonderful person to have on your side. With Bilal, a friend was a friend. For life . . .

Mr Joseph had been nodding encouragingly, if a little sceptically, throughout my long monologue. But when I got to the bit declaring Bilal my lifelong friend, he finally interrupted.

'Your friend for life? I wouldn't be so sure about that.'

He left the thought hanging in the air for a while. I fell silent.

He continued, 'Would you describe Bilal as a political sort of animal?'

'I'm not entirely sure what you mean by that. He is interested in politics, certainly. But he seems to prefer to observe it from a lofty distance. I definitely wouldn't call him an activist.'

'No, activist is certainly far too weak a word. How about extremist?'

'What on earth do you mean by that?'

Mr Joseph rummaged around in a brown leather briefcase he always carried with him and produced a sheaf of papers for me to look at. I flicked through them, trying to keep a disdainful frown off my brow. I tried to choose my words carefully.

'So, you have grainy surveillance photos of Bilal entering a mosque in Cambridge and talking to a fellow student. So what?'

'Did you know that Bilal was a regular mosque goer?'

I had to admit to Mr Joseph that I didn't. Bilal rarely spoke about religion but I had always assumed that he was an atheist or, at the very least, a trendy agnostic. Still, it didn't exactly prove anything, showing me a bunch of photos of him outside a mosque. Plenty of people went to mosques. They were called Muslims, not extremists. It was like saying that you had caught sight of a Christian outside a church, so they must be on the point of launching a holy crusade in the Middle East. I said as much to Mr Joseph.

'But don't you think it significant that he never mentioned his visits to you?' he asked.

'Not really,' I said. 'Bilal likes to talk about interesting things, not dull ones. He rarely tells me what he's eaten for breakfast, or how many times he's been to the loo that morning. Should I be suspicious about those omissions as well?'

Mr Joseph smiled. He is the only person I have met capable of smiling without showing any warmth at all. It actually made his face more unpleasant than usual.

'It's very good of you to stand up for your friend. Laudable, admirable, honourable. But would he do the same for you, I wonder. How much is he keeping from you? Look at that photo again. He is wearing a Palestinian *keffiah*. Have you ever seen him wear one of those before?'

'No,' I said. 'But I don't see what that has to do with anything. He is half Palestinian, after all. Maybe he misses home. Or perhaps he was just cold and wanted to wrap up warm.'

Mr Joseph sighed and jabbed the picture of the person Bilal was talking to with his left forefinger.

'Do you know who that is?'

'No.'

'If you'd taken the monitoring tasks I've given you so far a little more seriously you would. It's a Lebanese guy called Mustapha Ahmed. He's studying chemistry in Cambridge at King's. He also happens to be a known Hezbollah agitator, under constant surveillance by MI5. Why they let this sort of person into the country, let alone give them a place at one of the most prestigious universities, is quite beyond me.'

'Well,' I said, 'King's does have a very left-wing reputation.'

'Adam, I'm not sure this is the right time for jokes.'

'There's always time for jokes, Mr Joseph.'

Mr Joseph thumped his fist down on the steering column, making the car horn go off and making me jump. I'd pushed him too far – and not for the first time.

'No, Adam, there is no fucking time for jokes. No time for anything at all. This Ahmed guy is dangerous and if he's talking to your friend – if they have absolutely any contact at all, however fleeting or trivial – then your friend is potentially dangerous as well.'

'I can see that,' I said, trying to placate him. 'But if that's the case, surely MI5 will have their own interest in Bilal, their own operations. Much better to leave this all to them, surely.

They can investigate, discover nothing is wrong and we can all go about our business as before.'

'I wish it were that easy,' said Mr Joseph. 'But my sources in Five tell me that they would never dare put proper surveillance on to Bilal Tarikh. His mother's family is far too important, for starters. They would never risk the backlash. And if his father got to hear about it, there would be an outcry in the Arab world. The Tarikh family is one of the few moderates respected on all sides in Jerusalem. The British government would never do anything to rile them.'

'And the Israeli government?'

Mr Joseph smiled the same humourless, mirthless smile. 'Good, Adam. Very good. In this delicate case you will be the eyes and ears – and maybe even the hands – of the Israeli government. It will make your father very pleased and proud when I tell him all about it. And just think, this summer you will be able to tell him all about it yourself.'

I swivelled in my seat to look Mr Joseph directly in the eye. The windows, I noticed, had steamed up. We were pretty steamed up, too.

'And what would you like me to do?'

Mr Joseph turned on the car heater and met my gaze, levelly, speaking quietly and quickly. 'Do nothing rash. Continue your friendship as before with Bilal Tarikh, but every time you see him, every time he speaks, remember everything I have told you in this car. It's the small clues you're looking for, the tiny verbal slips, the changes in routine. Don't do anything suspicious. Whatever you do, do not compromise yourself at present. But, if the opportunity presents itself, try to search his room. Report everything you find back to me.'

'Fine,' I said. 'I'll do it. If it's that important, I'll do it. But remember, I'm only agreeing to this in order to clear any suspicions hanging over my friend's name. For the record, I think you're speaking absolute paranoid rubbish.'

Mr Joseph offered me a lift back to my college. I declined and climbed out of his car, slamming the passenger door behind me, unlocked my bicycle and pedalled into the driving rain and back into the centre of town.

Under surveillance

I had told Mr Joseph that I thought his suspicions were 'paranoid rubbish' and I meant it. But the problem with even the most paranoid garbage is that sometimes it sticks. Mr Joseph seemed so cocksure that it was difficult not to let some of that certainty rub off on me. I liked Bilal. I trusted him. But Mr Joseph had successfully planted a small, annoying voice in the back of my head which just would not vanish.

It chimed away, uninvited, the entire time during my cycle ride back to college: 'How well do you really know Bilal Tarikh? How long have you two been friends? Six months? Can you get to know a person – really know a person – in that time? Compare it to Richard Dempsey; you've known him all your life, you've grown up together and he still surprises you every now and again. So think how many surprises someone like Bilal Tarikh might have in store.'

By the time I had turned into King's Parade and was freewheeling past the Senate house I had successfully put all these stupid thoughts to the back of my mind. Yet I knew they were now there to stay, at least until I could prove Mr Joseph right or wrong. Until then, they would never entirely disappear.

I turned down Senate house passage, swung a leg over the saddle and started to lock up my bike. At that moment, Bilal emerged from the porters' lodge and came over to commiserate with me on the defeated game of rugby.

'I'm so sorry, mate,' he said, clapping me on the back. 'I was there watching with Richard. We didn't want to miss the last game of the season. But you shouldn't beat yourself up about it. There were any number of missed chances and minor mistakes in that game; you just happened to make the most obvious one. It's the price you pay for leadership: visibility.'

I smiled at him. Whatever Bilal was or wasn't up to, he was certainly a true friend.

'That's a complete load of bollocks, Bilal,' I said. 'But thanks for trying to cheer me up anyway.'

'I know something else that will cheer you up even more.'

'What's that?'

'How about two hundred bottles of champagne, four

hundred pretty girls and the best venue in Cambridge? How does that sound?'

'I think it sounds very good indeed.'

Bilal had secured himself a very cushy position as social secretary of the Hawks Club, the drinking den which, in theory at least, was only meant to be frequented by sportsmen and sportswomen who had achieved at least one Blue by representing the university at sport against Oxford. Bilal was so charming and gregarious a host that the committee decided to overlook the fact that he only had a half Blue in polo, and a fairly dubious half Blue at that, given that he had only lasted five minutes on the pitch before coming off and lying down until the previous night's excesses had worn off.

Like every other red-blooded man in Cambridge, Bilal well understood the concept of 'Blue tack', the rather unflattering term given to girls who hung around sporty types. Demeaning though it might have been, they were invariably extremely attractive. Bilal liked confident, brazen girls.

'Great,' said Bilal. 'I'll see you there at seven p.m. then and we'll drink your blues away.'

He laughed at the weakness of his joke, punched me in a friendly way on the arm and turned right in the direction of the River Cam, leaving me with my conflicting thoughts. So *this* was the young man Mr Joseph suspected of Islamic extremism? I actually laughed out loud at the thought. Girls, champagne, parties. Didn't the Koran have some pretty stringent things to say about all three? Mr Joseph was every bit as mad and paranoid as I had always suspected. Shaking my head, I finished locking up my bike and went inside for a very long bath.

Two hours later, the party in the Hawks Club was in full swing. Bilal wasn't exaggerating; there really were four hundred pretty girls and at least as many bottles of champagne. When the champagne ran out, there was as much wine and beer as you could drink. And when the pretty girls ran out . . . well, the pretty girls didn't run out. You could barely move for beautiful, intelligent women, none of whom seemed to mind too much that I had fallen over while trying to kick an oddly shaped ball between two posts.

There were so many people there that I barely even saw Bilal until after midnight, let alone got a chance to speak to him properly. It wasn't until 1 a.m. that we both found ourselves at the bar at the same time. He beamed at me, the most worse for wear that I had ever seen him. Bilal was always an excellent drunk – witty, loud and never violent or morose. But his head suddenly slumped forward into his gin and tonic before bouncing back up again. He beamed again. 'Just getting my third wind, mate,' he slurred. 'That's what I'm doing just in case you're wondering. Just getting my third wind, mate.'

A pretty girl walked past and Bilal miraculously recovered himself. 'Olivia,' he called out. 'Give me one good reason why I haven't yet danced with you tonight.'

She looked at him with a glacial smile. 'I can think of several,' she said. 'But number one is probably that you have no idea what my name is.' She started to walk away, then turned on her heel, walked up to Bilal and whispered in his ear, 'For the record, it's Nicola and dancing wasn't the activity I had in mind.'

I stood and gaped, open-mouthed and, quite frankly, jealous, at Bilal as he stared at the retreating figure of the girl he now knew as Nicola.

'Do you know what you are, Bilal?' I said. 'You're a bastard, that's what you are.'

Bilal laughed self-deprecatingly. 'Maybe, Adam, maybe. But there are girls and there are girls, and I know who my real friends are.'

We chinked glasses and downed their disgusting contents in one.

'Bilal,' I said, 'can I ask you a stupid question?'

'You don't normally ask permission before you do so.'

'Well, it's a bit sensitive.'

This, I reasoned, seemed as good a time as any to put some of Mr Joseph's theories to the test. Bilal was three sheets to the wind. Even if I did offend him, he would be unlikely to remember any affront in the morning. I could also put my own behaviour down to drunkenness. While I retained some degree of clarity due to the strange situation I was in, I was, nonetheless, almost as affected as Bilal.

'Of course you can,' said Bilal. 'I'm not exactly a sensitive type.'

I laughed. 'I know it's hardly the time or the place but I wanted to know how you squared your Muslim upbringing with your behaviour in Cambridge.'

Bilal stared at me, seemingly in shock. For a moment I thought he was going to hit me. Then his face relaxed again.

'God, mate, and I don't mean that blasphemously, you said it might be a slightly insensitive question, you didn't say it would be a bloody boring question.'

I laughed, too, with nervous tension. 'So is there a bloody boring answer?'

'What's come over you, mate? When did you suddenly become Adam Carter QC?'

I thought quickly, or as quickly as my drink-addled brain allowed. 'Oh nothing, really. I'm just becoming boring in my old age. Also, and you won't know this because you never come to lectures, but we've started translating Mohammed's *Hadiths* with Dr Anderson and it got me thinking about this sort of stuff.'

Bilal visibly relaxed again.

'Well, whatever, you're right, there is a bloody boring answer and it is this: I live two fairly separate lives. When I'm at home in Jerusalem and Ramallah I'm the good young Muslim, youngest son of a respected local dignity who would do nothing to bring shame on his family. But when I'm abroad

– and especially when I'm abroad at university – I have the freedom to become who I really am...' He trailed off, put his glass down and looked me directly in the eye. 'Adam, mate, the Bilal you think you know is the real Bilal. It's the English Bilal. It's me.'

His face had assumed an alien seriousness which scared me. The Bilal suddenly confessing to being the real Bilal was not the Bilal I knew. Then he smiled again and my old friend was back. 'Now, where has that girl, what's-her-face, got to?'

I left Bilal to go off in search of Olivia or Nicola or whatever his latest target was called. But I had to admit that our conversation had troubled me. Of course Bilal had spoken regularly about his time in the Middle East. He was proud of his family, proud of his roots. Yet, naively, I somehow imagined that he would behave exactly the same at home as he did here in Cambridge. A hinterland had just opened up and it was a hinterland about which I suddenly realised I knew nothing. It was unsettling.

This new side of Bilal was something I wanted to explore further, for my own curiosity if nothing else. Half an hour later, I was ready to leave the party but not ready for bed just yet. As I busied myself picking up my jacket from the cloakroom I made a great show of searching in all my pockets for my keys. Only five metres away, Bilal was locked in what might loosely be described as 'intense conversation' with Nicola. Catching his eye with a helpless look, I motioned to him to join me briefly at the bar.

'This better be good, mate,' he said, casting frantic, reassuring glances back towards Nicola.

'Oh, I think you'll thank me for it,' I said grimly. 'You see, I've lost my keys somewhere and I'm already in enough trouble with the porters so they'll kill me if I wake them up. So, I was thinking, perhaps you could lend me yours which might give you a perfect excuse...'

'The perfect excuse for what?'

Jesus, Bilal really must have been drunk if I was going to have to spell this out for him.

'You know, the excuse to go back to hers...'

'Aha!' The penny finally dropped.

Bilal joyfully made a great show of handing over his keys in front of Nicola who winked at me. As I walked down the steps of the Hawks Club and into the street outside I could hear him explaining, loudly and unnecessarily, 'You see, he'd lost his keys so it made sense for me to lend him mine. You don't mind, do you?'

Nicola could just be heard attempting to restrain her giggles at the awful amateur dramatics of the entire episode. I smiled to myself as I walked briskly back towards college. And we men still think we hold the cards!

Bilal was one of those people who signed out a night key for the entire duration of the term. I let myself in through the large wooden double doors which were always locked at 1 a.m. and turned instinctively right instead of left when I got into Front Court. Correcting myself, I doubled back and walked up Bilal's staircase until I got to his room: F7. The key turned easily in the lock and I let myself – the sanctioned, legitimate intruder – into a room I had visited a hundred times previously.

What was I looking for exactly? I already knew the room inside out: the large, vertical Palestinian flag hanging behind the door; the copious, empty wine bottles, many of them expensive, which he displayed as some sort of alcoholic's badge of honour; the numerous books, most of them original hardbacks, on subjects as diverse as philosophy, cookery and climbing; a couple of framed watercolours; the large Arab shisha pipe which was rarely used to smoke anything as weak as apple tobacco.

I started to search the room, having locked the door from the inside, left the key in the lock and wedged a chair under the door handle for safety. But obviously, I didn't really have any idea what I was doing. I felt like the kind of amateur detective you see on television, aimlessly rifling through drawers of unfiled receipts, used cinema tickets and other meaningless odds and ends.

It was a pretty gross infringement of privacy, even if I felt I had legitimate grounds for doing so. I became increasingly manic as my search continued to throw up no answers.

Despite his cavalier, seemingly carefree approach to life and work, Bilal was an extremely tidy person. Everything I messed up would have to be replaced exactly as I had found it.

I was just about to give up trying and collapse, gratefully and drunkenly, into a bed which looked significantly more comfortable than my own, when I saw a small chink of something reflective under Bilal's bed. Getting down on my hands and knees, I noticed a small, metallic cash box. I shook it and it rattled, although not with the sound of coins. Perhaps it was jewellery or something else valuable. And yet I couldn't see any way of finding out. I had already turned the room practically upside down and had seen no sign of a key.

Defeated, I got back down on my hands and knees to replace the cash box. As I did so, I slipped and the box fell on to the floorboard, making a strange, hollow sound as it landed. I moved the cash box to one side and tapped the floorboard lightly with my knuckles. It was definitely hollow. It also rattled when I hit it harder, suggesting it might be loose. Bringing Bilal's bedside lamp down to floor level so I could see what I was doing, I gradually prised the floorboard loose with my fingernails. Reaching into the semi-darkness, I pulled out what felt like a book. Holding it under the light, I saw that it was the Koran. Inside was a detailed architect's map of neighbouring Trinity College.

Mr Joseph reacts

'Well done, Adam,' said Mr Joseph, leafing, apparently absentmindedly, through the pages of Bilal's Koran. 'You did the right thing in calling me.'

It was 5 a.m. the same day. Mr Joseph had given me a special number which was linked to a pager system and told me I should call him, any time of day or night, if there were any significant developments. And this, apparently, was a 'very significant development indeed'.

'I take it you're referring to the discovery of the map,' I said, 'and not an innocent copy of the Koran.'

Mr Joseph looked at me very intently. I tried to focus on him, to stop my head from spinning from the earlier excesses if nothing else. 'Have you learnt nothing, Adam?' he said. 'Nothing is ever innocent in this business and nothing is *ever* as it seems.'

He took out a key ring fob from his pocket, swivelled the manufacturer's logo and out popped a tiny camera. Concentrating intently, Mr Joseph took as many pictures as possible of the plans of Trinity College before handing the sheet back to me.

'Aren't you going to take pictures of his Koran as well?' I asked, trying my best to keep the weary sarcasm out of my voice. It went undetected.

'No need,' said Mr Joseph. 'I'll be taking this copy with me and you can have a replacement. Hopefully, he'll never notice.'

To my astonishment, he reached into his bag and pulled out an identical copy of the Koran to Bilal's. 'The standard version? Excellent, just as I thought. Your friend is a clever chap.'

'You carry around spare copies of the Koran in the middle of the night on the off chance that you might have to drive somewhere and replace someone else's copy?'

'You have no idea what we are capable of, Adam. From the most mundane tasks to the most intricate, from huge-scale operations spanning several continents and even decades to the provision of a replica Koran (which, incidentally, is no less vital to the successful, smooth running of an operation than a superficially more important object) in the middle of the night in East Anglia – we do it all, and we do it better than everyone else.'

A large part of me wanted to start clapping sarcastically – I think I still felt somewhat drunk – but I managed to resist the temptation by sitting on my hands. In any case, Mr Joseph was paying scant attention to me. He was now in full spy mode, tapping a pencil on his teeth while staring alternatively at the map and the Koran.

'Now, tell me, Adam, why would a student studying Arabic want the complete architectural plans of Trinity College?'

'Perhaps he has a passing interest in architecture,' I said, lamely. 'As I've said, Bilal is very much the autodidact.'

Mr Joseph snorted. 'Come on, Adam, you can do better

than that. A passing interest in architecture which he hides under a loose floorboard under his bed? I don't think so.'

I had to admit, it did look pretty suspicious. What on earth could Bilal have wanted these plans for? All the suggestions I could come up with sounded increasingly ridiculous. Trinity was famous for its wine cellar; perhaps Bilal was trying to work out how to break in. Students always try to steal the coveted bowler hats of Trinity's porters before they graduate. Maybe Bilal was plotting his escape route (this last suggestion was so ridiculous that I didn't bother sharing it with Mr Joseph).

'No, Adam, one thing is for sure: this map, and the way it was hidden, stinks. Bilal, like you, is a member of the university at large as well as Trinity Hall. If he wanted to, he could simply walk through the main gate of Trinity and leave again, unmolested, at any time. So why this double dose of secrecy?'

I had no answer there and then but I was relieved to see that neither did Mr Joseph. After sighing and tapping his pencil a few more times, he decided to leave me in peace. He tucked Bilal's copy of the Koran under his arm and gave what I think was meant to be a conspiratorial wink. 'Let's see what gems this throws up, shall we?'

As Mr Joseph stood up to make his excuses, I presented him with a Blu-Tack impression of Bilal's key. 'I thought you might be able to use some of your sources – perhaps the same sort of sources who can provide you with a replica Koran in the middle of the night – to make me a copy of Bilal's key. Bilal might come back at any time tomorrow morning – very early indeed if his usual morning-after routine is observed – and I probably wouldn't have time to make my own copy, even if the local locksmiths were willing.'

Mr Joseph stopped in his tracks and tried to smile one of his warmest smiles. It was still entirely mirthless. 'Well done, Adam. Very well done indeed. Your father will be very proud when I tell him.'

The mosque

Mr Joseph and I had a lucky escape. Characteristically, Bilal returned to his room around 6:30 a.m. Deeply asleep by this stage, it took several minutes for his drunken hammering on the door to wake me up, by which time most of the corridor was also awake and angry. Bilal stumbled in, muttering something unintelligible before collapsing on to his bed. I didn't even bother to pretend that it was now sufficiently far into the next day for me to go to the porters' lodge and ask them to let me into my own room to which I already had the key. Bilal had passed out.

If anything, I found that the events of that evening helped to cement our friendship still further over the next few days and weeks. Bilal appeared to have fallen head over heels for Nicola, whom he took great delight in pursuing vigorously. 'It's love, mate,' he said on more than one occasion. 'And you've helped make it happen.' (For what it's worth, my personal opinion is that Bilal's relationship with Nicola at this stage was nothing of the sort. He had merely met his match and was having to work for it for once.)

Either way, it helped form a new bond between the two of us, as I became Bilal's number one wingman, forever accompanying him on slightly awkward double dates with Nicola and an assorted range of her friends, none of whom I really hit it off with. Still, it was amusing to watch Bilal tongue-tied and occasionally floundering.

He had not forgotten the other part of our conversation that evening at the Hawks Club. On Thursday evening, about a week later, the two of us were returning from yet another double date which had concluded with Nicola demurely telling Bilal she would see him the next day, when Bilal suddenly stopped and laughingly said to me, 'The irony is that, given Nicola's current behaviour, and despite the impression she gave when I first met her, she would make a first-rate Muslim wife.'

I looked at him quizzically, awaiting an explanation. It came quickly. 'Don't think I don't remember our drunken conversations, Adam. It's one of my strengths, as well as one of my great weaknesses. Sometimes I wish I could forget certain things that happen whilst drunk. Laura in first term, to give just one good example. But I certainly remember our conversation at the Hawks Club bar. Don't feign amnesia. The two Bilals, remember? Well, if you want to meet the one you don't know yet, why not come along with me to midday prayers at the mosque tomorrow? You might find it interesting. You could put the experience in your next essay, or something.'

The following day I met Bilal at the porters' lodge and we set off together for the mosque. I did my best to put on an air of cultural inquisitiveness, playing the part of the interested naif.

'So, explain it to me,' I said as we walked. 'Last night you ate roast pork, washed down with two bottles of Chateauneuf du Pape, and tried in vain to get into a pretty girl's pants. Today, you're popping into a mosque to say sorry?'

'Adam,' replied Bilal, patiently, 'do you believe in God?'

'Not really.'

'Do you go to church at Christmas?'

'Yes.'

'Why?'

'Because I like singing carols. And listening to the old, familiar readings.'

'Exactly! That's *exactly* it. That's why I like going to the mosque every now and again. When I hear the call of the *muezzin*, I'm no longer a student at Cambridge but a freedom fighter running around the old walls of East Jerusalem. I listen to the *fatihaah* – the chanted opening to the Koran – and I'm back at home, sitting on my grandfather's knee in our house in Ramallah as he intones the beautiful words. I bend down to touch my forehead on the mosque's heavily carpeted floor and, catching the eye of a fellow supplicant, realise that none of us is alone in this world.'

I looked at him sideways as we removed our shoes at the entrance to the mosque. This was certainly a new side of Bilal, a side I hadn't seen before. But in my eyes, it made him more interesting, more rounded, more real. It certainly did not constitute extremism.

Some of this magic rubbed off on me during the *Jumaah* prayers. Even I was captivated once again by the glorious sound of the recitation of the Koran and transported back to my recent visit to Jerusalem. Christians say that the Bible is the word of God, when what they really mean is that it is divinely inspired. For Muslims, the Koran actually *is* the word of God, His exact words. I do not believe this, of course, but the language, even the sound of the language, is undeniably beautiful, even if you do not understand a single word of Arabic.

My reverie ended at the conclusion of the service when the voices around me became harsh and English. Snapping back to reality, I suddenly noticed that Bilal was deep in conversation with Mustapha Ahmed, the Lebanese student I recognized from the surveillance photos Mr Joseph had shown me in the car.

They were too far away for me to eavesdrop on their conversation so I decided to bite the bullet. Attempting to be a lot more confident than I felt – at the back of my mind was the reminder from Mr Joseph that MI5 was watching Ahmed; I did not want to be on the radar of more than one intelligence agency – I walked up to the two of them and introduced myself. Ahmed, a large man in his mid-twenties with stylish slicked-back hair and dark, friendless eyes, was cold and hostile.

'Oh great,' he said, sarcastically, after Bilal had given an effusive introduction. 'Another Lawrence of Arabia figure studying Arabic before joining the British Foreign Office. You're just what the Middle East needs right now.'

'Oh great,' I retorted, conscious of my fingernails digging into my palms. 'Another smug, middle-class Arab who is happy to slag off the West while taking advantage of our education system and our freedom. You're very welcome in my country. *Ahlan wa sahlan*. Very welcome indeed.'

I probably should have counted to ten and bitten my tongue but people like him make my blood run cold.

'*Ahlayn fiik*,' he mumbled, evidently startled, before sloping off to find a friendlier face.

Bilal grabbed me by the arm. 'Come on, mate, let's get you out of here before you cause any more trouble.'

People stared at us as Bilal frogmarched me out of the mosque. I was incensed; incensed by the scene Bilal was causing and even angrier that some of Mr Joseph's suspicions seemed to be rooted in fact. As we stomped home, I rounded on him. 'Why do you associate with people like that?' I shouted. 'Why do you give him the time of day?'

Bilal stopped on the spot, absolutely still, put a hand on my shoulder and said, very quietly and very seriously, 'Because, Adam, to understand the enemy you have to know the enemy. People like Ahmed pose as much threat to my people as they do to yours, as much threat to my father's side of my family as to my mother's. It is people like him who stop the West trusting the Arabs, people like him who make it easy for you to write us all off as extremists. So, that's why I speak to him, so I can influence him. I associate with him so I can keep my friends close and my enemies closer.'

Another meeting with Mr Joseph

Mr Joseph and I had got into a curious cycle whereby he would send me off to acquire information to confirm his suspicions, I would return with facts which I believed allayed them and he would sigh and send me off again with a whole new set of suspicions.

Or, at least, so it was with my report on Bilal's behaviour in the mosque. Perhaps naively, I felt that what Bilal had told me gave us sufficient grounds to stop keeping tabs on him in this slightly despicable, underhand way. Mr Joseph, of course, felt the exact opposite.

'How can you be so immature in your logic, Adam?' he asked with a slightly wistful, sad shake of his head. 'Your friend tells you that he goes to the mosque because he feels homesick? He wants to imagine himself, and I quote from your own account, "as a freedom fighter running around the walls of East Jerusalem"? He associates freely and openly with known extremists because he "wants to know what they're thinking"? Come on, Adam. Isn't it all just a little bit *too* convenient?'

I tried my best to look indignant but it was difficult to argue with Mr Joseph when he was in this sort of mood. He made very strong points. 'I imagine Bilal finds a lot of his situation highly inconvenient,' I attempted to argue.

Mr Joseph, however, ignored me and reached instead into his leather bag, pulling out the copy of Bilal's Koran which I had stolen a week earlier. 'I had a few tests run on this and it threw up some very interesting results,' he said, flicking through to the relevant page. 'Here, take a look at this.'

He handed me the book.

'What am I looking for?'

'No, Adam, turn that round. Not what are *you* looking for, what was *Bilal* looking for? Our boffins have a clever machine which lets them take any given document or book and see which bit was being looked at the most. It's quite beyond me of course – something to do with pressure points – but here, look at the extracts they've marked up in Bilal's Koran. Let's just take one at random, shall we? "I will cast terror into the hearts of those who disbelieve. Therefore strike off their heads and strike off every fingertip of them." Whoever has been reading this Koran has run their finger over that verse a thousand times or more. You can see from the indentation when we zoom in. There are a hundred or so similar verses, all of which have something to do with jihad. It is a topic with which Bilal appears to be intimately familiar.'

I shook my head in shock. I didn't want to believe Mr Joseph but what choice did I have? The evidence was overwhelmingly hostile. I tried again to put up some sort of defence on behalf of my friend but I could sense how weak it sounded even as I tried to articulate it. The Bible had hundreds of similar passages, as did, of course, the Torah. But how many people went through these books focusing on just the most vengeful parts? It looked worrying, and I said as much to Mr Joseph.

'What do I do now, then?' I asked, a little helplessly.

'You carry on exactly as you have been doing already and you report back to me on a daily basis now.'

Mr Joseph produced a shiny new brass key from his pocket. 'In the meantime, your first task is to get back into Bilal's room and see what else he has in his treasure trove.' Mr Joseph reached into his other pocket and produced four tiny eavesdropping bugs. 'And while you're there, you might as well plant these. Young Tarikh has started being pretty indiscreet in his conversations with you recently. Let's see how talkative he gets when you're not there.'

It wasn't difficult to gain access to Bilal's room this time. I had a key, I was even more determined than before and he was, by now, often staying over at Nicola's. The evening after seeing Mr Joseph, I waited until Bilal was visiting Nicola and let myself into his room again. The 'treasure trove', as Mr Joseph called it, still contained the plans to Trinity College but nothing new. I secreted the bugs as I had been instructed – under the desk, the bed, the telephone and the table lamp – and left as quickly as I could.

Bilal Tarikh and David Horovitz

My daily meetings with Mr Joseph quickly became tedious. It was difficult enough being civil to him on the relatively rare occasions that I had seen him in the past. Once a day was altogether too frequent for my liking. He probably felt the same.

Nothing much appeared to happen for a time, in any case. The bugs in Bilal's room revealed only 'alarming nocturnal sounds', as Mr Joseph put it coyly. I smiled to myself at the thought of Mr Joseph, or some other boffin, fast-forwarding through the transcript with a look of disgust on their face.

Then, two days later, Mr Joseph arrived with another letter from my father. There was no need for him to go through the elaborate charade again of delivering it to my pigeon-hole. He simply turned up at the arranged time and handed it over, watching me intently while I read it.

It is too long to transcribe here and I know you already have a copy in the files but it is worth summarising its main points for the record. According to my father's letter, Dr Jamal Tarikh, Bilal's physician father,

I could find no record of this

HP

was not all that he seemed. 'Adam, he and I have what you might call "form",' he wrote.

My father claimed that Dr Tarikh was influential during the intifada. In public, Tarikh always protested his neutrality, portraying himself as a unifying figure who stood apart from, and above, partisan concerns. Yet my father believed him

The first intifada, or uprising, a mass Palestinian protest against Israeli rule, is generally considered to have lasted from 1987 until 1993. A second intifada started in September 2000 when Ariel Sharon controversially visited the al-Aqsa mosque

HP

responsible for much of the influential work behind the scenes.

'We met several times,' he wrote, 'but I never pinned the bastard down. He was so slippery, so urbane. Yet I knew he was guilty of everything he denied. I've never found any proof, but I know for absolute certain that the outfit he controlled masterminded what we call in Hebrew *Leil HaGilshonim* or "Night of the Gliders", which took place on 25 November 1987.'

My father went on to give a lengthy description of what happened on the Night of the Gliders. In summary, two Palestinians took off from South Lebanon in gliders powered by engines no bigger than a lawnmower. One landed in the security zone and was killed immediately while the other evaded detection by flying at tree level, landed in an Israeli army camp where he killed five soldiers and wounded seven others before being shot dead himself. David Horovitz's brother had been one of the people murdered.

'If the end result wasn't so shocking, one might have admired the actions of these Palestinian terrorists,' wrote my father. 'They had courage; it is the sort of outlandish stunt that Mossad might have attempted. But the people behind it had no courage at all. Rich cowards, armchair generals, pontificating at home into their whiskies before sending braver men to their deaths. One day, I'll get Jamal Tarikh.'

My father's letter concluded by pointing out that, from what he had heard, Bilal Tarikh was every inch his father's son. 'Do not trust someone just because they are charming,' he wrote. 'Some of the most dangerous psychopaths in the world have been charming. Neither should you trust someone because they are likeable. Your own instincts are often wrong. Intelligence does not equate to compassion. Worldliness does not equal goodliness. Keep your wits about you.'

I re-read the letter a third time, looked up and saw Mr Joseph had still not taken his eyes off me.

'Pretty powerful stuff, eh?' he said.

'I suppose so, yes.'

We sat quietly for a bit and then he spoke again.

'It's almost the end of term. What do you have planned for the holidays?'

I've already mentioned in this report that I wasn't too keen on going back to Fleetwood House over Easter. Relations had been slightly strained with my mother, I think, since I stopped keeping her updated with what was going on. She suspected something, I'm sure. Worse still, Lucy had recently sent me a particularly vitriolic letter. I wasn't that keen on seeing her either. But there might just be an escape route of sorts. Bilal was trying to organise a ski trip. Richard Dempsey would probably be going too and I hadn't seen enough of him recently. Nicola and a few others would also be going.

'You absolutely must go,' said Mr Joseph. 'Where is it?'

'Courchevel. In the French Alps.'

'Perfect. I'll be in touch.'

Courchevel

Every Christmas holidays there was a huge 'Varsity ski trip' with around five hundred students from Oxford and Cambridge descending on a small Austrian ski resort. Bilal, who had gone on this holiday for the full fortnight, wanted to organise a 'smaller, more intimate trip' at Easter. I had imagined it would be just him, Nicola, Richard, me and maybe a couple of other girls. In the end, there were forty of us, staying in a huge catered chalet in Courchevel 1850, the highest of the Courchevel resorts and part of the Three Valleys network with Meribel and Val Thorens.

Courchevel is a beautiful place to go skiing, as yet untouched by the hordes of British tourists who invade the likes of Val d'Isère and Meribel every winter. The resort is high and vast, the snow is excellent and the bars are open a lot later than they are in England. We spent a perfect first three days there. It snowed every night. By morning, the skies had cleared into a brilliant dark blue as we whizzed down freshly powdered slopes.

Although we were a large party, we normally split up into smaller, more manageable groups to go skiing and then attempted to meet up in the same place for lunch. The first couple of days, Bilal did his gentlemanly best to put up with a dawdling Nicola. However, by the end of day two, they had both driven each other mad so Bilal came to ski with me and Richard instead. It was a dangerous, testosterone-fuelled threesome as we all tried to outdo each other to be the fastest and most foolhardy. I had been skiing with the Dempsey family since I was a small child so I knew what to expect from Richard. We always secretly thought we were both pretty good but nothing had prepared us for the kamikaze approach Bilal took to every piste. Even to use the word 'piste' is misleading. Bilal loathed pistes; he scorned them. Pistes were 'Muppet motorways', as he called them. Even the hardest blacks were only fit for beginners and cowards. Bilal liked to ski off piste. He brought a whole new definition to the phrase 'fall line'.

And so we jumped off cliffs, set off avalanches and tore down the mountain, generally acting as irresponsibly as possible. Cambridge, work, my father, Israel, Mr Joseph – it all seemed a very long way away.

One of Bilal's favourite games was for us to take the cable car as high as possible at the very end of the afternoon, settle down in a restaurant at the top of a mountain and drink ourselves silly on *glühwein* until it began to get dark and we were thrown out. Then we would strap on our skis and race back down into the valley – a competition that Bilal called 'Chinese racing', i.e. there were no rules. You could push someone over, cut them up or even steal their skis. The only limit on your deviousness was your own imagination. It was great fun.

We were first introduced to this game on the third day. Bilal won easily, helped in no small measure by being the only person to grasp fully the one and only rule: namely, that there were no rules. On entering the restaurant, and before explaining the game to us, Bilal had cunningly hidden our skis.

Richard and I eventually found them and narrowed the gap but Bilal made good his head start and arrived at the bottom shortly before us. All of us were out of breath, drunk and beaming from ear to ear.

'This is the life,' declared Bilal.

It was difficult to argue with him.

The other two left to continue their après-ski drinking in the Calico bar while I went off in search of a postcard to send home, promising to join them as soon as I had finished. I was flicking through the usual rubbish – a mixture of naked skiers and weak French puns I barely understood – when I heard a distressingly familiar voice behind me. 'Looking for a postcard for your mother?' it said. 'Or for the Dempseys?'

I spun round. Behind me stood Mr Joseph, wearing an all-in-one black ski suit. He didn't even try to smile this time as he spoke. 'Adam, we need to talk. Now. Watch where I go and follow me ten paces behind.'

I observed Mr Joseph in the shop mirror as he clunked off down the corridor in his ski boots and followed at a discreet distance. He turned right at the tourist information booth, climbed a flight of stairs and let himself into a small apartment which he double-locked behind me.

'What's this all about? And what are you doing here?' I was extremely angry at having my holiday interrupted.

Mr Joseph ignored the question. 'You're an excellent skier,

Adam. That could come in handy. Seriously, you're very fast. I've been finding it difficult to keep up with you.'

'You've been trailing me on skis?' I sounded more surprised than angry now. You get used to bumping into the same people on the slopes but I had seen no sign whatsoever of Mr Joseph.

'Yes,' he said, a little smugly. 'It's not something I've done for a long time but it's a relief to know I can still do it.'

'And Bilal? Have you clocked him as well?'

'Yes. He's also a remarkable skier. Yet another tribute to his international upbringing. And, of course, the real reason why I'm here.'

Mr Joseph fumbled around in a suitcase which looked like it had been packed in a hurry and produced a cassette tape. 'Here, you better have a listen to this.'

Again, I know MI5 already has the transcript to this tape. Everyone is now familiar with its contents. But I sat, open-mouthed, in that tiny overheated

There is no record of this

HP

apartment for two hours, listening to the taped conversation between Bilal Tarikh and the Lebanese extremist, Mustapha Ahmed, barely able to believe my ears. To say it was explosive would be an understatement. Ahmed talked about his hatred of the West, his refusal to recognize Israel's right to resist and his desire for violent jihad. This much was to be expected. The worst thing was that Bilal could be clearly heard sympathising with, and even echoing, his views.

In the last half-hour of the conversation, they moved from rhetoric to reality, from random theorising to practical measures they might take together to implement their belief system.

'Let's make it something big, something massive and unexpected,' said Ahmed eagerly. 'Let's make it something next term in Cambridge.'

And with that, the tape ran out.

We sat in silence for a while, letting the full impact of what we had just heard sink in. The voice was undeniably Bilal's, but it was a Bilal I hardly recognized. He sounded harsh, pumped up even. It was a million miles away from the laid-back friend I thought I had grown to know.

Mr Joseph met my gaze, evenly. I detected a hint of triumphalism that I had finally come round to agreeing with the suspicions that he had held since the beginning. My capitulation must have been clear from the look of shock on my face.

I tried to be calm but as soon as I opened my mouth the questions started tumbling out. 'So, that's it, I guess. We've got our evidence, we've got our smoking gun. What do we do now? Hand it all over to the police? He won't know that I betrayed him, will he?'

'Woah,' said Mr Joseph, holding up a hand to stem the verbal barrage. 'We'll do none of those things.'

'Why not?'

'Because they are all stupid ideas, that's why. For starters, there's no point handing over a transcript to anyone. Recorded surveillance material is entirely inadmissible in a British court. A grave error, if you ask me, but there you go. There's nothing we can do about it. And, in any case, we can hardly approach the police and tell them that we've been conducting our own private surveillance operation. They would inevitably start asking questions and the finger would point at me and, ultimately, you. I don't mind being implicated; they know about me already, of course. But you're a clean skin and a very good one at that. We need to keep it that way.

'Plus, there is the danger that they won't believe us at all. Remember how well-connected Bilal's mother's family is? They might just laugh us away. And then there is the consideration that we are already barging in on MI5's operation with Mustapha Ahmed.'

'So,' I said a little impatiently, 'what *do* we do?'

'Let's look at what we know and what we don't know. We know that Ahmed is an extremist who has got Bilal on his side. We know that they are planning a significant atrocity within the next ten weeks, probably in Cambridge. The way I see it, we have two options. One, we could wait and see what happens. You're friendly with Bilal. You could stay close to him and try to foil whatever happens before it does. That might work, but it's a risky option.'

Mr Joseph fell quiet, looking at me as if he expected to be prompted. Eventually I did.

'And the second option?'

'I've just looked at the weather forecast for the next few days. It's going to be a whiteout, not many people on the slopes, poor visibility, lots of avalanches . . .'

Mr Joseph tailed off and looked me directly in the eye. I wanted to look away but I held his gaze, feeling that to do otherwise would be a sign of weakness. It was me who finally broke the silence.

'You're asking me to assassinate Bilal Tarikh?'

'Assassinate is a strong word. Let's just say that people have accidents in the mountains the whole time. It would be a much easier solution for everyone.'

'Easier, maybe. But is it the right decision?'

'You have my assurances that you would be in no way implicated.'

'You're asking me to kill my friend.'

'To save the lives of countless others.'

'We don't know that.'

'I think we do. I think *you* do. It's the right thing to do, Adam. The only thing.'

Mr Joseph stood up and moved towards the door. As far as he was concerned, this conversation was over. The abruptness of what had just happened startled me. I had been ordered to kill a friend within the space of a sentence or two.

'Is this a test?' I asked, suddenly suspicious. 'One more training exercise to see if I'm "up to the job"?'

Mr Joseph put his hand on my shoulder again and attempted that same unsettling smile. 'All of life is a test, Adam. All you have to do is make sure you pass it.'

And with that cryptic answer I was shown the door.

I rejoined my friends in the chalet and told them that I had bumped into an old school friend while buying a postcard. As we settled down for supper that evening a blizzard started outside. It looked as if it was settling in for the long haul so we started playing drinking games. They got increasingly wild as the night continued.

'Might as well push on through until dawn,' said Richard Dempsey, sticking his head out briefly on to the balcony and returning looking like the abominable snowman. 'There will be no skiing tomorrow. All the runs will be closed.'

'Bollocks to that,' said Bilal. 'I'm not missing the best snow of the season. I'll climb up the mountain if I have to.'

Nicola groaned.

'And I'll climb up it with you,' I said, raising a glass.

'You won't be going anywhere if you carry on drinking like that,' said Nicola.

Avalanche

Bilal was one of those annoying people who never got hangovers. The next morning, I was woken up at 8:30 a.m. by him shaking me. Inside my pounding head, it felt like the entire chalet was trembling.

'Come on, mate,' he said airily. 'We're going to miss the first lift.'

I looked outside. As expected, it was still a complete whiteout. Several trees had come down in the night and the wind was still whistling round ferociously, making the snow fall almost horizontally against the windowpane. I brushed away the condensation to get a better look. Only one lift was moving. There was no one on it.

Regardless, we put on our ski clothes and stomped down towards the cable car where we were stopped by a gruff lift operator.

'*Vous êtes fous?*' he said. '*C'est fermé.*'

'Mad dogs and Englishmen,' said Bilal in his fluent French. 'We're only here for a week and we want to get our money's worth. Anyway, isn't that someone just getting into a cable car now?'

'Yes,' said the lift operator. 'It's one of the mountain rescue people, off to make the runs safe for tomorrow when the snow stops. Come back then.'

Bilal wasn't going to give up. 'And what about the guy behind him?'

'He owns the restaurant at the top of the lift. He's going up there to salvage his food.'

'Perhaps he needs a hand,' said Bilal. And before I knew

it, he had grabbed my arm and propelled the two of us into one of the bubble cars. The lift operator made a half-hearted attempt to stop us but Bilal had timed it just right. The doors closed as he reached us, the bubble car disengaged and we swooped up into the great white unknown.

At the top we were met by a second lift operator, his radio chattering away excitedly. This one, at least, had a sense of humour. 'My colleague is very annoyed with you,' he said. 'He wants me to send you straight back down in the cable car and confiscate your ski passes.'

He leant forward. 'But between me and you, my colleague is a complete arsehole. I told him it is rare to see some English people who actually want to ski properly. So, off you go and enjoy yourselves. I'll tell him you overpowered me, or something.'

We smiled gratefully at him, our teeth already chattering with cold. Were either of us really up there to 'enjoy ourselves'?

As if our behaviour wasn't sufficiently kamikaze already, Bilal suggested walking further up the mountain in our ski boots, carrying our skis, so we could ski down the infamous couloirs.

'Come on, Adam,' said Bilal. 'We've made it this far. There's no point just skiing back down again. It's a boring, simple blue. Just imagine how amazing the snow will be up there.'

The couloirs are one of the most dangerous series of runs in the world. To get to them normally, you have to ski along a path which is no more than a metre wide. Either side is a sheer drop. After a hundred metres or so, you get to the end of the path and have the choice of dropping down into one of three steep, almost cliff-like corridors – or couloirs – formed by the natural contours of the rocks. The moguls are huge, the pistes very narrow and the snow unpredictable. In normal conditions, they are for genuinely expert skiers only. In a blizzard whiteout – well, it was suicidal.

Mr Joseph would have deemed it perfect.

We started to trudge up the hill. Bilal and I were both in good shape but it took almost two hours. The wind and snow bit into any exposed skin on our faces and we started to notice the altitude as we climbed. Occasionally, Bilal would turn to me and grin, fully and happily alive. I had to grit my teeth and continually remind myself of the shocking revelations I had heard in Mr Joseph's apartment. This was no longer my friend, this was an enemy. Bilal was a threat to my country; his father a threat to my father. There was unfinished business between our two families.

Finally, we reached the top. I looked at my watch. It was 11:20 a.m. and the weather showed no sign of turning. We were completely and utterly alone on the mountain.

We clambered over to the start of the path where it was a relief to be able to put on our skis. If Bilal went first my job would be easy. All it would take would be a simple push and he would tumble to his death. No one would find him for weeks. But if I went first, well, it would be altogether harder.

Bilal started off in front. This is it, I thought. But then he suddenly stopped and looked up at me, an uncharacteristic expression of fear on his face. Did he know? Did he suspect anything?

'Adam,' he said. 'Would you mind going first? It's just that you know this run better than I do.'

There was a split second in which to decide whether or not to do as he asked. I had already lost the benefit of surprise. He was standing very upright and solid, facing me. If I rushed him and grappled unsuccessfully, how would we deal with the aftermath? I decided to keep him alive, for the time being.

'Sure,' I said, squeezing past him on the narrow path and taking the lead. The wind was particularly vicious on the top. It buffeted us from all sides, whipping up the snow around our skis.

We were halfway down the path when Bilal stopped behind me and called out loudly, 'Don't go all the way to the end. Let's do the steepest of the three.'

I stopped where I was and we both peered over the edge. I thought quickly. What next?

'After you, mate,' I shouted out into the gale. There wasn't much I could do if I was downhill of Bilal. I needed to maintain my height.

'Rubbish,' shouted Bilal. 'Let's race. You take the left side, I'll stick to the right.'

'OK.'

I counted down. 'Three, two…'

Bilal had already set off. I tore after him, closing the gap on his red jacket. The wind and the snow whistled past my frozen ears. If I could just nick the edge of his skis, they would cross and he would tumble to the bottom.

We had both taken a very direct line but I was out of sync with his turns. The steepest couloir was also the narrowest of the three. I needed to be turning into the middle at exactly the same time as him for my plan to come off.

I adjusted to take a more direct line and sped up significantly. As I did so, I hit the next bump at an awkward angle and somersaulted. I heard Bilal laugh below me as I got groggily to my feet and picked up the ski that had released. It was a lucky escape. My fall had been cushioned by a second mogul. If I'd fallen a couple of inches further down I could have gone the whole way to the bottom.

Bilal was now a good thirty metres ahead of me. I stamped my ski boot back into its binding and set off again in pursuit. I was skiing faster and better than ever before in my life. The red dot of Bilal's jacket grew larger as I gained ground.

Then, as I dug in my edges for one particularly sharp turn, I noticed that I had dislodged more than the usual amount of snow. I watched in horror as the lump gathered pace, slowly but surely, collecting more and more snow until I was floating above a giant, deadly river. I had started an avalanche and it was heading straight towards Bilal.

Just as I became aware of the full horror of what was happening, I heard the huge bang of a dynamite explosion behind me. The man we had seen going up on the lift before us was doing his job, making the pistes safe for the next day. As far as he was concerned, they were empty.

I stopped where I was and looked back towards the top of the slope. The clouds were thinner now and I could just make out a huge slab of snow breaking off and beginning to gather speed. We were both in grave danger. I was trapped between two avalanches. Bilal was in the path of both of them.

'Bilal,' I yelled.

He had already heard and seen both avalanches and was doing his best to out-ski them. It was typical of his arrogance. Most people know that it's impossible to ski faster than a moving wall of snow. Bilal must have thought that, if anyone could do it, he could.

There was no time to think about Bilal. The avalanche triggered by the dynamite gathered pace into an almighty roar and bore down on me. There was only one escape route: sideways. Crouching down into a tuck position, my ski sticks folded tightly under my arms, I took the most direct route possible down the mountain. It meant hitting the bumps at speed, my skis leaving the ground as I flew from one to another. There was no time to choose a route. I just had to get the hell out of there.

The roar behind me became deafening. In a matter of seconds it would be upon me and there would be no way out. I was now in the narrowest part of the couloir and would be dashed against the rocks.

But there was a glimmer of hope ahead. If I could just make it another twenty metres, I would be out of the bottleneck and into the more open piste, where I would have more chance of survival. I crouched lower, willing myself onwards. I could feel the snow beginning to lift my skis. A few more metres. The piste widened and I turned sharply left, flattening myself against a rock and hanging on for dear life.

The avalanche rushed past me. I took a deep breath, praying silently in several languages to whichever God would listen, and cleared as much space as possible around my mouth and nose. For what felt like hours, but can't have been more than a few seconds, the world turned even whiter as the snow pounded around me and into the valley below. I had had a very lucky escape.

I clambered gingerly to my feet and checked myself all over for broken bones. It wasn't just snow that had hit me; there had been rocks and bits of ice, even branches and small trees swept up in the avalanche's path. The skin on my hands had rubbed raw where I had been holding on to the rock. I had also broken my nose during my initial fall, a fracture that had been disguised at the time by the adrenaline. Otherwise, I was unharmed.

I did one careful turn so I could get a better view of the valley below. It was a distressing sight: the avalanche had continued nearly all the way to the bottom. The trees which had been there on our walk up were completely obliterated. Even the restaurant was half covered. There was no sign of Bilal.

But wasn't this what I had wanted? I hadn't even killed him, had I? It was his idea to come up the mountain in the first place, his idea to go stomping up to the top in suicidal conditions. I had thirty-eight witnesses from the previous evening to attest to that. I might have set off one small avalanche but it probably wasn't the one that had got him. The killer, huge one had been detonated by the man above us. It wasn't the guy's fault; he was just doing his job. It was our fault for being there, Bilal's in particular.

As far as anyone in authority cared, it was an accident. But for anyone else of importance in my life, it could be considered a clever stroke of genius. Mr Joseph would be appeased, my mother safe forever and my father reconciled. I would have ended one guilty life in return for saving countless other innocents. And as for me, I could have my old life back, if that was what I wanted.

But no! I was suddenly shaken out of this ridiculous thought process. Yes, it had been a horrible, stressful few years. My mother had been threatened, my life turned upside down by the strange and sudden appearance of Mr Joseph and an unknown father. But still, was this any way to behave? Was I no more than the hired thug of an amoral controller, the vigilante, deniable arm of a foreign power, dealing out arbitrary justice on the harshest possible terms?

What if Bilal was innocent? What if there was some other explanation? And even if he was guilty of Mr Joseph's accusations, it was not up to me to play God. This was no way to go about dealing with the situation. What about international law? The right to trial? Due process? Habeas corpus? Maybe there was a reason audio transcripts were not admissible in British courts.

I experienced that sudden terrible burst of guilt when you know you have done something horribly wrong.

Tearing off down the mountain, I called out Bilal's name as loudly as I could. Perhaps it wasn't too late. Perhaps I could still find him and make things right again.

I slowed down as I neared the area where I guessed he might be. As I stopped to look around, I noticed a bright red cord lying on the surface of the snow. I almost laughed with relief. Bilal is the only person I know who would bother to go and buy avalanche equipment and get the most old-fashioned device possible.

'Bilal,' I called out again.

This time, there was an answering, muffled shout. I took off my skis and used them to dig frantically, guided by the rope. Bright iron markings, a metre apart, indicated how far I had to go.

'I'm coming, Bilal,' I yelled, encouragingly. 'I'm coming. Just hold on.'

Eventually, I reached my friend.

'Did I win the race?' he asked with a weak half smile.

'Yes, you did.'

'And you have saved my life.'

'Yes, Bilal, I have.'

Back in Cambridge

After the excitement of that day in the couloirs, the rest of the holiday seemed fairly tame in comparison. The sun shone, the wind dropped and Bilal and I decided we would stick to marked pistes that were open. It wasn't a story that required much exaggeration but Bilal did his best anyway. By the end of the week, most of the party believed that I had dug him out over the course of three hours, with my teeth.

The day after our near fatal encounter with the avalanche, I saw Mr Joseph again at an agreed meeting point on an empty chairlift in Val Thorens. He seemed disappointed, but not all that surprised, that our plan had not come off. I didn't tell him about my last-minute change of heart. I thought it better to keep my ammunition dry and to keep everyone on my side for as long as possible.

'It's a shame, Adam,' said Mr Joseph. 'But it's not disastrous. We'll just have to get our man back in Cambridge instead.'

Before going back to Cambridge, I had decided to return to Fleetwood House for Easter. On landing at Gatwick airport, Richard and I were surprised to be met by a tearful Sarah Dempsey. Richard and Lucy's father, Simon, had died of a severe stroke that morning.

We travelled back home in silence and were met with an oppressive atmosphere. For the first time in my life, I felt like an intruder at the Dempseys' and the worst type of intruder at that: an intruder on their grief. I, too, felt the pain of loss intently. Simon Dempsey had been the closest person to a proper father I had ever known. I owed all my opportunities in life to his generosity. But it wasn't the same. He was Lucy and Richard's real father, not mine. The situation was not made any easier by the fact that Lucy and I had not spoken for over a month.

I know that my mother felt similarly isolated at this time. In recent years, she had always got on much better with Simon Dempsey than with Sarah. I think she was worried about what would happen to us next.

After I had ensured that my mother was OK, it was with some relief that I returned to Cambridge for the summer term. For most students, the summer meant one thing: exams. However, Bilal and I were fortunate in that Arabic was considered so difficult that the exams at the end of first year only counted as 'preliminaries'. The result did not go towards your final degree.

Bilal and I therefore spent a great deal of time together while everyone else jostled for position in the library. As far as Bilal was concerned, our friendship was now cemented for life. Every time I met one of his friends for the first time, I was introduced as the 'hero who saved my life'. I would smile politely, trying not to think how different it could have been.

And yet, and yet . . . I still couldn't get that transcript out of my mind. What had that all meant? I continued to keep a close eye on Bilal, monitoring any suspicious behaviour. But there was nothing to go on. He didn't even see his friend, Mustapha Ahmed, for the first week of the summer term.

One day, we were sitting in Bilal's room after lunch trying to cheer up Richard. All the talk in the first week of term had been about which May Ball we were going to attend. 'May Week' is something of an institution in Cambridge – an entire week of debauched black-tie parties in different colleges which take place at the end of term. This being Cambridge, May Week was always in June.

Trinity Hall traditionally held a fairly low-key May Ball. Trinity, our richer, bigger neighbour, hosted the party which everyone wanted to attend. Its budget was almost as big as the GDP of a small African country, the food and drink were lavish and limitless and the entertainment was normally provided by the biggest band around. There was only one small problem: tickets were almost impossible to come by.

'Are you sure there's absolutely nothing you can do, Richard?' I asked.

'Honestly, mate, I would if I could. I'm actually in Trinity and it's been pretty bloody hard to get tickets even for myself.'

Bilal started rustling around under his bed.

'What are you doing?' asked Richard.

'I think I might just have a solution to get me and Adam here into Trinity. I've been working on this for a little while.'

There was the sound of tapping and scraping under Bilal's bed. Eventually he emerged, triumphantly holding a copy of the Koran aloft.

'What the hell is that?' said Richard.

Bilal looked at the Koran, evidently somewhat embarrassed. 'Oh, that's a Koran which an old friend of my father's gave me when I first came to England. He's a bit of a religious nutter, but essentially harmless. This Koran is meant to be very old and valuable so I keep it hidden away under my bed so no one steals it or pours coffee over it by mistake. But this, well, this is altogether more valuable.'

Bilal opened the Koran. Inside were the architectural plans to Trinity College which I had seen a few weeks earlier, removed and passed to Mr Joseph to copy. He unfolded them and laid them out on his bed with all the relish of an ancient archaeologist discovering forgotten treasure.

'Yes,' he said enthusiastically, 'I think you'll like this. As you guys have probably heard already, one of the most fun things about May Week is crashing the parties. Sure, some of them aren't worth crashing at all. Trinity Hall's for example. And some are very easy to get tickets for. But where's the fun in simply handing over your money and walking in the main gate?

'When it comes to oversubscribed balls like Trinity, you have to use ingenuity. It's the holy grail for crashers. A significant proportion of their budget goes on security which is ironic when you consider that most May Ball committees actually want people to crash as it is a sign that their ball is some good. Adam, you'll know about this. They often use the university rugby team to keep out interlopers. And some of these crashers are so stupid, I'm told, that they all try to get in the same way. So to stand a higher chance, you have to use that little bit more cunning. Hence, these plans.'

Bilal gave the map a loving thump to finish his speech and beamed at the two of us. I think he might have been expecting a round of applause.

'Bilal,' I said, 'where the hell did you get these plans from?'

He looked at me nonchalantly. 'There is a tiny, secret university society which specialises in crashing May Balls. It was founded about ten years ago by my elder brother when he was here. He was an architect, incidentally.'

'I would never have guessed,' said Richard, wryly.

'Well, can I join this society?' I asked.

'Adam, you saved my life. It would be a pleasure.'

Richard groaned. 'Oh God, if you two are about to embark on a mutual backslapping exercise, I'm out of here.'

We tried to protest but Richard really did have to go to a lecture. 'Seriously, guys,' he said, 'I wish you luck planning your illegal entry into my college. It's just a pity you didn't apply there in the first place and so ended up in this dump instead.'

After Richard had left, Bilal babbled away enthusiastically about the best route to get into Trinity but I wasn't really paying attention. All I could think about was the fact that every time Mr Joseph's suspicions had been put to the test they crumbled completely. If he'd been wrong about most things so far, what other facts had he – wilfully or otherwise – misconstrued?

'Bilal, tell me seriously, what is the real reason that you're making friends with Mustapha Ahmed?'

Bilal broke off abruptly from his enthusiastic musings about the weak surveillance spots in Trinity's South Court.

'What?'

'You told me a little while ago that you were friendly with Ahmed because you like to keep your friends close and your enemies closer. You felt you could influence him by maintaining a dialogue with him.'

'Yes,' said Bilal. 'That's true.'

'But is it the whole story?'

Bilal went very quiet as if he was wrestling with his conscience. He stared at the floor, then at me and then at the floor again, holding his head in his hands. It was very unlike him.

'I just don't think I can tell you, Adam. I'm sorry.'

'Come on, Bilal. You can trust me.'

He let out a large sigh and looked me directly in the eye. 'OK. OK. I was meant to tell no one but I know I can trust you. You're an intelligent man and a loyal friend. Adam, the truth is that I was approached by MI5 in the first term and asked to spy on Mustapha Ahmed.'

I almost laughed with relief. Bilal, however, had never looked so serious in his life. I tried to cheer him up by enthusing naively that everything would be OK. 'But that's great,' I said. 'You're obviously doing a brilliant job. And how exciting to be working for the Security Services.'

Bilal shook his head sadly. 'Yes, Adam, it would be great if Ahmed hadn't vanished. No one's seen him for two weeks and he's gone completely off the radar. I'm terrified about what might happen next.'

Finding Mustapha Ahmed

A large part of me wanted to tell Bilal everything as soon as he revealed that he was working for the British Security Services. The revelation was a relief more than anything else. The friend that I had trusted, admired, loved even, was not a traitor but a patriot. Suddenly, it all made sense.

It was good to know that I could trust my own instincts, although it made me shudder to think how close I had come to acting against them. I learned a valuable lesson that summer. I would never make the same mistake again of doubting myself.

And yet I decided not to tell Bilal the whole story for the same reason that I decided not to tell Mr Joseph that Bilal was working for MI5. As I was slowly discovering, knowledge was power in the game of espionage. There was no point revealing what you knew before you had to.

And so, when I saw Mr Joseph a few days after Bilal's revelations, I simply said that I felt that Bilal's flirtation with extremism had been short-lived. I wanted to see how Mr Joseph reacted. Two days later, I received another handwritten letter from my father in which he again stressed the supposed extremism of Bilal's family. 'I sense from Samuel Joseph that your enthusiasm for, and conviction about, this project is waning,' he wrote. 'It must not. Let me remind you how duplicitous the Tarikh family is. I repeat: they are not what they seem. Bilal Tarikh must be terminated at the earliest possible opportunity. He is a danger to both you and me.'

The more Mr Joseph – and by extension, my father – tried to convince me of Bilal's guilt, the more I became convinced that he was innocent. It was not simply that I liked and trusted

Bilal more than Mr Joseph, although that was obviously the case. My judgement was based on a sober consideration of proper evidence. Everything that had been pinned on Bilal had a rational explanation. All that my father and Mr Joseph had come up with appeared circumstantial and grossly subjective. I began to get the sense I was being used. Worst of all, I had no idea why.

Meanwhile, Bilal was deeply concerned about Mustapha Ahmed's disappearance. I was further convinced of the legitimacy of his story when I noticed what I imagined were his two MI5 handlers pay him a visit in his room one afternoon. I watched them leave again two hours later and they stood for a while in Front Court in their stiff suits, neatly pressed white shirts and club ties, pretending to admire the view and looking every inch the British civil servant. I immediately ran into Bilal's room and asked him how it had gone. He looked weary and unsurprised that I had guessed the identity of his visitors.

The sartorial standards of the British civil servant have slipped somewhat in the last 16 years

HP

'Not too bad,' he said. 'They're not angry with me. They said it wasn't my fault that I had lost Ahmed, that I wasn't a professional, that I couldn't be expected to know where he was or what he was thinking or what he would do next, etc., but I could tell they were secretly disappointed. Most of all, I think they're really worried. Imagine how stupid we will all look if Ahmed does something dramatic and the press gets hold of the fact that he slipped away from under our noses.'

'What exactly do you think he might be planning?' I asked.

'That's the worst thing,' said Bilal. 'We have no idea at all. But the fact he's suddenly gone to ground makes it look very worrying indeed. It suggests an attack is imminent. And all we're doing is jabbing around in the dark. We even got the university calendar out and started checking for any significant debates at the union involving Jewish people. We've looked at any high-profile Zionist students or sons and daughters of VIPs with links to the Middle East. But it's all desperately blind amateur stuff. There's next to nothing to go on and what little we do know or suspect simply opens up more possibilities. There are no fewer than three relations of cabinet ministers in Trinity College alone. In the university at large, there are two sons of senior executives at a large weapon-making company, dozens of Israelis and high-profile Jews and five close relatives of Arab Gulf sheiks traditionally loathed by the likes of Ahmed and Hezbollah. Where on earth do we start?'

'And you have absolutely no idea where he is now?'

'We know he's in the country. Or at least, we're pretty sure he's in the country. There has been a full-scale alert at ports and airports since he disappeared. But well, as you know, it's a pretty big country…'

Bilal and I spent most of the rest of the summer term in a state of almost constant nervous tension. In some ways, it was easier for him. He had done nothing wrong and he had the full backing of the state. I, however, had an ongoing conflict of loyalties. I had my doubts about my father – a man who wanted one of my best friends dead – but I still wanted to meet him. And although no direct threats had been made recently against my mother, I still did not feel that she was out of danger. Mr Joseph knew who she was and where she lived.

It was a delicate balancing act, to say the least, keeping him happy without endangering my friend. In the end, I just had to come out with it. 'Bilal is a good person and I don't suspect him of anything,' I finally said to Mr Joseph at one of our regular meetings near the end of May. 'And even if I did, I wouldn't be capable of killing him. I'm sorry, but if this is a test, then I'm happy to fail it. I don't even care if it means disappointing a father I still haven't met. I will not do your dirty work for you in this instance.'

Mr Joseph shook his head sadly. 'That's a shame, Adam. A very big shame indeed. Because if you don't, I will have to find someone who will.'

Suicide Sunday

May drew towards its end. Everyone else finished their exams, the sun came out and the party season started in earnest. And yet neither Bilal nor I were really in the mood for celebration. We didn't feel as if we had earned it, for one. Partying was much more satisfying if you had just been through the hell of exams. It was the contrast that made it worthwhile.

Furthermore, Bilal was still worrying constantly about Mustapha Ahmed and my thoughts were taken up with Mr Joseph's veiled threat concerning Bilal. It was one thing to stand up for one's principles, it was quite another to realise the stand might all be in vain. I became paranoid. I started to see shadows everywhere.

Then we entered June, the sun burned still stronger and nothing went wrong. We started to forget about Mustapha Ahmed. Perhaps he had simply returned home, aware of the obtrusive surveillance he had been under. The longer, balmy days stretched out, seemingly endlessly, in front of us. We had three months of the summer holiday to look forward to. Bilal invited me to come and stay with his family in Jerusalem. 'My parents are dying to meet you,' he said. I accepted readily.

Marking the start of May Week was an entire day of garden parties known as 'Suicide Sunday'. It used to be the date on which exam results came out. Those who had done badly threw themselves from the top of the nearest tall building. Results now appeared in a more staggered fashion but the day had kept its adjectival prefix due to the huge amounts of alcohol consumed from breakfast onwards. It was, indeed, 'suicidally' debauched.

The day in Trinity Hall started with a champagne breakfast at 7 a.m. We had to be up early as ours was always the first and, we liked to think, the best garden party of the day. Bilal was back to his usual, ebullient form, marshalling the troops setting up the alcohol and the entertainment with cheerful, almost manic, bonhomie. The garden party was a strange mix of louche and refined, stylish and cheap. A string quartet played at the bottom of the garden while the first years were initiated into the drinking society with vodka shots. Meanwhile, four hundred plus guests mingled in the sunshine, eating economy peanuts. Everyone seemed happy, no one more so than Bilal who would doubtlessly have made a large profit on the £5 tickets.

The day continued as it had started as we moved from garden party to garden party, getting steadily more sunburnt and tipsy.

'I bloody love Suicide Sunday,' declared Richard Dempsey in the late afternoon, lying on his back on the lawns in Pembroke College and promptly passing out.

I chuckled. Next to me, however, Bilal had suddenly gone pale. He grabbed my arm, suddenly sober. 'That's it, Adam.'

'That's what?' I asked, looking around to check that no one was listening.

'That's what Ahmed will be planning: a suicide attack. I remember him saying it once with a chuckle after Friday mosque. "I love suicide bombers." And he did. He admired them, envied them even. He said they were Hezbollah's greatest weapon in the modern world and should never be relinquished as a method of warfare. I remember talking to him earlier this year about the attack on the American Embassy in Buenos Aires. He thought it was his organisation's finest hour.'

It was during Lebanon in the 1980s that the modern concept of suicide bombing as we now know it first took hold. Between 1982 and 1986, 41 Hezbollah suicide attacks killed 659 people. The attack to which Bilal Tarikh refers took place on 17 March 1992 in Buenos Aires. A pickup truck was loaded with explosives and driven by a suicide bomber into the Israeli Embassy. Twenty-nine people were killed.

HP

I tried to take in what Bilal was saying. I think I went as white as him.

'Are you sure?' I asked.

'Of course I'm not fucking sure,' he snapped. 'But it's better than anything else I have to go on.'

At my insistence, Bilal drunk several cups of strong coffee and called his MI5 handlers to share his suspicions. To my surprise, he reported back that they had almost laughed at him. No one would try that kind of stunt over here, they had said. And especially not in Cambridge. It just wouldn't happen. Ahmed had just vanished for a while. He should stop worrying about it.

'We'll see about that,' said Bilal, grimly.

Trinity May Ball

The next day, Monday, 19 June, we both woke up feeling terrible in more ways than one. Neither of us had slept much. Later that evening was the Trinity May Ball.

'I have a dreadful feeling about this,' said Bilal. 'You've definitely checked there is no Mustapha Ahmed on the ball ticket list?'

I assured him for the twentieth time that I had asked a friend on the Trinity May Ball committee to run their eye down the list on the pretext that Ahmed was a friend of mine who had fallen ill and was no longer able to use his ticket. 'Nice try, Adam,' my friend had said. 'But Ahmed doesn't have a ticket either.'

'Why are you so sure that Ahmed will target Trinity?' I asked Bilal.

'I can't be sure,' he said. 'But I just have a gut feeling about this one. I knew the guy pretty well, remember. He wanted to do something spectacular and he wanted to do it in Cambridge. There's nothing bigger or more dramatic here than tonight's party. All the bigwigs among the university fellowship will be there, along with the largest number of students you're ever likely to see crammed together in one small space. It's the perfect target. I've even heard that the Foreign Secretary is attending as Trinity is his alma mater. And have you heard which band is playing? Right Said Fred.

'Ahmed is a nihilist,' continued Bilal, 'but you have to remember that his principal driving force is an extremist distortion of radical Islam. Picture the Trinity May Ball

According to my research, this band had a number one hit in April 1992 and were, briefly, very big.　HP

and its rich, drunken, fornicating students. Imagine the press coverage any attack would have. The more I think about it, the more I'm convinced that this is the only way Ahmed would consider taking his own life.'

'Then we have no choice,' I said. 'If the Security Services aren't going to take the threat seriously, then we must. We have to be at that party.'

'Adam, I'm not in the mood for a party.'

'We're not going there to party,' I said. 'We're going to protect nine hundred people who don't deserve to die.'

There are many apocryphal stories about the best attempts to get into May Balls, many of which Bilal's elder brother had relayed to him with glee. A member of the university air squadron reputedly parachuted into John's and was allowed to stay by the Ball committee. Another favourite is the story of a student who swam up the River Cam in his dry suit, left it under a tree and entered the ball in his immaculate dinner jacket. When he returned to the tree at the end of the evening, his dry suit had been stolen. The dry suit cost £150 to replace. Buying a ticket for the ball would have cost £60.

Neither of these luxuries were available to us. We had to enter that ball in the least conspicuous and most secure way possible.

According to friends in the year above, most crashers chose the obvious route of punting down the river which divided the two parts of the party and making a run for it when the security guards weren't looking. If a group of you went at the same time, it improved your chances, but the odds were still very much stacked against you. Trinity had a well-known zero tolerance policy when it came to crashing. The first time, they took your name, your college and your photo. The second time, they would report you to the police. Bilal and I just couldn't take the risk.

We spent the afternoon poring over Bilal's architectural plans of the college, trying to find the weak spots in the college's security. As the shadows lengthened on the River Cam and the city's clocks struck 9.30 p.m., we were ready.

We met in our own college, dressed in a bowdlerised version of black tie. On the bottom half, we wore black jeans which were much tougher than dinner jacket trousers and would be indistinguishable now that night was falling. On our feet were sturdy black army boots which we would need for climbing. Bilal had found an oversized white shirt, under which he had secured a bag packed with rope, nails and a hammer. The bag was kept in place with an ostentatious crimson cummerbund. In one of my inside jacket pockets I had hidden the architectural map of Trinity College. In the other were wristbands in a variety of different colours which a medical friend of mine had secured from the local hospital. Once we were in, we would observe the bands worn by the paying guests and adjust accordingly. It wasn't a fail-safe option but it was the best we could do.

First, however, we had to gain access to the college. Sticking to the mantra that it was best to work with what we knew, we decided to approach Trinity from neighbouring Trinity Hall. We went up to my room in S staircase and opened the window. New Court in Trinity was only five metres away but to get there we first had to cross over Garret Hostel Lane below. I tied the end of the rope into a lasso knot, waited until no one was passing underneath and flung it at one of the many chimneys poking up above Trinity. It caught first time and the knot tightened correctly and securely.

I smiled at Bilal. 'A wasted childhood,' I said.

'It looks like a childhood very well spent to me.'

Bilal swung across and then threw the rope back so I could join him. Although we were now inside Trinity we were still only halfway there. New Court was joined to the rest of the college but sealed off as far as the ball was concerned.

We started to make our way carefully around the roofs, ducking down every time one of the huge spotlights from the main stage swung our way. A massive security guard wandered in from the adjacent court and had a quick look around to check that everything was OK. We ducked down even further, mercifully sheltered by the huge tree in the middle of the court, a tree that Cambridge legend suggests bore the apple which fell on Sir Isaac Newton's head and prompted him to think about gravity in a little more depth. The security guard moved away again and we continued inching round the top of the court until we arrived at the opposite side to the one we had come in by.

Below us the party was already in full swing. It was quite a sight from our vantage point high above. As you looked east, you could see the final stragglers in a queue that snaked round into Great Court, the largest open-air courtyard in Europe. You could then follow that long, elegant line of ball gowns and dinner jackets to the entrance of the ball where they were met by fire jugglers and a full pipe band. Once inside, the party opened up into the splendour of Neville Court where there were numerous punts filled with champagne and ice. Continue through Neville Court and you were on the backs of the River Cam and within spitting distance of the main stage. All around were numerous smaller tents containing everything from comedy acts to smaller bands to hypnotic dogs. A bouncy castle jiggled in the distance alongside a dodgem cars construction. I could even make out several hog roasts. Everything was decorated with the highest degree of detail. It was one of the most glamorous sights I had ever seen.

Bilal turned to me and smiled. 'Next year, Adam, we're going to come back here and enjoy this party properly.'

Bilal reached into his shirt and pulled out a couple of nails and a hammer. Waiting until the pipe band below became particularly loud, he set about banging four nails into cracks in the stone, timing his blows so that he was in perfect sync with the bass drummer. I looped the rope round the nails, gave it a quick tug to check it was secure and started to lower myself over the side into a quiet tree-lined spot between the river and Neville Court.

I dropped quietly into the undergrowth and gave the rope a little twitch to signify to Bilal that it was OK to follow. He joined me at ground level and we decided to leave the rope in place. It might get discovered but there were almost a thousand people at the ball. No one would be able to pin it on us. And we might want a quick, unexpected escape route.

As it turned out, we almost needed the escape route straight away. We were just silently congratulating ourselves on successfully gaining access to the restricted part of the college when we heard a voice in a nearby tree and saw the sweeping flash of a torch.

'Woah, who goes there?'

Bilal put his head between his knees and started to retch violently while I patted him reassuringly on the back. We had already planned for this eventuality.

'My mate's not feeling too well,' I called out. 'Got stuck into the champagne a bit too early. He just needs some air.'

A person materialised at the end of the torch. 'Wristbands,' he grunted. 'Show them to me.'

We were already wearing the default blue wristbands we'd agreed on. We knew from Bilal's brother that Trinity had used yellow the year before, and red, black and white respectively the years before that. Bilal extended a trembling hand. The security guard grunted approval and shuffled off again. He hadn't seen the rope behind us. It was a lucky escape. We could now, at least, look relaxed as we moved around the ball, knowing that we were unlikely to be thrown out on any spot check.

Relaxation was, of course, the last emotion we were feeling when we first joined the ball, but it was difficult to maintain a constant state of nervous tension in the midst of so many people having such a good time. Eternal vigilance might have been our aim but it was a high ideal to aspire to as merry couples weaved in and out of the throng, swigging liberally from champagne bottles.

I turned to Bilal. 'We have to concentrate,' I said. 'We can't let ourselves get caught up in the atmosphere.'

'Don't worry, Adam,' said Bilal, more serious than I had

ever seen him before. 'It's to protect the special atmosphere of nights such as this one that I'm running around joylessly with nails and hammers strapped to my stomach. Mustapha Ahmed might have his grievances. And God knows, the West has often treated Islam in general and the Middle East in particular with shocking disdain. But if Ahmed is planning what I think he's planning, then there is absolutely no excuse for such a reaction. I don't subscribe to Islamic extremism any more than I subscribe to Western imperialism. No "isms" do it for me, full stop. If I believe in anything, then I believe in tolerance.' Bilal gestured with a wide, expansive movement of his arm.

'Take this evening, for example. It may not be to every-one's taste. Many Muslims would be offended by the amount of alcohol being drunk. But take a closer look, look properly at the happy faces of the people here. Are they really causing any harm? Or are they just enjoying themselves with their friends? Likewise, I could show you scenes in the Middle East which might offend Western eyes. But is it any of your business? And is this any of Ahmed's business? To both, I would say an emphatic no. There is altogether too much intolerance and censure in this world and far too little laughter and enjoyment. Live and let live. And live fully. That's what I say.'

Bilal gave a little chuckle as he finished. They were fine, noble words. They would turn out to be the last I heard Bilal speak.

We separated, as planned, and fanned out in different directions to circulate around the ball. One obstacle we hadn't envisaged in our amateur surveillance preparation was that Bilal and I would have a lot of friends among the other guests at the ball. The first person I bumped into was Richard Dempsey who jokingly threatened to report me to the committee and have me thrown out. Looking over my shoulder, I could see that Bilal had been similarly detained by a friend of his from the Hawks Club. We did our best to keep on moving but we didn't want to arouse even more suspicions by acting strangely. Several times I used the false excuse that I didn't have a wristband and therefore had to keep on moving in case security caught up with me.

By midnight, the whole charade had become tiresome. The crowds were getting more and more boisterous while I grew weary and annoyed. What were we doing there exactly? Atoning for our own failings? The fireworks came and went but little of their undoubted magic rubbed off on me. I was too busy using the extra reflected light to get a better look at the faces in the crowd. But it was no use. I had already spent the last two hours staring as subtly as I could at every Middle Eastern person I walked past. It seemed a futile task. I had only met Ahmed once and he could have changed beyond all recognition in the intervening months. Disillusioned, I put the chances of him even being in the ball at around 10,000 to 1.

But then, nearing 1 a.m., the main act geared up to take

its place on the principal stage. The rest of the ball thinned out as all the guests congregated in one place to hear the music. My sluggish senses began to wake up again as I tried to get myself into Ahmed's mindset. If I were him, and he was here, this would be the ideal moment.

The band started playing and the atmosphere shifted up several notches. Pretty girls, now shielded against the cold by their boyfriends' jackets, were held aloft on shoulders so they could punch the night sky in time to the music. The volume became deafening. A second round of fireworks greeted the end of the first song. As the band launched into one of their biggest hits, I caught sight of Bilal on the opposite side of the crowd to me, looking anxiously at the River Cam behind him.

I followed his gaze. Approaching in two punts were eight of Bilal's friends who I knew formed part of the secret society that prided themselves on crashing May Balls. I looked over to the security guards who appeared to have given up doing their job and were enjoying the music. Suddenly one of them noticed the impending intrusion and reached for his radio. Ten seconds later, three of them were converging on the riverbank in an attempt to stop the intruders getting on to dry land and losing themselves in the crowd.

Initially, it all looked like a good bit of spectator sport. Some of the people at the back of the crowd watching the band nudged each other and turned round to enjoy the spectacle. The first two crashers leapt off the punt, waded the last few metres and managed to evade the first security guard before being brought down in a crunching double tackle by the second. A larger section of the crowd now gave a cheer as more security guards came over from keeping an eye on the band to lend a hand.

It was at this moment that I saw a third punt approaching, unnoticed, from the opposite direction, and gliding towards the unguarded section of bank recently vacated by the other security guards. It contained a tall, strong solitary figure.

Decoy.

I started to run towards the river, pushing my way through the crowds. But there was no way through. People turned on me angrily, thinking I was simply trying to get a better view of the band. I thought about warning everyone by shouting out 'fire' but was worried about what might happen in the ensuing panic. The last thing I wanted to do was to drive them towards the danger.

I turned and sprinted round the circumference of the crowd, giving me a clear run. The figure in the punt was now very close to the bank. Once he had disembarked, there were only fifteen or so metres until he reached the thick of the crowd. I made a rapid calculation. I should be able to cut him off before he reached anyone.

I clenched my fists and pushed harder, my heart thumping against my chest and my lungs screaming in pain. I could feel every muscle in my body taut and ready for action. *God forgive me if I didn't make it in time.*

I reached the gravel and felt it crunch underfoot as I pushed myself for one final burst of speed. Now that I had a clear view of the bank, I could see that Bilal had also clocked the third punt and was running towards it himself.

The tall man jumped off and landed on the bank. Now all three of us were converging on the same point at the western edge of the crowd, racing to get there first.

Then I suddenly noticed a familiar face emerge from the throng. It was Mr Joseph, immaculately turned out in evening dress. There was no time to warn Bilal. He had never met Mr Joseph and never saw the blow coming. It struck him with murderous, professional accuracy in the jugular. Bilal crumpled to the wet ground in a heap.

I was within five metres of the man who had just arrived on the bank. For a brief moment, he paused and looked me directly in the eye. There was no doubt it was Mustapha Ahmed. He was wearing a beard and his figure was unnaturally contorted by the suicide belt packed with explosives he wore round his chest. But I would have recognised those dark, cold eyes anywhere.

His path to the centre of the crowd was blocked off, but I saw his hand inch towards a cord trailing near his leg. I ran and lunged simultaneously, tripping him with a hand round his ankles. We rolled as one body towards the river, wrestling with the cord and the belt. Ahmed made one final effort to stand up and I knocked him backwards into the river, pulling the cord as I did so.

I felt the explosion but did not hear it as I had already dived into the river myself. Taking a deep breath, I swam for almost three minutes before surfacing near where Bilal and I had entered the college three and a half hours previously. I climbed up the rope, which was still in place, pulled it up after me and returned to my own college the same way I had left it.

I let myself into Bilal's room with the skeleton key provided by Mr Joseph. I rifled through his possessions until I found a contact number for Bilal's handler in MI5. Bilal had always been the absent-minded sort, the type who would write something like that down. I had known him well, to the very last.

I was picked up within five minutes by your Cambridge contact and taken to the safe house where I currently reside writing this report.

This report is now finished.

Adam Carter

6
Operation Abraham

Note from Harry Pearce

At first, I was at a loss as to where to look next to see what happened. Adam's remarkable report left many questions unanswered. What had happened to Bilal? How did Mr Joseph justify his actions to the authorities, if at all? And, most importantly of all, what happened next? Even if Adam had willingly put himself into MI5 custody, he was, in theory at least, guilty of treason.

Again, I went through all the files but could find no details of Adam's debrief. Not even the briefest hint.

Then I suddenly remembered with a jolt of pain my old colleague and friend, Clive McTaggart. Clive had been my boss on section D before retiring in January 1991. In November 2005 he was murdered by British agents acting on the orders of Juliet Shaw, the National Security coordinator. The appalling reason given was that Clive had been working on his unauthorised memoirs which contained explosive revelations on MI5's operations. His breach should have been dealt with in a more sensitive manner.

After leaving section D, Clive had retired to the village of Grantchester, just outside Cambridge. In the summer of 1992, he would therefore have been the ideal safe pair of hands – no longer directly connected to the service but retired sufficiently recently to retain clarity of thought – to debrief a volatile young man such as Adam Carter.

Following this hunch, I went to visit his delightful widow, Elspeth, who was well into her late seventies but still extremely active. She greeted me like a long lost friend outside their cottage.

'Harry,' she beamed, stretching out both hands. 'How good of you to come. I heard about Adam and wondered how long it would be until you knocked on my door.'

She led me upstairs and into an oak, book-lined library. Moving carefully over to one of the bookshelves, she plucked out a copy of Ian Fleming's *From Russia With Love* and pressed a button. The bookshelf revolved. Behind it stood a small shelf containing some expensive jewellery, a few rolls of banknotes and a large, bound, handwritten book.

Once a spook, always a spook, I thought.

Elspeth picked up the book and handed it to me. 'Clive always believed in keeping duplicates,' she explained. 'I hope you'll find whatever you're looking for in here. Adam Carter was an exceptional young man. I remember the night they brought him here, so dashing in black tie, so seemingly unaware of the heroic thing he had just done and unafraid of what might happen next…' She tailed off. 'Oh, for the confidence of youth again.'

We smiled comfortingly at each other.

I took myself to a quiet corner of Clive's old study and

started to read his memoirs. They were gripping, gossipy, salacious and well written — everything a good memoir should be. And yet they were also illegal and dangerous. Did he really intend them for publication? Were they worth dying for?

I found the relevant part about Adam Carter near the end. Every detail, including in-depth, verbatim conversations, had been faithfully recorded.

Understandably, Elspeth was reluctant for me to remove the documents from her house for security reasons, so I am unable to reproduce Clive's account in its entirety. I can, however, draw on it as an additional source material to describe what happened after Adam Carter foiled a suicide attack and turned himself over to MI5, still wet and stinking from the putrid waters of the River Cam.

The account I present here is, therefore, in my own words, drawn from Clive's unfinished memoirs as well as my own interviews with the key players in the mission that came to be known as Operation Abraham.

This is its only surviving record.

Adam's new handler

Wisely, I think, the first thing Clive made Adam do when he was dropped by an MI5 pool car at his cottage was to write down the report we have just read. According to Clive's memoirs, Adam was talking so fast and so wildly, about everything from Mossad to his mother, that Clive could think of no other way to stem the flow. He got the bare, salient facts of the case out of Adam, checked that no one else was in immediate danger, and then gave him a pen and a large pad of paper and left him in peace.

While Adam wrote, Clive and his former colleagues checked up on the situation back at Trinity. The police had already been notified, the ball closed down and the college sealed off. Mustapha Ahmed's lifeless body was retrieved from the river and taken for a post-mortem. Adam was extremely fortunate in that the detonators had failed to ignite the rest of the explosives. He doubtlessly saved a lot of lives that night while coming within a whisker of losing his own.

Bilal Tarikh was pronounced dead at the scene at 1:14 a.m., killed by the direct punch to his neck. Samuel Joseph, who had delivered the fatal blow, willingly volunteered himself to the local police for interview, claiming that he had acted in self-defence. According to his testimony, the unnatural shape of Bilal's figure made it look as if he, too, was concealing explosives under his clothing. Tarikh was of Middle Eastern origin and a known associate of Mustapha Ahmed's. The fact that nails were found on Bilal's person made Joseph's testimony even more convincing. He was an influential man in Cambridge, in London and in the world at large. He was released without charge while Bilal Tarikh's death was covered up as a tragic, collateral accident. If the police had suspicions as to why a middle-aged man such as Joseph was capable of delivering an expert, fatal punch to a young, fit man, they didn't voice them.

Adam, meanwhile, remained unaware of these developments as he sat in Clive's study writing up his report. When Clive finally told him that his friend Bilal was dead, Adam broke down — for the first time, I imagine, in his adult life — and cried for hours.

'It's my fault,' he wept. 'All my fault.'

Clive was sympathetic towards Adam — the two of them were similar personality types and had struck up an immediate bond — but having read his report, Clive also felt the need to ensure that Adam was aware of the seriousness of his predicament. Ultimately, Adam might have acted heroically, saving the lives of potentially hundreds of people. He had also withdrawn from the brink and shown great moral courage in refusing to follow Joseph's orders in Courchevel. Yet it could not be simply forgotten that he had spent almost two years in the employ of a foreign, albeit superficially friendly, intelligence agency.

'I had one driving force from start to finish,' Adam told Clive. 'It was to protect my mother.'

'I believe you,' said Clive. 'And it's the reason we're willing to give you another chance. We're offering to protect your mother until you've carried out the task we're about to give you to our satisfaction.'

'You have my mother under protection?' asked Adam, wide-eyed with astonishment.

Clive handed Adam the following letter.

[spooks]

Undisclosed location
21 June 1992

My dear Adam,

As you know, things have not been easy at the Dempseys' since Simon died. Sarah and I have had an argument which resulted in her asking me to leave the estate. I had no other choice but to go.

Just as I was about to leave Fleetwood — a friend had offered me a room in London — I was picked up by someone from the Security Services and placed under their protection. Darling Adam, I know you have been keeping aspects of your life from me and I understand, really I do. Do whatever it is you have to do and come back safe. That is the only thing that matters.

I have been told that this letter will be passed to you. I hope it finds you well and happy. Always remember that I love you.

Mum

According to Clive's memoirs, Eleanor gave the young officer who picked her up more details about her forced departure from Fleetwood. Mrs Dempsey had grown less fond of her over the years, partly because she was jealous of every success Adam notched up compared to Richard, but mainly because she always suspected, but never proved, that Eleanor had been having an affair with her husband. His death was the opportunity Sarah had been waiting for to get rid of her rival.

Clive, who never met Eleanor, decided not to tell Adam the full story due to a laudable desire not to cause any more anguish to this anguished young man. Instead, Clive simply confirmed that they had picked Eleanor up and were looking after her very well.

'You're holding my mother to ransom?' said Adam.

'I wouldn't put it like that,' said Clive. 'If what you've told me is true, I have no doubt that she is still in danger. Even more so if she's not living with the Dempseys. I trust you, Adam. I like you. But until we know you entirely, I don't think you can blame us for taking a few extra precautions. For all our sakes.'

Adam smiled at his new handler. 'Very sensible,' he said. 'I would do the same.'

Clive smiled back. 'And that's why you'll make an excellent British intelligence officer one day.'

'I was hoping you might say that,' said Adam. 'What can I do to make things right again?'

'I'd like you to come and meet a couple of old friends of mine in Six,' said Clive. 'I have a feeling they might be very interested in this father of yours.'

Adam Carter joins MI6

One of Clive's friends in Six turned out to be Dr Mark Roupell, the 'trendy don' who had interviewed Adam for a place to read Arabic at Trinity Hall. I met him for the purpose of this account and Adam's earlier description of him was spot on. The other was an up-and-coming young MI6 officer called Diana Jackson, an expert on Middle Eastern politics in general and

Israeli counter-intelligence in particular. According to Vauxhall's files, she is currently serving abroad and I was unable to track her down.

This triumvirate had been carefully chosen by Six's resident psychologist to appeal to Adam on a variety of different levels. Clive was the authority, father figure. Roupell provided the intellectual weight. And I don't think it needs me to spell out the appeal of Jackson, one of Six's most noted beauties.

The four of them met in Roupell's rooms in N staircase, Trinity Hall. If Roupell felt any sense of surprise that the promising young candidate he had interviewed for a place over a year previously was now sitting in front of him as a former Mossad, and potential double, agent, he didn't show it.

'You know, Adam,' he said wryly, 'I wondered the first time I met you whether you might be MI6 material one day.'

Adam nodded at Roupell and smiled across at Jackson. She pretended to ignore him.

'Right,' continued Roupell, looking slightly annoyed at Adam's drifting attention. 'Tell me everything you think you know about your father.'

'I have already written everything I know in my report,' said Adam.

'I don't care,' snapped Roupell. 'Tell me again.'

The three of them listened in polite, attentive silence while Adam related the facts that pertained to his father. When he had finished, it was Diana Jackson who spoke first.

'Do you have any proof of David Horovitz's friendship with Samuel Joseph?' she asked.

'None,' said Adam. 'I can only go on what the two of them have told me, both in letters and face to face. I know from my mother that most of the facts about my father's life tally with her own memory. But that's it, I'm afraid.'

The three of them asked Adam to leave the room briefly while they spoke among themselves. Twenty minutes later, they called him back in.

'OK,' said Diana Jackson, taking charge. 'We've made a decision. You are to accept your father's invitation to attend the Mossad training "Factory" in Israel this summer. Once there, you will ascertain who he is, which rank he holds and what his intentions are. We will provide you with secure communications so you can report back to us on an ongoing basis. Depending on the intelligence we receive, we shall give you further instructions. Is that clear?'

Adam looked a little taken aback by the directness of her approach. 'Sure,' he said. 'But I have to ask, do you guys have any idea what's going on here?'

Jackson spoke again. 'Much of what you've said makes sense. Samuel Joseph is well known to us, as are his favourite recruitment methods. But we've drawn a complete blank when it comes to David Horovitz. We're familiar with most senior Mossad agents. We work closely alongside them as often as we work against them. Horovitz, however, is a mystery.'

'And I'm to unravel the enigma?' asked Adam.

'Exactly,' said Jackson, a little more gently. 'Horovitz is clearly using you as bait. In the absence of anything more concrete to go on, I'm afraid you're going to have to nibble.'

'There's nothing I like more than a good nibble,' said Adam.

'I bloody well hope you're taking this seriously,' interjected Roupell.

'Of course he is,' said Clive. 'Give the man a break. Now, Adam, is everything going to be OK with Samuel Joseph?'

'I think so,' said Adam. 'As far as he's concerned, we were working as a team that night at Trinity. He took out one "terrorist suspect"; I took out the other. He probably imagines that I had finally come round to his point of view. I can't see any reason why he wouldn't trust me.'

'And will you be able to keep your emotions under control when you next see him?' asked Jackson. 'He did kill your best friend.'

Adam stared at the floor. 'My revenge will come from completing this mission successfully and seeing Mr Joseph brought to justice,' he said through gritted teeth.

The other three took this as a sign to adjourn the meeting. Jackson stood up and extended a well-manicured hand. 'Good luck, Adam. We have every confidence in you.'

'Will you not be coming with me, Diana?' asked Adam, holding on to her hand a little longer than was strictly necessary.

'No,' said Roupell firmly. 'This is something you have to do alone.'

Clive and Adam returned to the cottage in Grantchester to prepare for the mission.

'Tell me more about Diana Jackson,' said Adam mischievously in the car.

Clive laughed, relieved to see Adam in better spirits again. 'I'm afraid you'll have to join the back of a very long queue,' he said. 'And anyway, she's going out with some unemployed writer chap in London called Hollingsworth.'

Adam sees Mr Joseph again

Before Adam could fly out to Israel, he first had to arrange a meeting with Samuel Joseph. The two of them had not seen each other since Joseph delivered the fatal blow to the neck of Bilal Tarikh and Adam had dived into the River Cam to escape the blast of Mustapha Ahmed's explosion. The Cambridge police, on the request of MI5, had deliberately kept Joseph in the dark as to the well-being of Adam. They wanted to keep their options open and there could have been advantages in Joseph thinking Adam had died along with Bilal and Ahmed.

As it was, it was deemed safe — for the reasons Adam discussed with Roupell, Jackson and Clive — for him to make contact with Joseph again.

Joseph must have been mounting an ongoing, surreptitious surveillance operation on Trinity Hall because not long after

Adam returned to normal student life, another note appeared in his pigeon-hole, requesting a meeting in the same car park they had used on previous occasions. When Adam climbed into Joseph's black Mercedes, he immediately found himself with a gun in his face and forced to answer a barrage of suspicious questions.

'Where have you been for the last week?' demanded Joseph.

Adam tried his best to remain calm and remember the training given to him by Clive.

'I've been recovering from the blast wounds,' he said.

'Where? I checked Addenbrooke's Hospital and they had no record of you there. And you haven't been to see your local GP either.'

'I've been recovering in my room,' lied Adam. 'The wounds were pretty minor. Shock really, more than anything else. The college nurse came to see me.'

'And have you had any contact with any British law enforcement agencies?'

Clive had prepared a very careful answer to this question. 'Yes,' said Adam. 'The police came round to talk to me while I was recovering in bed. I told them as close to the truth as possible, namely, that I had crashed the party in order to have a good time and had simply acted on instinct when I suspected something terrible was about to happen. The police have accepted that story.'

Joseph nodded, apparently satisfied. 'And have you spoken to anyone else? The media? Your mother? Where is your mother, by the way?'

'She's gone on holiday,' said Adam, trying to keep his annoyance that Joseph was still keeping tabs on Eleanor out of his voice. 'She's staying with friends in Scotland.'

'And the press? Have they been sniffing around?'

'They've tried to,' said Adam, truthfully. 'But they're hampered by the fact that no one apart from the police is entirely sure who tackled Mustapha Ahmed. It all happened so fast that night that no one managed to identify me. I don't appear on the named guest list for the party so the journalists bribing the May Ball committee haven't got anywhere. Only Richard Dempsey knows for certain — he would recognize me anywhere — but I've sworn him to secrecy. I've had a few calls from particularly persistent journalists but it's all tailed off now.'

Joseph lowered the gun and stowed it in the glove compartment which he locked.

'I'm sorry about that, Adam,' he said, gesturing at the glove compartment. 'But you can't be too careful. Your father is now a very powerful man in Mossad and I have to make sure that every security angle is covered before you meet him.'

'I'm going to meet him?' said Adam, trying to keep the excitement out of his voice.

'Yes,' said Joseph, handing him another letter from David Horovitz.

Tel Aviv
25 June 1992

Dear Adam,

I'm just writing you a short note to offer my sincere congratulations for your behaviour at the Trinity May Ball. Your actions were nothing short of heroic. Samuel Joseph is very pleased with you and I am more proud than I can express in words.

This is just to confirm that I shall definitely be around for the Factory when you visit.

I cannot wait to meet you.

Regards, Your Father

Adam read it and carefully folded it into his pocket. Later, he passed it to Clive, who reproduced it in his memoirs.

Joseph smiled at Adam. 'It's really happening. You're going to meet your father and he's going to be very pleased that there is one less Tarikh in this world.'

Adam dug his fingernails into his palms to stop himself saying anything.

Joseph continued, 'Now, you're going to need some kind of cover story when you go to Israel, both for the British authorities and the Israelis. Mossad is much respected over there but that doesn't mean you can just turn up at Ben Gurion airport and ask the customs officials to give you directions to the Factory.'

'So, what should I do?' said Adam.

'Didn't the *Daily Mirror* promise you a spot of work experience over the summer?'

Foreign correspondent

Having checked with Clive McTaggart, who thought it an excellent idea, Adam rang up his old nemesis of a news editor, Rob Helen, at the *Daily Mirror* to ask if his offer of summer employment still stood.

'Of course it does, Carter,' said Helen. 'If you'd care to grace us with your presence again, then I'm sure we'd be delighted to have you. My editor can't stop talking about you. But I rather imagined you would spend your summers in Cannes, or Tuscany at the very least. I can't admit to not feeling a pang of disappointment at your decision to come back to our lowly offices.'

At the beginning of July, Adam returned to the *Mirror* and Helen's jibes, just under a year after he had last been there. Maxwell had died — in the strange circumstances I have already described — the previous autumn, leading to many departures and a change in atmosphere at the *Mirror*. However, on a daily basis, it was Helen that Adam had to deal with and there, at least, little had changed. Within a few days, Adam was back on data entry, despite having proved himself so spectacularly the year before. The clash of personalities between Adam and Helen was irreconcilable. More out of curiosity than anything else, I managed to effect a seemingly random meeting with Rob Helen in a bar near the office where he still works. It is enough to say that, as always, Adam was an excellent judge of character.

As July drew to a close, Clive became increasingly anxious about the deterioration in Adam and Helen's relationship. The only real point of Adam working at the newspaper was to persuade them to send him out to Israel in August so that he had a decent cover story while working on behalf of Six. Joseph had similar fears as, on this point at least, his goals were identical to Clive's. Yet since Maxwell's death, Joseph no longer exerted the same influence at the paper.

Fortunately, Adam pulled himself together at the last moment, befriended the foreign editor and bypassed Rob Helen altogether. That the foreign editor was an attractive and extremely well-preserved forty-year-old might have helped Adam's case. In whatever way he persuaded her — Clive's memoirs become rather coy on this point and I had no particular desire to investigate further — Adam was duly dispatched at the beginning of August to write three feature articles in Israel: the first on the plight of Israeli Arabs, the million or so Palestinians who had taken Israeli citizenship but were treated in a fairly second-class way; the second on the declining influence of the kibbutz movement; and the third on the situation in Gaza now that the intifada appeared to be coming to an end.

The article on kibbutzes was intended for the travel supplement. The others were to fill the hole left by the recent departure of the *Mirror*'s Jerusalem correspondent.

Helen appears to have been delighted to see the back of Adam, although he couldn't resist one last dig before he left. On his final day in London, Adam found a handwritten note left on his desk: 'Good luck, William Boot. I do hope you don't get shot, stoned or kidnapped. All the best, Rob Helen.'

> A reference to Evelyn Waugh's bumbling, accidental foreign correspondent in his novel Scoop.   HP

On a more serious note, Adam was also allowed to write a final letter to his mother before he left.

Undisclosed location
31st July 1992

Dear Mum,

I hope you can forgive me for keeping some things from you over the last year. I'm glad you understand. This is something that I have to do alone.

I'm not allowed to say much right now but I will, I promise, tell you everything as soon as I return. I'm going away for a short while. There's nothing to worry about and I'm glad you're safe. Soon, we both shall be.

I love you very much indeed.
Adam

Adam joins the Factory

Adam finally left for Israel on 2 August 1992. Before his departure, Clive had debated whether or not to equip him with the full field kit of an MI6 agent. In the end, it was decided that it would only make him too vulnerable. Instead, Adam checked in at Heathrow airport for his British Airways flight with only the tools of his supposed trade in his bag — notepads, pens, a Dictaphone and a few spare changes of clothes. Locked away securely in his mind, however, was one very important detail: the name, address and phone number of MI6's Jerusalem station chief, a man called Edward Black who, incidentally, is well known to me. If at all possible, Adam should make contact with Black who would serve as his immediate superior in the chain of command. If further decisions were required, Black would communicate securely with Clive and the others in the UK.

Adam passed through both British and Israeli security without any hassle. On arrival in Tel Aviv, he met Joseph, as expected. Adam noted that the man seemed infinitely more relaxed and confident in Israel than he did in Britain.

Joseph and Adam climbed into a waiting, chauffeur-driven car, which set off north in the direction of the Galilee. While they drove, Joseph told Adam about the infamous Factory course he was about to attend.

'In the CIA in America, they call their training camp for new recruits the Farm. Here in Israel, we call it the Factory. The Farm and the Factory are very similar, except that the latter is ten times as tough, ten times longer and ten times more difficult to pass. Only one in twenty new recruits graduates. Last year, there was one death; the year before, two.'

'Are you trying to scare me?' asked Adam. 'Because if so, it's working.'

Joseph laughed, humourlessly. 'Relax, Adam. You're here as an observer. It's just as your father said in that letter. We thought it would be a good way to show you a little bit more about Mossad's work.'

At that moment, a large van swerved in front of them, blocking their path and forcing them off the road. Masked gunmen leapt out and shot the driver and Joseph twice each through the forehead. Adam was hit on the back of the head with a rifle butt. He was then tied up and bundled into the back of a van.

When he came round, his ribs aching from the kicking they had given him to wake him up, Adam found himself in a tiny dark room with no windows and no natural light. Two huge guards stood over him, barking questions to which there could be no right answer.

'Name!' shouted one.

'Adam Carter,' replied Adam.

'Wrong answer,' shouted the guard giving him another hefty kick.

'Job!' shouted the other one.

'I'm a student and I'm in Israel as a journalist.'

'Liar,' yelled the thug, stamping on one of Adam's fingers.

'Are you working for the British Intelligence Services?'

'No,' said Adam, biting his lip through the pain.

The guards stamped on his other hand.

This brutality continued for almost two days, with Adam only getting through the ordeal because he guessed, correctly, that this roughing up was all part of the Factory's first test. Before he had left the UK, Clive had warned Adam that everyone, however hard they might think they are, has a breaking point. Aware of this and conscious that he must be seen to break at an opportune moment, Adam decided at the end of the second day that enough was enough. The last thing he wanted to do was give away information which the thugs did not already know.

So, when they asked for the hundredth time what he was really doing in Israel, he looked them straight in the eye and said, clearly and evenly, 'You know as well as I do that I'm here to take part in the Factory, the name given to Mossad's initial training course.'

One of the guards stepped forward, smiled and shook Adam's hand. 'Welcome to the Factory, sir,' he said. 'You've held out longer than anyone else this year.'

The Factory

After his initial ordeal was over, Adam was allowed a bath, a change of clothes, a medical check-up and an uninterrupted sleep. When he woke again, in daylight, thirty-six hours later, he found himself in a small tent in a clearing in the middle of a densely forested area. All around were similar tents, housing other candidates who had made it through the first stage. As soon as he emerged, Adam was approached by a smiling man in his late forties who held out a hand for Adam to shake.

'Hello,' he said. 'I'm Daniel but everyone calls me Danny. I'll be your lead instructor whilst at the Factory.'

Adam smiled back and shook his hand. 'Tell me, Danny, where can I get a decent cup of tea around here?'

Danny laughed. 'They told me they had an English person this year, but they didn't warn me just how English he would be.' He looked Adam up and down, noting the bruises on his skin. 'Still, they do make you pretty tough over there. Congratulations on passing your first test, by the way. It's not one I particularly support, I must admit. I think it gives out the wrong impression of intelligence work. But they seem very keen on it here.'

'You're not—'

'No,' said Danny. 'I used to work in military intelligence and now I work for Shin Bet which is the Israeli domestic intelligence agency. They've got me here on secondment. And I must say, you're lucky to have me as lead instructor. I'm not going to go easy on you, but I promise not to be gratuitously violent like some of the others.'

With this strangely unreassuring promise, Danny shook Adam's hand again and told him to go and explore the camp.

There wasn't much to see on first glance. He discovered that it was about two miles across, hidden from the surrounding villages by the natural slope of the valley. To provide extra security, a twenty-foot-high electric fence had been erected around a perimeter patrolled by guard dogs and monitored by closed-circuit television. There was no way out or in.

At midday, Adam congregated, as instructed, with the other recruits in the centre of the camp. There were, he noted, about fifty other young people, thirty-five of them men.

A large, powerfully built man in his fifties with cropped hair walked to the front of the group and called for silence.

'Welcome to the Factory, ladies and gentlemen. I'm going to speak in English for the benefit of our British friend. For the next four weeks, the Factory will be your home. You will train here, you will sleep here, you will eat here and, if you don't do as I say, you will die here.'

There was a small ripple of nervous laughter.

'My name is Omar and I am in charge of the camp,' he continued. 'Twenty years ago, I sat where you are sitting now. I had the same fears and expectations that you are probably feeling now. So let me reassure you, if reassurance is what you need, of two things. One, you have already done very well to reach this stage. You have been chosen from almost a million of your contemporaries as the best and brightest of your generation. You will not be aware of this yet, but five hundred people started at this camp and four hundred and fifty of them have already dropped out before the end of the first test.'

'The other thing I want to say is that all the training here is intended for your own good. Why did we put you through such pain at the start, you might ask. Are we sadists? Do we get a sense of enjoyment out of watching you suffer? The answer, of course, is no. But we have to make you fully aware of the kind of career you might be entering. Mossad agents often work alone, undercover and in situations of extreme danger. We would be doing you a disservice if we did not make you aware of this at the earliest possible stage. Train hard and you will fight and live easy. Train badly and you will die. If you wanted a quiet, easy life, you should have stayed in the army. Is that clear?'

'Yes!' chorused the recruits.

'Good,' said Omar, more softly. 'Let me leave you with a final thought. Our history is thousands of years old but our country has yet to reach its fiftieth anniversary. If it does, it will be thanks to people like you who have struggled to maintain its security. Israel is in a state of perpetual war. Our enemies want our destruction. So we do not fight because it gives us pleasure or because we are a particularly pugnacious people. We would happily live in peace with our neighbours, but until our neighbours want to live in peace with us, we shall take the fight to them. Be in no doubt, it is a fight for our very existence.'

The group dispersed and broke up into their smaller training units of five for a more detailed briefing. Over the next fortnight, Adam learned how to use a gun as well as to acquit himself well in hand-to-hand combat. There are many ways to kill a man, as the poem states, and Adam was quickly familiar with most of them. Mossad favoured taking the best parts of the different martial arts and combining them into a lethal whole. When he returned to the UK, Adam was able to share what he had learnt with the training instructors at MI5 and MI6.

They were also instructed in all the basic techniques of espionage. Recruits learned about signal intelligence, dead letter drops and how to encode and transmit a message securely. There was also a daily schedule of lectures and written tests. However, in this first half of the course, the emphasis was principally on the physical side of being an undercover operative. Recruits were regularly woken in the middle of the night and required to perform gruelling endurance tasks. Interrogations were also commonplace.

Almost everything took place within the fenced-off confines of the Factory itself. On occasions, however, they would venture into the surrounding countryside on a particular task. One of these involved stealing cattle from a nearby Arab village and killing them without being seen. When one young recruit was caught by an Arab farmer and chased away with a shotgun, he was swiftly given his marching orders from the Factory.

The dropout rate was slow but steady. Some gave in on the interrogation; others collapsed during night exercises or proved themselves incapable of handling a gun properly. By the end of the second week, there were only thirty people left.

While Adam learned a lot during this period – skills which we were able to put to good use when he returned (not to mention the more general intelligence he could share on Mossad's recruitment and training exercises) – he was none the wiser as to what he was doing there as far as Mr Joseph and his father were concerned. Joseph, it could be safely assumed, had not really been shot dead in the roadside ambush as it appeared at the time. But where was he? And what was he doing?

As the Factory continued into its third week, Omar drew the camp together again and announced that they should make everything ready for a very special visitor the next day. 'It's quite an honour,' he explained. 'The new acting head of Mossad himself will be visiting to check on your progress. And he's bringing a colleague and old friend, who has been running our UK station single-handedly for years and has just been made head of Mossad operations in Europe.'

Adam did his best not to jump at this news – his counter-interrogation training over the last fortnight had, at least, helped him to maintain an even expression at all times – but it wasn't easy. These two colleagues and old friends must be his father and Mr Joseph. Hadn't his father mentioned in one of his letters that he had missed Adam's last trip to Israel because of a trip to the States to secure CIA approval for a significant senior appointment in Mossad?

The recruits were given the afternoon off, partly as a reward and partly so that they could get the camp in good order for the arrival of the VIPs the next day. After doing the bare minimum to tidy his tent, Adam sought out Danny who was reading a book outside the instructors' digs. He checked there was no one else around and sat down next to him on the ground.

'Danny, can I ask you a question?'

'Of course, Adam,' said Danny, putting down his book.

'What's the name of the new acting head of Mossad?'

Danny shook his head and smiled. 'That's classified, Adam. And to tell you the truth, I don't even know myself. But even if I did, I'm afraid I wouldn't be able to tell you. Maybe you'll find out tomorrow.'

He picked up his book again. The conversation was over.

According to Adam's report, as summarised in Clive's memoirs, it was at this moment that Adam had the sudden revelation he needed. *His mother's long letter*. He kicked himself for not thinking of it earlier.

'Danny,' he said, trying to sound as natural as he could. 'Where do you normally live when you're not in a tent in the middle of nowhere?'

Danny laughed. 'It's a good question. I never seem to spend any time at home now. But when I do, home is a small kibbutz not far from here. I share it with my wife, Hannah. She's English. I think you'd like her.'

'And how long have you lived in this kibbutz?' asked Adam, barely containing his excitement.

'Oh, forever,' laughed Danny.

'Do you know a man called David Horovitz? And a girlfriend he used to have called Eleanor?'

The smile fell from Danny's face.

'Oh my God. Is it you? Eleanor's son? I saw a fleeting resemblance when I first met you and then told myself to stop being stupid. What are you doing here?'

'I've come to find my father,' said Adam.

There was a long, awkward pause while Danny worked out how to phrase what he said next.

'Adam,' said Danny, gently, 'I'm afraid your father died five years ago.'

'What?' shouted Adam, leaping to his feet.

Danny motioned to the instructors' tent and succeeded in calming Adam down. They moved away to a quieter part of the camp.

'You have to be careful,' whispered Danny. 'And I have to be careful too. First, tell me everything about your mother.'

It's difficult to imagine that Adam was thinking rationally at this stage as there were so many unanswered questions going round in his mind. But he seems to have decided that Danny was a man he could trust. He told him, as calmly as he could, everything about his mother that he felt necessary to prove to Danny that he was who he said he was. Danny nodded as Adam spoke of his mother's time at university, her frustration with teaching in London afterwards and her decision to travel to Israel with her friend Hannah and work in a kibbutz. However, when Adam got to the point where Danny entered the story, Danny finally interrupted.

'Yes, in retrospect I think we acted a little hastily, fleeing the country like that.'

'What do you mean?' said Adam.

'Your mother was upset, obviously, and I think she overreacted slightly to David Horovitz. I think we both perhaps overreacted. I was younger then and more easily scared. I got to know David afterwards and he was a good man, your father. I genuinely believe he was acting with the right motives in trying to find your mother before she left the country, even if he went about it completely the wrong way. Their affair had been so intense and so quick that I think neither of them really knew what to do when your mother became pregnant. It panicked them. It panicked me, too.'

'So why would my mother say otherwise?' said Adam.

'Did she? Well, maybe she felt embarrassed. Or perhaps she just wanted to forget about the whole episode. But I imagine that, most of all, she wanted to protect you. I said that your father was a good man but he was a hard one too, in a dangerous business. He certainly felt guilt and remorse about how he had treated your mother but the fact still stood: he did treat her badly. I imagine Eleanor was trying to scare you off ever trying to find him. Was this a world your mother wanted you to grow up in?'

Adam laughed suddenly. 'But look at me,' he said. 'I have grown up into it.'

'Do you want to tell me how?' asked Danny.

'Do you mind if I don't?' said Adam.

'No, although it might help me if I did know.'

'I just can't.'

'OK. You've put your trust in me so I shall also trust you. Do as you see fit.'

Adam looked at Danny. This man was so different from everyone else in the Israeli intelligence community he had dealt with so far. This was no Mr Joseph with his bumbling, furtive manner and horrendous threats that were often carried out. Nor did Danny display the aloof arrogance he had first encountered with the security officials who had blackmailed him at the airport. So he took a deep breath and gambled on telling him everything. If Danny were a danger to him then he already had Adam at his mercy. And if not, Danny might be able to help. Better one person on his side than nobody, Adam reasoned. Danny was his godfather, after all.

So, Adam quickly told Danny an abridged version of the entire story — how he was recruited, Mr Joseph, the letters from David Horovitz, Bilal and his mission on behalf of MI6 to Israel — while Danny listened in open-mouthed astonishment, swearing repeatedly in Hebrew. When Adam had finally finished, Danny succinctly summed up the situation for him. 'Oh my God, you're fucked.'

Adam found it difficult not to agree with Danny. He was stranded in a Mossad training camp in the middle of nowhere. The next day, the acting head of Mossad, who appeared to have been masquerading as Adam's father for the past year with God knows what motive, was arriving in the camp along with Adam's UK handler, Samuel Joseph. They were fairly certain of one thing: Adam had been selected and used to get to Bilal Tarikh.

That had been their main aim. But there were two outstanding questions. Why? And what did they plan on doing with him next?

Neither of them could think of a decent answer to either question.

'I have to get to Jerusalem,' said Adam. 'If I could just talk to my contact there, he might be able to give us more of an inside track on who this mystery Mossad man is.'

They sat in silence for a long time until Danny finally broke it. 'The new acting head of Mossad is called Joshua Coen. And my main reason for being here is to investigate him on behalf of Shin Bet.'

It was Adam's turn to look astonished. 'The internal security service is investigating the man who is about to become head of the external security service?'

'It's not quite as simple as you make it sound.'

Danny tried to explain. Mossad had been going through a rough patch recently. It was no longer the invincible saviour that had been lauded and feted in Israel's early days. High-profile mistakes had been made and a handful of its senior officers had resigned in disgrace. So what Mossad really needed next was a safe pair of hands and there were many – in the army, the cabinet and, most significantly, in Shin Bet – who suspected that Joshua Coen was a very unsafe pair of hands indeed.

His reputation was that of a maverick who believed he operated outside both domestic and international law. Stories of mistreatment of suspects abounded. There were even rumours that he had once walked drunkenly into a Palestinian refugee camp and fired at random on women and children. He was an inflexible man who bore grudges. In desperate times the service was turning desperately to exactly the wrong sort of person — a grave error, in the view of Danny and many others, when Mossad had plenty of alternative options in men of great character and moral integrity. Danny's job, then, was to get as close as possible to Joshua Coen, report back on any dirt he found and block the finalising of Coen's appointment before it was too late.

Joshua Coen

Little of this conversation offered Adam much comfort as he tried to go to sleep that evening. True, he did at least have one ally now. But how much help could Danny really be? His hands were tied by his own mission and the overriding imperative of not getting caught. He could keep half an eye out for Adam but little more than that.

Most of all, Adam lay awake thinking about his father. It was some comfort to know that he hadn't been quite as much of an ogre as his mother had made out. Yet the more he began to see him in a better light, the more it upset him that he would never get to meet him. The letters from 'David Horovitz' had moved and affected him more than he had perhaps realised.

To be duped in this facile way made Adam especially angry. Was it all for nothing that he had been led on this wild goose chase over the last two years?

But where could he direct his anger? Where was the outlet? He wanted to kill Mr Joseph, of course, several times over. But what about this mysterious Joshua Coen? Had this man known his father? Danny had thought they might have served together abroad but he couldn't be certain. There was no way of checking while within the confines of the Factory.

This unproductive, destructive thought pattern was suddenly interrupted by Danny who burst into Adam's tent at 2 a.m.

'We can't just stay here to wait and see what happens,' said Danny. 'Both of us are impotent. You, in particular, will be a lamb to the slaughter when Joshua Coen turns up, whatever it is he wants from you. I've been thinking about it non-stop. We have to leave.'

'They'll notice if we do anything, surely.'

'Adam, you forget that I'm an instructor here. I can do anything I like. Now come on, hurry up! We've got to get out of here. We'll think of something en route.'

Danny chucked a bundle of clothes at Adam, who followed him out to the perimeter of the Factory where they were stopped by a guard with a large Alsatian.

'Hey, Yuri,' said Danny. 'I've got one more flunker here, I'm afraid. I'm just going to walk him up to the main road and make sure he gets a bus OK. Then I'm going to stay with a friend who's in town. I'll see you tomorrow.'

Yuri let the two of them through without a challenge. As soon as they were out of sight and earshot of the camp, Danny and Adam doubled back to where Danny had left his car.

'Why are you doing this for me?' asked Adam, as Danny started the engine.

Danny turned to face him, deadly serious. 'I'm doing it because you have been treated badly by unscrupulous individuals in a country that I love. I do not want you to think that this is the real face of Israel. It is not. I am also helping you because your mother is a great woman who, by chance, brought the love of my life out here to meet me. Hannah and I have enjoyed a happy life and your mother deserves one too.' Danny stopped, as if surprised by himself. 'Is that a good enough answer for you?'

Adam nodded.

Danny continued, 'So, I assume you want me to take you to the house of Edward Black, MI6's station chief in Jerusalem?'

Adam looked across the steering column, startled by his godfather's knowledge.

'Oh, come on, Adam, don't think that we don't know the name and the address of every single foreign diplomat, undercover or not, friend or foe.'

At 5 a.m. exactly, they pulled up at Black's luxurious residence in the Arab quarter of East Jerusalem.

'Are you not coming in?' asked Adam, who had opened the door before the car had even drawn to a halt.

'I think it's better for all of us that I don't,' said Danny. 'Black is known to me socially by a completely different name and there's no point my confusing him by suddenly showing up on his doorstep in the early hours with you. I'll wait around the corner and make a few discreet telephone inquiries of my own. And Adam, a word of warning. Black is a little eccentric to say the least, so don't be too surprised if you don't get much out of him.'

Danny wasn't exaggerating. Black was the worst example of the Foreign Office types I wrote about earlier in this report – the type who go native as soon as they enter the Middle East. All the other British diplomats and spooks lived in West Jerusalem. Black preferred the East as it was 'more real', by which he meant more Arab. I was unable to interview him for this account as he died of liver cirrhosis in 1995. However, the descriptions given by both Adam and Danny tally with my own unpleasant recollections of dealing with Black in the 1980s.

Certainly, Adam was about to find out why Danny had warned him not to expect too much. Black opened the door readily enough and he appeared to be aware of who Adam was and what he was doing in the country, but that was about it as far as his usefulness went. Adam mentioned, rather mischievously, to Clive that Black was dressed in a full Arab robe in place of more traditional bedclothes. If the situation hadn't been so serious, it might have been amusing.

Adam repeated his story and his suspicions to Black as quickly and as succinctly as possible. Black replied that he had never heard of either David Horovitz or Joshua Coen as he 'didn't take much notice of what was going on in the Israeli intelligence services'. Adam looked at him aghast. How had this man risen to a position of such prominence within MI6? he asked himself. The answer, of course (which Adam would not have known then), is that Jerusalem is a sinecure pre-retirement posting for ageing officers who have somewhat lost their way It mainly involves liaising with a nominally friendly country that only really cares about the CIA. The real power in the Middle East lies in the positions in Beirut, Damascus and Cairo. Still, it was outrageous that Six should have sent a young, essentially undertrained man out to Israel with so little support.

Adam eventually snapped at Black. 'Well, if you don't have any way of helping me, perhaps you could put me in touch with London so I can get a proper decision out of them.'

'Oh, I can give you a decision myself,' said Black. 'It's exactly the same as the only decision I have ever taken my entire career: save your own skin. It's always stood me in good stead. Believe me, young man, they don't care two jots about you back at headquarters. They only sent you here for their own ends, so they could find out more about the future head of Mossad and its station chief in London without risking any of their own skins. You see, you're a deniable, Adam. Who's going to believe a university student if it all goes wrong? It's a win-win as far as they're concerned. Get out while you can. That's my advice, if you want it. You're out of that bloody Factory, or whatever it's called. Stay out of it.'

'That may well be,' said Adam. 'But I'm not the sort of person who can stay out of anything. I also have my own agenda. Several agendas, in fact. Revenge. Curiosity. Atonement. Security for my mother.'

'Very well,' said Black. 'If you feel that strongly about it, I'll lend you my secure line of communication.'

Black led Adam through to his study where he expected to see a large red telephone or some form of radio transmitter at the very least. Instead, Black gestured towards a rather forlorn-looking rock sitting on the mantelpiece.

'What the hell is that?' said Adam.

'It's just in, so we're not sure how well it's working yet. But basically you speak into the side of the rock and it encrypts and records your message. The rock thing goes into the diplomatic bag and is sent back to London before the end of the month, as long as it doesn't get mistaken for rubbish, that is. Then, assuming that the recording has worked OK, they listen to it and try to record a message of their own to send back in the diplomatic bag the following month… Adam? Where are you going?'

Adam had turned on his heel and was heading for the front door. He had heard quite enough. Black didn't even bother to follow him.

'Nutter,' said Adam, climbing into Danny's waiting car. 'Just as you bloody said. Have you made any progress yourself?'

'A little,' said Danny. 'I've made a few phone calls and found out that Joshua Coen and Samuel Joseph are expected at the Factory at two p.m. sharp so we still have some time to play with. As long as we're back before then, I can come up with something convincing to explain your absence.'

'Great. Thanks.'

'But listen, here's the real breakthrough. I never told you how your father died. There was a night in November nineteen eighty-seven which we call in Hebrew *Leil HaGilshonim*. This translates into English as the Night of the Gliders—'

'I've heard of it,' interrupted Adam excitedly.

'Hear me out,' said Danny. 'Your father was stationed temporarily at the Gibor camp in northern Israel that year. It was meant to be a staging post for him to rest and recuperate on the way back from a gruelling undercover mission in southern Lebanon. Something to do with Operation Wrath of God. But two hang gliders took off that evening, piloted by Arab terrorists. One of them showed up on the radar in the room in which your father was relaxing. He was tired and grumpy after his long tour and told the junior soldier to ignore it as it was probably only a bird or a technical error with the radar machine. Forty-five minutes later, your father was shot dead by the terrorist. Five others were killed, seven wounded.

'All this, of course, I knew already, but I didn't want to burden you with it earlier. The reason I mention it now is that I have just called a very trustworthy contact in Shin Bet and made a startling discovery: Joshua Coen had a brother who was killed in Gibor camp that evening and a sister who was shot in the spine and remains in a wheelchair to this day. Most startling of all, there was also a Joseph among the dead that night. It appears to have been a nephew of Samuel Joseph.'

'Oh God,' said Adam. 'One of the letters supposedly sent

from my father said that *he* had a relative killed that evening.'

'There you go,' said Danny. 'Coen and Joseph have used you as bait.'

'And if they can't get their revenge on my father, they're going to take it on his son?' said Adam.

'Precisely.'

Adam already knew exactly what they had to do next. 'Have you heard of someone called Dr Jamal Tarikh?' he asked.

'Of course,' said Danny. 'Everyone knows Dr Tarikh. We could do with a lot more Palestinians like him.'

'Then please drive me to Ramallah,' said Adam. 'I desperately need to speak to him and I'll explain why on the way.'

Dr Jamal Tarikh

Bilal Tarikh had often described his family home in Ramallah – the Tarikhs always spent much of the summer there – but Adam had never been there and didn't really know where it was. They were gambling on finding someone who could direct them to the house of such a well-known family.

As they approached Ramallah, Danny looked increasingly anxious. It was clear that neither he nor Adam were Arab and the yellow Israeli number plates on their car made them stick out even more. The town was just waking up and an angry mob surrounded the car as they drew into the centre of the town.

Fortunately, a year of studying Arabic had given Adam sufficient confidence to communicate convincingly with the crowd. '*As salamu alaykum*,' he announced in greeting as they jostled and harried him. '*Ana sadiq Bilal Tarikh min Inglaterra. Laazim min atakallim ma' abuhu, sayeed doktoor Jamal Tarikh. Wayn yaskun?*'

It was enough to placate the angry gathering. If anyone was a friend of the Tarikhs, then they were a friend of that town's. There was suddenly no shortage of people eagerly pointing out conflicting directions to Dr Tarikh's house.

A slightly shaken Danny climbed back into the car and drove Adam to the large Tarikh villa on the outskirts of the town, which was tastefully concealed from the main road by olive groves and palm trees. Danny killed the engine and they walked up together to the front door where Danny rang the bell.

It was opened by a young man in his middle twenties who was the absolute spitting image of Bilal. Adam started, as if he'd seen a ghost. It was Bilal's elder brother, Isa.

'Hello, Isa,' said Danny. 'Is your father home?'

Isa smiled and nodded, gesturing for them to come in.

'How well do you know this family?' whispered Adam, as Isa disappeared upstairs to find Jamal Tarikh.

'Oh, pretty well,' said Danny. 'We moderates on both sides have to stick together.'

They were interrupted by the sound of someone coming down the stairs. Jamal Tarikh, a slight, tall, elegant man with swept-back grey hair and a friendly, open face, walked into the room.

'Daniel,' he said, holding out both hands in greeting. '*Ahlan wa sahlan*. You are always welcome in my home.'

He turned to Adam. 'And Adam, how nice to see you again. I remember you from Bilal's funeral. What a wonderful, moving speech you gave that day.'

He motioned to them to sit down. Isa came into the room with coffee and left again.

'Now,' said Tarikh. 'Daniel, I know you well of course, and Adam, I have heard many good things about you from Bilal. But I must admit to being somewhat surprised at seeing the two of you together in my house in the West Bank at nine a.m. on a Friday. I'm sure one of you will enlighten me.'

Adam, who had by now got rather good at telling the story as succinctly as possible, gave Tarikh a rapid, edited rundown of the facts. 'So,' he concluded, 'we were hoping you might be able to provide the missing piece in the jigsaw. What is your history with Joshua Coen?'

Tarikh, who had been looking thoughtfully out of the window throughout Adam's account, sat in silence for a long time. When he eventually spoke, it was in a voice cracked deep with emotion.

'So, that is why my son was killed. I *knew* it was a cover-up by the British authorities. And I *knew* that Coen would one day reappear to blight our lives.'

'I don't understand,' said Adam.

'Neither do I,' said Tarikh. 'Much of human behaviour is far from understandable. But let me try my best to explain. You mention the Night of the Gliders. Of course, I am familiar with this event but however much I tried to persuade Coen otherwise, he would not accept that it had absolutely nothing to do with me. I don't know why he has always had it in for me. Maybe he doesn't like the fact that I have influential friends in the West. Or perhaps I don't fit his stereotype of how an Arab should act under occupation. But the truth is this: I am no terrorist. Neither have I ever been involved with funding terrorist organisations. My work on behalf of my people, the Palestinians, is humanitarian. I run several charities in Ramallah. I help families who have fallen upon hard times. I give free medical care to those who need it and also help with municipal government. I have no interest in violence of any kind.

'I explained all this to Coen, even as he detained and tortured me, even as he threatened my wife and children. Maybe Bilal never mentioned this to you, Adam. He, like me, was a proud man. But, unlike me, he was more taken with the concept of violent revenge. When he found out what Coen had done to me in that dark prison, he wrote to him saying that, as long as he walked this earth, he should watch his shadow for Bilal would be lurking around the corner. Coen did not take kindly to this and visited me again at home with more threats. I told him that he was being ridiculous, that Bilal was just a hot-headed young man who didn't mean what he said. Coen ignored me and said that he would hunt my son down, even if it meant going to England to do so.'

Dr Tarikh sat back in his armchair, emotionally exhausted by his revelations.

'And as you now know,' he concluded, 'I made the mistake of not taking him seriously.'

'And that's where my story and Bilal's overlap, I suppose,' said Adam. 'Here was the chance to kill two birds with one stone. I was the guileless puppet on a string, lured by the prospect of meeting someone I thought was my father, who, in turn, almost succeeded in setting me against my friend and his sworn enemy. The sins of the fathers would then be visited on their offspring—'

A silenced gunshot rang out from the front door. Adam's coffee glass splintered in his hand. There was another muffled bang and Danny clutched his right hand, which had been inching down towards the pistol he kept taped to the inside of his leg.

'Don't anyone move,' said a familiar voice from the door, 'or the next one will hit where it hurts.'

The three of them slowly raised their hands above their heads and turned to see Samuel Joseph standing in the doorway, covering them with two automatic pistols. He smiled, his face contorting into an unsightly, smug grimace. There was no trace of the occasionally bumbling demeanour that Adam had noted on previous occasions.

'You say two birds with one stone,' he said. 'How about three birds with three bullets?'

'How...' Adam managed to say.

Joseph shook his head in mock sadness. 'Two years you've known me, Adam, and you still underestimate me. You really think I was stupid enough to leave you in the Factory without supervision? Omar alerted me that you'd left. It wasn't very difficult tracking you down to Edward Black's house given that we have it bugged and we assumed it would be the first place you went to. After that, we simply had you tailed to Ramallah.'

He moved closer to where they were sitting.

'It's a great shame, in many ways. I think Joshua Coen would have taken great pleasure in watching the son of David Horovitz die. We had it all planned. Omar was going to arrange a special training demonstration to show off to the new acting head of Mossad. During this, you would have been tragically and accidentally shot by a rubber bullet. Still, Joshua will be delighted when I tell him that I've also bagged his least favourite Palestinian and his least favourite Israeli at the same time. Three bullets, three targets. One gentleman terrorist with a family grudge and the ability to blackmail Joshua in his future posting; one weasel of a left-wing Shin Bet agent attempting, and failing, to investigate him; and one young Brit whose father destroyed mine and Joshua's life. It's not a bad tally for one day.'

Joseph cocked the hammer on one of his pistols and took aim. 'Now, which one of you would like to go last and watch his friends die?'

'You've got it all worked out, haven't you?' said Adam, frantically playing for time.

'Indeed I do,' said Joseph, never lowering his aim. 'But I mustn't take all the credit. You played right into my hands, Adam. The errant young youth looking for a noble father? The strong young man hoping to protect his mother? It's *pathetic*. That's all it was. Pathetic. Who was the man you knew as "David" at Ben Gurion airport? It was Joshua Coen, of course. After your father died, we had access to his files. When they were stationed together in Beirut in the nineteen eighties, Horovitz spoke to Joshua about Eleanor on so many occasions that we were able to get all the details right. You know who wrote those letters from "your father"? I did, of course. I set up your job with the *Mirror* because we needed a decent cover to lure you out to Israel so we could kill you. We patted you on the head and punished you in equal measure so you became our tool. We helped you get into Cambridge so you would come into close contact with Bilal Tarikh. You were the ultimate deniable. Joshua and I were in it together, from the very start. We are old university friends, just as I pretended I was with Horovitz. We were lucky to stumble upon you in the first place but everything else has been planned out very carefully. We—'

Joseph broke off, following Adam's glance over his shoulder, just in time to see Isa Tarikh bringing a chair smashing down on his cranium. Simultaneously, Adam threw one of the shards from his splintered coffee glass. It struck Joseph just above his eye.

Adam leapt to his feet, disarmed Joseph and pointed both guns at him.

'No,' called out Jamal Tarikh. 'It would not be the right thing to do. Gandhi was right. An eye for an eye and the whole world will go blind.'

Adam turned and looked at Dr Tarikh, without lowering either gun. According to Danny, Adam looked like a fully grown man for the first time.

'I respect you, Dr Tarikh,' he said. 'And I respect your philosophy. But with all due respect, it is no longer a creed I can live by.'

And with that, Adam dragged Joseph outside, pushed him to the ground just beyond the boundaries of Dr Tarikh's land and shot him twice in the head.

'Now,' he said when he rejoined Danny. 'How do I get home?'

'If we can just get you as far as Haifa, I have a very trustworthy fisherman friend,' said Danny.

Endnote

Adam Carter returned safely to England where he was given a hero's welcome by Clive, Roupell and Jackson. His report was, however, never written up officially for fear of damaging relations between the UK and Israel should it ever be uncovered. Its only surviving record was, until now, contained within Clive's unpublished memoirs. It is possible — although I cannot be certain — that Clive was murdered by a Mossad *kidon* unit tasked by Joshua Coen to find the memoirs. Coen was not a man to forgive a grudge.

In Israel, however, Danny's report on behalf of Shin Bet was enough to stop Joshua Coen being confirmed as head of Mossad. Instead, his next posting was abroad, in Nigeria. He died last year of cancer. A small paragraph written by a Press Association journalist mentioned that Samuel Joseph, a success-ful businessman with dual British and Israeli nationality, died in a car accident in the Occupied Territories.

The new head of Mossad, a much respected former general, wired Adam a large sum of money by way of apology. Much to Rob Helen's delight, Adam used some of this to reimburse the *Daily Mirror* for the cost of his (apparently) wasted flights to Israel. The rest he used to pay back the Dempsey estate for his school fees and to buy his mother a house in Blackpool — a house that Daniel and Hannah visited regularly on their trips to the UK. Daniel, who now holds a senior position in Shin Bet, made himself available for interview for this book, as did Dr Jamal Tarikh.

Adam was immediately offered employment with MI6 as soon as he graduated, on condition that he never breathed a word about anything that had happened. Only his mother, who subsequently changed her name again, was ever told the full story. Adam later gave her the copies he'd kept of his correspondence with 'David Horovitz' which she passed to me. It was also Eleanor who pointed me in the direction of the *Hans Wehr Dictionary of Modern Written Arabic* (edited by J. Milton Cowan) on the second floor of the Trinity Hall library to find Adam's report on Operation Bilal.

The rest, of course, we know. Adam was a first-rate officer — the very best of the best — both at MI6 and, later, at MI5. His funeral was well attended by many valued colleagues and friends, some less expected than others. On re-examining MI5's official photos of the event, an elderly Jamal Tarikh can just be made out, comforting a distraught Danny.

Adam Carter went to Israel to find his father. He ended up finding several father figures. He also found his own vocation.

It is to preserve the memory of this remarkable man that I have felt it my duty to uncover the true story of his early life. It is my wish that this manuscript be placed in a secure location within MI5 for at least fifty years, at which point it may be declassified and released to the public. In the meantime, it is my recommendation that, on reaching the age of maturity, and subject to appropriate security checks, Adam's son, Wes, should be given full access to this story of his father's early life.

I do not want another admirable young man to grow up not knowing the true nature of his father.

Harry Pearce

London, February 2009

Postcard from Adam Carter
Dated 21 August 1992, Cyprus

Cyprus
21 August 1992

Dear Mum,
I've bumped into a few old friends of yours in Israel who send their best.
I'm coming home.
I'm safe and so are you.
Love from Adam

MI6 Application Form

Surname

Carter

Forenames

Adam Henry

Date of birth

31.10.1972

Place of birth

Wimbledon, London

Nationality at birth

British

Permanent Address

Trinity Hall,
Cambridge University,
CB2 1TJ

Current occupation

Student

Date of availability for employment

June —
from graduation

Do you hold a full, clean driving licence?

Yes, but 9 points for speeding

Medical

Do you have any conditions – either physical or psychological – which might affect your employment?

Broken leg — sustained during a
rugby match — which required setting
under general anaesthetic in 1988.
No subsequent problems

Father's name, address and occupation

David Carter, 42 West Kensington
Road, London SW10

Retired diplomat

Mother's name, maiden name, address and occupation

Lucy Carter (nee Johnson), 42 West
Kensington Road, London SW10

Architect

Brothers / Sisters (with names and D.O.B.)

Jack — 12.9.1971

Olivia — 24.5.1975

Secondary Schools / Colleges
Dates : Names : Town

1985—1990 : St. Paul's School :
London

GCSEs or equivalents

3 A* (French, German, English
language), 5As (History, Geography,
Maths, English literature, Biology),
2Bs (Chemistry, Physics)

A levels and AS levels or equivalents

French — A

German — A

English language — B

MAP|06.fa|vii.1

Gap Year

How did you spend any break during your education?

Spent seven months teaching English in a Palestinian school in the West Bank

University or Further Education

Cambridge University — 1991–1995

B.A. (Hons) in Arabic — pending (2:1 — predicted)

Awards

Please give details of any other awards (e.g. music)

Grade 3 guitar

EMPLOYMENT

Dates	Employer	Position
Summer 1994	MRKG	Intern

Have you served in HM Forces (including Reserves)?

Officer Cadet in Cambridge University Officers Training Corps, 1991–1995

Do you have applications pending for other jobs?

This is the one job I want. If I don't get it, I plan to travel and re-apply next year.

PERSONAL QUALITIES AND SKILLS

SUMMARY

Provide a pen-portrait of your life to date

My father was in the Foreign Office so I spent much of my early life either abroad or in English boarding schools. My childhood was idyllic but it was short-lived. I felt as if I had to grow up faster than I would have liked.

I was always happy at school as well as quite hard-working. I'm outgoing and laid-back, and I don't like to plan ahead too much.

I studied Arabic at Cambridge University — mainly so I could use it to travel — and I've spent most of my holidays travelling. I am rarely happier than with a rucksack on my back and meeting new people. However, there is nothing I love more than returning home again at the end.

MAP|06.fa|vii.2

MOTIVATION

Why do you think you would be suited to a public service career?

- My family upbringing instilled a love of public service in me
- I am politically highly aware
- I am well travelled
- I quickly adapt to new environments
- I speak Arabic, as well as French

POLITICAL CURIOSITY

Give three political topics (historical or current) which interest you

- Israel vs. Palestine conflict — time spent teaching there
- Islamic fundamentalism in Egypt — spent 3rd year of university course in Cairo
- Balkans — father stationed in Sarajevo

ADAPTABILITY

Give an example of a time when you had to adapt to unexpected circumstances

I spent seven months after school teaching in the West Bank. I had a bit of time in the holidays to travel and decided to go up to Syria. Unfortunately, I travelled via Jerusalem and so my passport was stamped with an Israeli entry and exit visa.

When the lady in the Syrian embassy in Amman told me that this would prevent me from entering Syria I ignored her. A group of Australians were heading north and offered me a ride to Damascus if I hid in the back of their truck.

Initially, the plan worked fine. I spent two weeks travelling around Syria, but I faced problems getting back into Jordan again. The Australians were heading up into Lebanon but I had to get back to catch a flight from Amman.

In the end, I had no choice but to brazen it out at the border. The confrontation started well, but the guards on the Syrian side started to doubt my story. Then I recognised someone on the Jordanian side who I'd met during my time in Amman. He gave me the nod; I moved round to an unguarded side of the fence; and he let me through unmolested.

A bit of extra tipping persuaded him to leave my passport alone as well.

MAP|06.fa|vii.3

RESPONSIBILITY

What positions of responsibility have you held – at school, university or otherwise?

```
School — Head boy; captain of rugby
University — Captain of rugby
Officer Cadet in Cambridge University Officers Training Corps,
1991–1995
```

FOREIGN LANGUAGES

Please indicate level of competence

```
Arabic — fluent, verging on bi-lingual
French — fluent
German - functional
```

OTHER INTERESTS

```
Rugby — training twice per week; weekends
Socialising
```

TRAVEL

Give details of all foreign travel in the last 10 years, including reason for travel

```
Lived in Sarajevo and Paris (through father's work), and
Egypt (year abroad)
Visited for interest, mainly backpacking — Jordan, Israel,
Syria, UAE, Morocco, Algeria, Spain, France, Peru, Ecuador,
Bolivia, Mexico, India
```

EQUAL OPPORTUNITIES

This information is not used as part of our selection procedures

Gender	Ethnic origin	Disabilities
(Male) Female	White British	None

REFEREES

Please give details of three referees. One of these should be a contemporary who knows you well

```
1. Dr Nick Lampen, Lecturer in Arabic, Cambridge University
2. Michael Wynne, Director of Audit, MRKG
3. Sam Edes, childhood friend
```

SIGNATURE

DATE

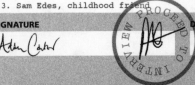

2nd February 1995

MAP|06.fa|vii.4